"A story of the human heart and the tortured mind. Jonah's plight will touch your soul."

—Tabitha Suzuma, author of *Forbidden*

★ "An affecting, well-crafted story that will stay with readers long after the final page."

—*Booklist*, Starred Review

"An intense portrait of the unpredictability of schizophrenia and the toll it takes on those close to those who have it."

—*Publisher's Weekly*

"Jonah's paranoia, symptoms of schizophrenia, and thwarted attempts at treatment are raw yet sensitively depicted."

—*School Library Journal*

"Readers are carried o ~~coaster~~, which is often thrilling and beautiful

—*VOYA*

# RULES OF RAIN

## ALSO BY LEAH SCHEIER

*Your Voice Is All I Hear*

# RULES OF
# RAIN

## LEAH SCHEIER

sourcebooks
fire

Chapter 2, study in Ethan's journal, page 27: Megan A. Jones, "Deafness as Culture: A Psychosocial Perspective," *Disability Studies Quarterly* 22, no. 2 (Spring 2002). Used by permission.

Chapter 29, study in Ethan's journal, page 295: Claus Wedekind and Sandra Furi, "Body Odour Preferences in Men and Women: Do They Aim for Specific MHC Combinations or Simply Heterozygosity?" *Proceedings B* (October 22, 1997). Used by permission of the Royal Society.

Published by Sourcebooks Fire, an imprint of Sourcebooks, Inc.
P.O. Box 4410, Naperville, Illinois 60567-4410
(630) 961-3900
Fax: (630) 961-2168
www.sourcebooks.com

Library of Congress Cataloging-in-Publication data is on file with the publisher.

Printed and bound in the United States of America.
VP 10 9 8 7 6 5 4 3 2 1

*To my sisters,*

*Anna, Dinah, Sarah, and Tammy*

"Let food be thy medicine and medicine be thy food."

—Hippocrates

# Cooking with Rain
## SERENITY THROUGH YOUR GUT

*Where I answer all your burning food-related questions!*

**Dear Rain:** I really want to impress my boyfriend. What snack should I bring to the office party tonight?

—Lovesick Girl in Reno

**Dear Lovesick:** We've all heard that the way to a man's heart is through his stomach. So don't squander this opportunity by bringing chips and dip! Instead, knock him dead with a double dose of aphrodisiac. How about *avocado chocolate mousse with agave nectar*? Both avocado and chocolate are packed with libido-boosting fats and vitamins. Did you know the Aztecs forbade virgin women from leaving their houses during the avocado harvest because they feared the sexually overwhelming powers of the avocado? That Casanova snacked on dark chocolate before romancing his date? Well, you can use these ancient food secrets to make your boyfriend hot for you!

# ETHAN'S JOURNAL:

Researchers have recently discovered a cranial nerve that they believe is the route through which pheromones are processed. This secret nerve, present in animals and people, could be how pheromones turn us on. (Notes from R. Douglas Fields's *Sex and the Secret Nerve*.)

**Note:**

This may explain the Hope phenomenon.

**Proposed experiment:**

Attempt communication with subject during day four of upper respiratory tract infection (when congestion most interferes with the olfactory process).

**Alternative:**

Stuff cotton balls in nose next time she visits.

# Chapter 1

There's a gigantic hologram of a human colon sitting where the refrigerator once stood. I stare at it for a moment and lean my head back to appreciate the flickering image. With veins, without veins, with veins…it's almost hypnotic, the tilting shift of images on the shiny board.

I'm not surprised to find it there. Most people would be confused if they came home from school to find a major kitchen appliance missing and a six-foot diagram of guts resting in its place. I am a little annoyed, I guess, but that's only because I'm really hungry, and the refrigerator has been replaced by a detailed poster of a man's lower intestine.

"I need to eat, please!" I call out—not too loudly (so as not to upset him), but loud enough to make my point.

There's no answer at first, but I'm not worried. If I'm patient, he'll eventually appear on his own. Worst comes to worst, I could try to find the refrigerator by myself (how far could he have dragged it?), but that wouldn't be a healthy solution for either of us. "We have to teach Ethan to take responsibility for his actions," my mother likes to tell me. "If we treat him like he's different, he'll never learn from his mistakes."

She says stuff like that less often now but not because anything much has changed recently. I think she's realized that for every mistake Ethan fixes, there are twenty fresh ones just waiting to pop out. Today is a perfect example of this. I'm used to finding pictures of unappetizing body parts taped to random places in our home. This is, however, the first time the refrigerator has gone missing.

"I need to eat!" I repeat, more insistently this time. "You have to help me find the refrigerator."

This time there's a vague rustle from the second floor and then a soft padding on the stairs. A moment later, my brother comes into view and without a word brushes past me and opens the side door. "Hello, Rain," he says simply, his eyes fixed on a distant point. "I put it in the backyard." Then, without further explanation, he turns around and moves to leave the room.

"Just a second," I say, holding out my hand. I'm careful that my fingers do not touch him. No one touches Ethan without warning, not even me. "Can you tell me *why* you moved the fridge outside?"

The truth is, at that moment I'm too hungry to care about the answer. I'm just hoping the food in the fridge hasn't spoiled because I really want a turkey sandwich. It's been an exciting day, and I need a healthy dose of tryptophan to de-stress. But this is a "teaching opportunity," according to my mother, and from force of habit, I need to get an explanation for this millionth bit of strangeness from my twin brother.

"It was making noise," he states, his eyes still fixed on some point far behind me. "The sound was bothering me."

"Efan," I say. I still call him by the name I used when we were toddlers together. I've long outgrown that speech impediment, but he never outgrew his sister's baby voice. I can never call him by his real name. "*Efan*," I say again, louder, hoping he will take the cue and look at me.

It works this time. He starts suddenly, as if remembering an old lesson, and abruptly raises his eyes.

"Thank you." I smile, more for me than for him. "Why didn't you just unplug the fridge? Why drag it to the yard?"

I don't bother asking why the noise bothered him so much that he felt the need to throw the refrigerator out of the house. That is Ethan's number one rule. He gets overstimulated by loud noises, crowds, and strong smells. But asking *why* those things bother him would be like asking someone why the sound of nails on a chalkboard or a baby shrieking is disconcerting.

"If I left it in the house, it would leak all over the floor when the food in the freezer melted," he tells me.

"Oh." It's hard to argue with that logic. "And the guts hologram?"

He shrugs. "There's no more space in my room."

"Well, you could always take down the eyeball dissection diagram," I suggest as I step out into the backyard to rescue my thawing lunch. "That poster really freaks me out."

He doesn't reply. When I return to the kitchen, he's standing in front of the hologram, completely engrossed.

"Would you like me to make you something?" I pull out the hospital antiseptic and roll up my sleeves. My skin stings as I rub the soapy sponge over my palms.

"Have you had your lunch yet?" I persist when he doesn't respond.

It's a silly question, and I know it. Ethan has lunch every day at 12:15. I prepare it for him and leave it on the counter before I go to school. He has dinner at 6:15. He's shockingly flexible about the contents of the meal as long as I've performed the surgical hand scrub and then cooked every item from scratch. But he's not flexible about time. It's now three o'clock in the afternoon. Eating a meal at three o'clock would be madness, plain and simple. But I ask the question anyway because sometimes I say stuff just for the hell of it, to fake normal conversation.

He doesn't call me on it, doesn't even notice I've asked a silly question. "It's three o'clock," he tells me, simply, as if I'm new to his routine. "Dinner is at six fifteen."

"I know it is," I say indulgently. "I was just playing with you."

He gives me a quizzical look and then a little smile dawns. "There are eleven cranial nerves!" he states triumphantly.

Well, okay, then.

I stare at him. Non sequiturs are a part of everyday conversation with Ethan. Sometimes it feels like he's talking next to me, rather than to me. At least he's making eye contact today.

He looks disappointed by my nonreaction. "Only eleven?" he prompts, and raises his eyebrows, or the part of his forehead where his eyebrows are supposed to be. He's so blond that his brows are hard to see, and the effect is just a general wrinkling of very fair skin.

"Whatever you say, bro."

It's not the answer he's hoping for, obviously. His shoulders slump, and he sighs loudly. "I was *playing* with you," he says. "There are actually *twelve* cranial nerves."

I nod, understanding suddenly. He'd been trying to make me laugh, had tried to joke with me, as I'd just joked with him. I'm generally the only person who understands him, and even so, I miss the mark quite often. I force an amused chuckle and watch as the shadow lifts from his light blue eyes. Sometimes, it takes so little to make him glow.

"Actually, some scientists think that there are really thirteen cranial nerves," he continues eagerly, encouraged by my little laugh. "Cranial nerve zero was discovered in 1913, but no one really knows what it does. But I just read a theory—"

I nod again, halfheartedly, and let my attention wander. I have my own news to think about today, and there's no need to listen to my brother now. Ethan has launched into a lecture about his favorite topic, human anatomy, and he won't stop until he's exhausted himself. I don't have the energy to redirect him today. Besides, my brother's reedy, monotone voice is a nice background to my own thoughts, and I'm happy to indulge him. He'll never notice that I've stopped listening. He can't pick up on those cues like other people can. As long as I'm still physically in the room, in his eyes, I am his captive audience.

I can't help wondering how Ethan would react if he heard my news, even though I know I can't share it with him. I've never even told him about my crush on Liam. Would he care at all if I did tell him? Would he just stare blankly at me before going off on some irrelevant tangent about fallopian tubes? Or would he freak out completely, terrified at the thought of sharing his twin with some stranger? Ethan doesn't deal well with change. But if I introduced Liam very, very gradually, could my brother get used to the idea of my first boyfriend? I really have no idea. It's not like it's ever come up before.

I glance absentmindedly at my watch and take a bite of my sandwich. I'm expecting my best friend, Hope, at any minute. She texted she was coming by after I sent her an emoji-splattered, all caps message. We were having a meeting in my room to discuss unprecedented developments in my love life. Top secret.

Only problem is, Ethan is still firmly planted on the kitchen stool opposite me, and he's barely finished with the fifth cranial nerve. (There's seven more to go, right?) I have to get him to wrap it up and head back to his room before she comes. It's not that I'm embarrassed by him or anything. The way I see it, if my friends can't handle my brother, then they can't handle me either. We're a package deal. Besides, Hope has known Ethan for a couple of years, so I don't have to explain his quirks to her; she's used to him by now.

But lately Hope has been getting very weird around my brother. And by weird, I mean hopelessly in love. If he's in the kitchen when she comes, she's not going to want to send him away. In fact, she'll probably try to include him in the conversation. Hope has this crazy idea that my autistic brother is trapped in some kind of mental tower, like a male Sleeping Beauty, and that all he needs is a spark of love to melt his heart and free him from his "sleep."

Her crush on Ethan is a pretty recent development, and it's freaking me out a bit. She used to just give him a friendly wave (which he ignored) and then forget about him. But a few weeks after her breakup with Grayson, her douchey boyfriend, I noticed a change in my best friend. At first there was this creeping shyness I couldn't understand, then a strange insistence on meeting at my house, and finally such obvious attempts at flirting that even Ethan picked up on it. He didn't respond, of course, unless hiding in his room could be counted as a response.

So, to spare both of their feelings, I've been trying to keep them far apart from each other. I even bought a giant box of graham crackers to try to smack down her hormones a little.

*(From the blog: In the early 1800s, the Reverend Graham urged his congregants to eat dense crackers and whole grains, as a remedy to suppress sexual urges. His preaching inspired the modern day graham cracker.)*

I haven't had a chance to test this out on Hope because she just said no thanks, heavy carbs make her bloat. Maybe I should find a less passive-aggressive way to tell her to give up and find another project, but the crackers were the best idea I had. I generally prefer subtle food manipulation to actual verbal confrontation. If I try to discourage her directly, I'll just end up hurting her feelings.

I look up from my lunch and smile brightly at my brother. He's so animated now, so obviously eager to tell me about the many wonders of the trigeminal nerve that I feel almost sorry interrupting him midsentence "—and it's actually the mandibular branch that controls chewing, or mastication of that sandwich you're eating—"

"Efan—"

He responds by picking up speed. "—and allows you to feel the food on your gums and teeth, but it has nothing to do with taste, that's actually the seventh and the ninth nerve, so if you were bleeding in your mouth, you would feel the blood with the fifth nerve but taste the blood with the seventh—"

"Gross, Efan! Please stop."

He looks hurt and pauses to draw a ragged breath before concluding. "And maybe you would taste the blood with the ninth nerve—if you swallowed it—"

"Secret Rule!" I call out desperately. "Secret Rule."

He halts abruptly, like a record player hitting a scratch. There's a brief pause as he bites his lip to halt the flow of words. "What can I do?" he whispers finally.

"*Please* stop talking about drinking blood, okay?" I plead. "I really don't think Hope is going to want to listen to that when she comes over."

I try not to invoke the Secret Rule if I don't have to, but the topic today is making my stomach turn. Also I needed to warn him that my best friend is coming. I'm praying the mention of her name will make Ethan flee the room. But before he can respond, Hope appears behind me like a summoned genie (who apparently doesn't believe in knocking).

"I don't mind hearing about it, Ethan, if you want to talk about it," she says generously, addressing him in her quiet voice, a voice she reserves for him only. "Why were we talking about drinking blood?"

I turn to stare at her. She's sidled up beside me and slipped onto a nearby kitchen stool. I note that she was careful not to approach my brother too quickly; she's long ago given up her attempts to hug him or even touch him.

He appears momentarily stunned and then shoots me an accusing look. "You didn't tell me she was coming."

I pass over the bit of rudeness; it isn't his fault. I've just violated one of Ethan's rules. My brother needs to be warned hours in advance of any change to his routine. Some changes (haircuts, doctor's visits) need days of preparation. I can't spring Hope on him like this. "It's okay," I tell him in a soothing voice. "We're going to be in my room. You don't even have to see her. She's not staying for dinner."

Ethan puts his hand to his nose and begins to back away. Strangely enough, Hope doesn't seem offended. She slides off her chair and moves a step closer to him; he tenses suddenly and stares at the floor. "Is Rain's turkey bothering you?" she asks him, pointing to my plate. "It *is* pretty pungent stuff."

"No, it's you," Ethan tells her bluntly. "I'm doing an experiment."

"An experiment?" She shoots me a baffled look over her shoulder.

"No experiments today!" I say, ignoring her look. "Hope and

I are going to my room now." I try to link my arm through hers, but she slips past me and takes a step closer to my brother.

"I was hoping that you'd hang out with us a little too," she tells him softly. "If you're not too busy."

His eyes flicker over her, and he swallows loudly. One hand tightens around his nose, the other clenches at his side. Watching him now, teetering on the edge of panic, nearly undone by a simple question from my harmless friend, I wonder again why Hope wants him to stay. Maybe sixteen years of being Ethan's interpreter, therapist, and nurse has warped me a little. When I look at him, I don't see a tall, handsome young man with waves of white-gold hair and large, deep-set blue eyes. That's Hope's vision of my brother. All I see is the boy that sat stonily mute for years, who shrieked his frustration in wordless howls until I finally learned to speak for him, who rocked and bit and tore himself to pieces until I learned the magic charm to quiet him. The way I see it, despite all the progress he's made, he's still a hiccup away from a total breakdown, and I'm always hovering by his side, ready to pick up the pieces when he shatters. I need to stop this meltdown before it starts. "Ethan, why don't you boil up a pot of chamomile tea for Mom?" I suggest firmly, taking my friend by the arm and steering her away from him. "She's been stressed recently, and I'm sure she'd appreciate it. At four o'clock, you and I will go out for our run. Then I'll make dinner while Mom calls the fridge repairman."

The precise instructions and the confident tone with which

I dictate them seem to calm my brother. I see the tension in his shoulders ease; the worried pucker in his forehead relaxes.

*(Idea for the blog: Special Spices Edition—Harness the calming power of herbs to season your entire household with serenity! Spotlight: lavender, chamomile, and linden.)*

"I thought you forgot about our run," he says in a relieved voice.

"Of course not. I never forget about you," I reply.

I mean it too. I can never forget Ethan.

Not for a second.

## Cooking with Rain

### SERENITY THROUGH YOUR GUT

*Where I answer all your burning food-related questions!*

**Dear Rain:** Do you ever feel like your friends are getting all the action, and you're left sitting on the sidelines? What can I do to get people to notice me?

—Blah in Kentucky

**Dear Blah:** I hate to break it to you, but this is a cooking blog. I'm really just here to tell you what to eat. Today I'm recommending coconut oil! Slather yourself in the stuff, inside and out. Great for dull hair, blotchy skin, and flaky scalp. Try it as a substitute for gel when shaving your legs! As for your insides: toast up some coconut oil kale chips!

## ETHAN'S JOURNAL

### Re: The Antidote to Hope

The problem appears to be multisensory in nature. Next time, I should try closing my eyes.

# Chapter 2

"What's the Secret Rule?" Hope asks me as I shut my bedroom door behind us. "I heard you shout that at him as I walked in."

"Oh, that's nothing," I tell her vaguely. "It's like Ethan's reset button."

"How does it work?"

"It's hard to explain." I hesitate and consider changing the subject. I've never spoken about the Secret Rule to anyone. "I don't know if Ethan wants me to tell people about it."

"I'm not just 'people,'" Hope protests. "I'm your best friend. But whenever your brother is around, you act like I'm some dangerous stranger. Seriously, why couldn't you have invited him in for a little while?"

I laugh shortly and lean back against the wall. "No way. That would be way too weird!"

She sighs and climbs up to sit cross-legged on my bed. "Rain, you don't need to protect me from Ethan—"

"I'm not protecting you; I'm protecting him," I interrupt irritably. "I'm just trying to prevent a meltdown, okay?"

"Relax, Rainey!" She puts her hands up in mock surrender.

"I get it. I just feel sorry for him sometimes. He's here the whole day, all alone, while you're at school. He has no one to talk to. At least if he had some friends, someone to hang out with—"

I can't help smiling, despite my frustration. "We've *tried*," I tell her. My mother had enrolled him in every kind of social group that Mineral County had to offer. We'd been to the Child Development Center about a thousand times even though it's more than an hour away. And he'd gone to school with me until a couple of years ago. But public school was a total disaster for him, and homeschooling was the only other option in our little town. "He's happiest when he's surrounded by his drawings and his books," I explain. "Once in a while he hangs out with me and Mom, but that's as big as his circle is going to get. Trust me, Ethan will never get close to anyone else."

I say that last statement pretty loudly; I even shake my head at her and raise my eyebrows as a none-too-subtle hint. *He will never want you near him*, I'm trying to tell her silently. *Just stop trying already.*

She really doesn't hear me. "I think he's lonely," she persists. "I just want to help him. I want to be his friend."

I don't know what to say to that. *Help* him? What does she think I've been doing my whole life? Every breath I take is somehow related to my twin.

"You know, I've been reading about countertransference," I say, trying my best to sound casual. I'm a little proud of my ability to name the condition. "So I'd be careful if I were you."

"You've been reading about *what*?"

"Countertransference. It's when a therapist confuses his feelings for a patient with love. It starts innocently enough. You *think* that you're just trying to help—"

"God, Rain, where did you read *that*?"

I point feebly to the psychology tome on my desk. "I'm most of the way through—"

"Oh, I hate this new hobby of yours!" she exclaims, rolling her eyes. "What's next? Should I nibble on your signature ginseng pretzels to stay calm in case the Freud boogie monster comes knocking?"

I take a page from Ethan's book and ignore the sarcasm. "Actually, the high salt content of pretzels can raise your blood pressure and make you *more* nervous. And ginseng doesn't help with complex psychological issues. I don't think."

"Oh, so you're saying I have complex psychological issues? And that I'm some sort of confused therapist who thinks that Ethan is my *patient*?" I can't tell if she's pissed or amused now, but her crossed arms and raised eyebrows suggest a little of both.

"Well, no—not exactly—" I'm not sure what I was suggesting. I was just excited to diagnose something. That chapter on nurturing and carer's confusion had Hope's name written all over it. Or so I'd thought when I'd read it last night.

"I think *you're* the confused therapist, Rain," she says, pursing her lips. "And I don't like being your patient."

I just want to get off the topic already. It's not really going the way I expected.

(For the blog: *After you piss off your friends, try serving them chocolate-covered potato chips! Chocolate is the best cure for irritability, and potatoes are the ultimate comfort food. Only don't tell them it's for their cranky mood, or they'll just throw them at you. People used to throw food in my face a lot when I was younger.)*

"All right, all right." I clear my throat and slump back against my pillow. "Forget I said that."

She shrugs but doesn't let go of her righteous pout. "Fine, I will. If you promise to stop analyzing me. *Every time* I mention Ethan."

"Okay, I promise. I'm sorry."

The worry fades from her face as she shakes my brother from her mind with a toss of her head. "Let's talk about something else. Or should I say *someone* else?"

"Well, that *is* what I messaged you about."

"Yeah, but your text was really vague. What's going on? Did something happen between you and Liam?"

"You're not going to believe it." I take a deep breath, let the suspense build a little. "Liam asked me to be his lab partner this morning. He actually picked *me*."

She nods slowly and waits, silently, her green eyes wide with expectation. I wait for the rest of her reaction. I love Hope for many reasons, but the greatest thing about her is the way she brims over with excitement about *everything*. Half the pleasure of telling her anything is watching her features light up, her round cheeks glow pink, her curly blond head bob up and down in celebration with me. So after months of pining over a boy who had never once looked in my direction, I thought this news deserved a real bang of a response.

"Okay," she murmurs. "And?"

I hesitate. "That's it. I mean, he chose—there were other people he could have picked—I wasn't—" I splutter to a halt.

I'm completely baffled and a little frustrated. I mean, last week she'd squealed for fifteen minutes when I told her about a new flavor of ice cream at Manny's. I expected at least a small bubble of happiness from her now.

She seems to realize her mistake and her face colors a little. "No—that's great!" she stammers, a little too loudly. "I got confused, that's all. Your text said 'It's finally happening!' so I thought maybe he'd asked you out or something—"

"Asked me *out*?" My voice quavers, and I'm suddenly embarrassed. I should never have texted her at all. Maybe I'd gotten a bit overexcited about the whole thing. But it had seemed so momentous a few hours ago. "How could he have asked me out? I was surprised he even knew my name!"

She sighs and settles back against the wall. "It's Clarkson High School, not Caltech. There are thirty-five kids in the eleventh grade. Everyone knows everyone's name—"

"He could have picked Mike instead of me!" I interrupt heatedly. "Or Angel—"

"Angel barely passed the tenth grade," she says with a shrug. "As for Mike—" She makes a *pow* sound with her lips.

"Oh, that arson charge was like a year ago! And they could never prove that he set his dad's garage on fire."

"The class will be working with Bunsen burners, right?" She's smiling now, and I realize how stupid I just sounded. Of course Liam picked me. There were three people left to choose from after everyone had paired up—and I was simply Miss Process of Elimination. Not Miss Future Girlfriend. God, I really am an idiot.

Hope shrugs sympathetically as I slump against my pillow. "This could be a good thing, Rainey. You've had a crush on this guy for almost a year, right? Now you don't have an excuse anymore. You two have to work together on your science projects. So you'll *have* to talk to him. And you never know—"

I nod and sit up a little straighter. "Well, yeah. I don't know why it's been so hard for me to start a conversation. Talking to people is supposed to be my thing!" It's what I wanted to do with my life. My mom was always saying that psychology was my true calling.

"Sure it is," she remarks sarcastically. "If it means analyzing the crap out of people."

"But there's nothing to analyze about Liam. Don't roll your eyes! I know that everyone thinks that their crush is perfect. But he actually *is* the smartest guy I've ever met. Plus he volunteers with the paramedic team and is a lifeguard at the pool *and* tutors a bunch of ninth graders on the side—as if he's not busy enough staying at the top of the class—"

"Rain," she interrupts, holding up her hands. "I know the guy's resume. He's the class overachiever, future valedictorian blah blah blah. But I'm still trying to understand why you're so nuts about a guy who's never really looked at any girl at our school—"

"You say that like it's a bad thing! Maybe he has other things on his mind."

"He's sixteen. He shouldn't have other things on his mind." She shakes her head. "You know, sometimes I wonder if we're even talking about the same person. Liam isn't exactly—" She breaks off and plucks nervously at her sleeve.

"Yeah, I know you don't think he's cute," I say shortly.

She shrugs and looks away. "That isn't it. Everyone has their type. Just because I'm not into the skinny, curly hair, giant glasses look doesn't mean that you can't be. I'm just trying to figure out why you find it so hard to talk to him. You're really smart and pretty. He should be thrilled to talk to you!"

"Thank you." I can't help smiling at the compliment hiding behind her jokes. "I guess the problem is that I feel like a *nothing* when I'm standing next to him. So I freeze up. My mind goes completely blank."

"So just take it slow, okay? Maybe start with the science experiment and find a way to make it personal. Like—'Hey, Liam, those chemicals are pretty flammable. Aren't you glad that I'm not a pyromaniac who set fire to my dad's garage?' Like that."

"Ha. Very funny, Hope."

"Or how about…" She puckers her lips and sinks her voice into a hoarse whisper. "'Oh, Liam, my name may be Rain, but right now I'm hotter than the exothermic reaction in that beaker—'"

I smack her on the shoulder. "Shut up! That's just—"

"You can even use chemistry as an excuse to ask him out!"

She's shaking with laughter now. "'Wow, that lab made an awful sulfur smell, Liam.'" She fans her face in mock disgust. "'You want to go somewhere quiet and romantic where the air doesn't smell like fart?'"

"All right, enough!" I smother a smile and duck my head. "You can stop making fun of me now."

"And, you know, if all else fails," she suggests between a hiccup and a giggle, "you can just keep stalking him silently, like you've been doing all year."

"How can I be stalking him?" I protest. "He hasn't posted anything new on Instagram in three weeks and nothing on Facebook for seven." I pause for a moment as she bursts out laughing again. "Okay, fine. You've made your point."

She wipes her eyes with the back of her hand. "It won't be as hard as you think," she reassures me, her voice suddenly serious again. "What do you talk about with everyone else? I mean, besides your recipe fetish."

"What's wrong with that? Guys *like* food—"

"*No*, Rain."

"Just because you threw up that time—"

"You served me pancakes with hot chili sauce!"

"It's a thing! I swear—"

"You didn't even warn me! It looked like maple syrup."

"Syrup is *boring*. And I just thought—"

"Be boring, Rain. At least in the beginning. I'm serious. And don't mention the blog."

"It has twenty followers."

"Good for you. Forget the puke pancakes for a minute. Rain, you have so much going for you! Your future is all mapped out in your head. That's something to talk about. And then there's the 'rules' that you're always telling me about and your theories about everyone—"

"I thought the whole point was to make me sound normal."

"I'm working with what I've got," she says, grinning. "Don't look at me like that. I'm trying to tell you that you're awesome. I mean, you've practically raised your brother with those rules. That's pretty impressive, isn't it? You can talk about Ethan—the things you do to help take care of him—"

"No!" I cut her off before she can finish the thought.

She blinks at me, her eyes blank with surprise. "I just meant—"

"Ethan is not a topic of conversation," I say shortly. My voice comes out harsher than I intended, and the air between us suddenly goes cold. "I don't gossip about my brother. To *anyone*."

She looks genuinely hurt now, and her eyes narrow defensively. "I didn't think you felt that way," she mutters. "I never thought you'd be ashamed—"

"I'm not! That's not how I feel at all!" *No one* understands this part of my life. Everyone thinks that they get it, thinks that they can imagine what it feels like to be tied to someone you love, tied to him every minute of every day. But they can never understand. Even my best friend doesn't get it. She just thinks of him as a hot puzzle that hasn't been solved. "I have *never* been ashamed of

Ethan," I tell her, trying to keep my voice steady but failing. "He's the most important person in my life. But I'm not going to use him that way, all right? I won't use him to get a date."

She shakes her head and pushes herself off the bed. "You get a little crazy about this subject, you know that? If I even mention his name, your hair practically stands up like you're getting ready to pounce on me. I didn't say that you should 'use' him. But if he really is the most important person in your life, it isn't a crime to talk about him."

I don't answer her right away. This is the closest Hope and I have ever gotten to a real fight, and for a moment I'm tempted to take it all the way and have it out with her. How can she call me crazy? She moved to Clarkson two years ago, so she missed Ethan's four mute years, the doctor visits, the string of therapists, the awful transition into elementary school, the difficult choice my mother and I had to make when the principal insisted we withdraw him from the school. Hope wasn't there through any of that, so she has no right to judge me. I want to tell her that. But haven't I just watched her flirt with him? How does she expect me to discuss this casually with her now?

"Maybe we should change the subject," I suggest.

Hope sighs and wanders over to the window. "I'm sorry I upset you," she says in a gentle voice. "It's my fault for bringing it up. I know how sensitive the topic is for you."

I want to protest, insist that I'm not being oversensitive—but I know anything I say will only prove her point. I'm trying to think of a good response when we're interrupted by a sharp knock on the bedroom door. "Hello, Rain. Mom just came home," my brother says, peering into my room. "It's time for our run."

I'm a little relieved to hear him. Recently our forty-minute run had become kind of a burden to me. It was yet another unvarying activity in our daily routine. Every afternoon, come rain, shine, or Montana blizzard, Ethan and I would tie up our running shoes and do exercise therapy together. It was originally my idea when I'd observed that my brother was calmer and happier after physical activity. Rain and Ethan's daily run had been my solution, and now I was stuck with it. No matter what else was going on in my life, I had to be home at four o'clock for our jog. Today, however, I welcome the excuse to say goodbye to Hope. By tomorrow I'll probably feel better about our disagreement, but right now, my unsaid words are beginning to chafe.

Hope looks disappointed. "Okay, I guess I'll head home." She glances hopefully at Ethan, but he turns quickly and shuts the door behind him.

"Sorry about that." I grab my shoes and water bottle. "I have to go."

"Maybe one day I can join you two," she suggests brightly. "I could use the exercise. And it would shake things up a little."

I hope she's joking, but I decide to play along. "Sure, maybe one day." *Yeah, right*, I think. When we're a hundred years old and Ethan can't see too well. Maybe then he won't notice if we invite Hope along.

I call out goodbye to my mother who's standing in the kitchen and staring in bewildered silence at the giant 3-D colon hologram. "The refrigerator is in the backyard," I remark over my shoulder. I don't bother to explain. Mom will put together the pieces on her own.

## Cooking with Rain
### SERENITY THROUGH YOUR GUT

*Where I answer all your burning food-related questions!*

**Dear Rain:** Have you always been a foodie? I'm more of a mac 'n' cheese guy. The kind from the box.

—Wacky Mac from Missoula

**Dear Wacky:** Thank you so much for writing to me! Would you like ideas for recipes, or do you want to chat about food in general? I respect all lifestyle and culinary choices, but I hope you don't *really* prefer your cheese in dust form. How about trying Rain's super easy Mac 'n' Cheese recipe? The almond milk and pinch of nutmeg give it a little zest. Let me know what you think!

## ETHAN'S JOURNAL:

"Particularly within the past few decades, proponents
of deafness as a culture have asserted that deafness
is not a pathology and therefore does not need to
be 'fixed.'" (Megan A. Jones, *Disability Studies
Quarterly*, 2002.)

### My Observation:

I used to reject this. Not using modern advances
seemed silly and backward.

Recent experiences have led me to reconsider.
If I couldn't hear noise, I might find it easier to
leave the house. I wouldn't need to worry about
the roar of a busy restaurant, the squeal of a
baby on a train, the chatter of my classmates. I
could ignore my sister's voice through the thin
walls. I could forget Hope.

# Chapter 3

Ethan is already on the front porch when I finish tying my laces; he nods briefly when I join him and, without a word, bounds down the steps and takes off running.

We jog side by side in silence for a few minutes, our rubber soles thumping rhythmically against the sidewalk, the brisk October wind whistling in our ears. The road stretches quietly ahead of us, the distant hum of cars on the interstate and the silent majesty of the snowcapped Rocky Mountains are comforting and familiar. As my breathing quickens and my pulse begins to pound, I glance up and grin at my brother. I truly love these moments. I love the simple perfection of the two of us, all alone with no one around, no expectations or pressure or stress. Just the sound of running shoes, the clean mountain air, and the sweet, unspoiled smile on my brother's face. He's running as he always does, arms slightly akimbo, legs wide, like a toddler trying to keep his balance, but his face is peaceful and happy. His skin is flushed; the wind whips his long hair around his cheeks and open lips. We look like a strange team; no one would ever guess we were twins. Ethan is long and lanky, nearly six feet tall, with our mother's Nordic fairness and delicate features. I'm small—almost a foot shorter than my brother—olive-skinned with long, straight, dark hair and my father's strong, arched eyebrows and black eyes.

My breathing relaxes as my body falls into a comfortable running rhythm, and after a few minutes I call my brother's name. He startles and stumbles forward; I reach my arm to steady him, but he regains his balance and resumes a slower jog. "Sorry, I didn't mean to mess you up," I say, "I just wanted to tell you that I love our running time together."

He doesn't say anything for a moment, and I'm not sure if he's heard me. Sometimes you have to repeat yourself several times before it registers, especially if he's concentrating on another task. Right now I know that he's completely absorbed in putting one foot in front of the other and struggling to control the clumsy limbs that have troubled him since he was little. I'm not expecting a deep conversation under the circumstances. Still, there's something I've been dying to ask him.

"Efan, I was just wondering—"

He turns his head to me for a second and then looks forward again. He's listening.

"You don't have to answer right now. I was just curious about something."

We jog on for a few seconds and then he gasps out, "Curious about something?"

I know that it's hard for him to run and form sentences at the same time so I press forward, pleased he's at least registered my words. "Yeah. I was wondering what you think of Hope."

It's too vague a question, but I can't think of any other way to put it. I'm suddenly self-conscious about the whole idea. Maybe I shouldn't be; Ethan is sixteen, and it's perfectly natural that he would think about girls. Just because he's never spoken about it doesn't mean the feelings aren't there. And my mother is always telling me to relate to him as I would to a neurotypical brother. Plenty of siblings talk to each other about their crushes, so why shouldn't we?

He says nothing for a minute, and I think that maybe he's zoned out again when suddenly he slows his pace to a walk and turns in my direction. His eyes don't quite meet mine, but he's concentrating on his answer, and that's enough. "She's short, like you," he tells me finally, "and also fatter. She smells like licorice most of the time."

I suppress a sigh. Answers like that make people think that Ethan is mentally challenged even though he's quite intelligent. But literal responses tend to throw people off. I know I should have phrased the question differently. That's rule number three: When talking to Ethan, be as exact, truthful, and direct as possible.

He seems uncomfortable suddenly, and he shifts back and forth beside me. We've paused a few feet in front of Manny's Ice Cream Shop, which is our halfway point. He glances over his shoulder and gestures roughly with his hands. "We stopped running," he states loudly.

"I know. I need to rest for a little bit."

He doesn't say anything, but his eyes dart around the street, and he bounces nervously on his heels.

"Let's go inside, okay?" I suggest. "I could use a snack."

He stays quiet and continues to bounce.

"You like Manny's," I remind him patiently. "He does the sterile scrubbing procedure, exactly like you've shown him. I've checked."

He looks unconvinced, but after a moment he nods and follows me into the shop.

We settle down at the counter, and Manny saunters up to us to take our order. "Sweet potato cashew shake coming right up," he declares. "I ordered the sweet potatoes especially for you, Rainey. Not much demand for those in an ice cream shop."

"Manny, that's awesome! You tried my recipe?"

He grins. "Yup. And I licked the glass clean."

"It would be even better with a shot of bourbon," I whisper.

"I'm not trying to get arrested," he replies with a wink. "Let me guess, strawberry shake for Mr. Ethan?"

Ethan smiles, and his shoulders relax a little. This place is clean, quiet, and familiar; the smells are pleasant, and there is no one there but us. Perfect. No reason to worry, I tell myself. Ethan is breathing regularly, and the cornered rabbit look has left his eyes. Manny waddles off to fiddle with the smoothie machine, and I use the opportunity to pick up where we left off.

"Hey, Efan, can you look at me?" I suggest.

He focuses on a corner of my sleeve. Close enough.

"Back to what we were talking about—" I hesitate and take a deep breath. "I was just wondering—do you think that Hope is pretty?"

He blinks once before answering. "Yes."

His answer is so quick and definite that my mouth drops open in surprise. "Really?" I blurt out. "You do?" I'm both shocked and pleased, and for a minute I can't think of anything to say. It's not that I don't agree with him; Hope has always been pretty, and recently she'd graduated to stunning. She'd even dated Grayson, the class hottie. They'd been the "it" couple for most of sophomore year.

But none of that stuff had ever interested my brother before. So I can't believe Ethan has noticed her.

"Really?" I persist. "Well, that's—that's great."

"Why did you ask?" He looks confused. "I thought you already knew that. She's your friend."

"I do. It's just—I just—" I can't find the words to express my disbelief. "I just wanted to know how *you* saw her."

"Oh. Okay." The perplexed look vanishes. He seems to consider for a moment, then takes a deep breath. "Her eyes have thick, dark limbal rings," he declares. "This feature has been shown in studies to influence facial attractiveness. The theory is that because the ring tends to fade with age and medical problems, a prominent limbal ring gives an honest indicator of youth and is therefore preferred by the opposite sex. The distance between the pupils of her eyes in relation to the width of her face is about forty-six percent, which is considered to be an attractive ratio. Her nostrils are not too wide or thin or long, and they don't have hair in them. She has large, red lips, which are attractive except when she laughs, and her mouth gets very big. Her teeth are white and straight except for a chip on the left incisor. Her skin is clear but there's a three-millimeter birth-mark on her upper neck. Her hair is very curly and long with no bald patches or oiliness. So if you take all the facial features together and consider them as a whole, the good far outweighs the bad." He takes another deep breath and clears his throat. My mouth is still hanging open, and I'm fighting the urge to laugh. But Ethan isn't done yet.

"Her body proportions are also attractive," he continues, picking up speed. "She isn't bony or obese. Her waist to hip ratio is seven to ten, which are the preferred proportions in this country. Her breasts are symmetrical and the appropriate size for her height, which is—"

"Okay, okay!" I hold my hand out to stop him. "I don't want to hear about my best friend's boobs, thank you very much!"

He raises his eyebrows and turns his head away. "If you didn't want to hear about it—"

"Yeah, I know, I shouldn't have asked." I chuckle softly to myself. "I'm sorry, I just had no idea that you liked her. Or that you'd *analyzed* her like that."

He turns his head back in my direction and focuses on some point past my shoulder. "What?"

"Come on, *look* at me when I'm talking to you," I urge him quietly. "What are you staring at back there?"

There's a bothered, frustrated wrinkle between his brows, and he slowly lifts his head to meet my gaze. "I'm trying to hear what you're saying," he tells me softly. There's a pained look in his eyes. "It's easier when I don't look at you. What did you say before?"

"I said that I had no idea that you liked Hope."

"I don't like her." His response is sharp and automatic and feels like a slap in the face.

"Oh."

I turn away from him to hide my disappointment and focus on Manny, who's just walked up and set our drinks down on the counter. He places two napkins and straws in front of us, wheezes loudly for a moment, and then shuffles off. I run my fingers over the cool droplets on my glass and draw a sad face in the film of condensation. The doodle reminds me of a game I used to play with Ethan years ago, when we were trying to teach him what facial expressions meant. "Look at my mouth, Efan," I would say. "See how it's open and my eyes are all narrow? That means that my feelings are hurt."

I wonder if he remembers that now and if he can interpret the hurt look on my face. It seems like a lot to expect from him. My feelings don't even make sense to *me* at the moment. I don't understand why his abrupt rejection of my friend has upset me so much. It's not like I want them to be together. An hour ago, I was actively trying to discourage Hope from doing just that. So why does it bother me that he's rejected her?

"Why don't you like her?" I ask him after a moment.

He seems to consider the question. His forehead is furrowed and his long fingers pick nervously at the napkin in front of him. "I don't know what she wants from me," he murmurs finally, his tone unusually quiet and hesitant.

"That's it?" I ask. "Well, I don't think you should worry about that. I bet if you relax you'll actually enjoy talking to her. I'm pretty sure that she just wants to be friends with you. For now."

He shakes his head emphatically. "That's not what I meant," he says, his voice edged with frustration. "When she's near me I feel like I did at school. Remember how you wanted me to try to make friends? And I did. I kept trying. And I kept getting it wrong."

He's right about that. I remember watching Ethan walk up to a new classmate and introduce himself, a touch too loudly. I'd usually be a few paces behind him, smiling my encouragement and holding my breath. But then, before the kid had an opportunity to reply, Ethan would rattle off a slew of random questions. "What's your favorite color? Do you like dogs? Did you see the Learning Channel's program about heart transplants?" The person would step back a pace, their eyebrows would go up—and Ethan just wouldn't take the cue.

The nicer people would simply answer politely and walk away as quickly as possible. The less-nice people—well, they're the reason Ethan is being homeschooled now.

"But you know Hope already," I reassure him. "She's been over a bunch of times. So it shouldn't be worse than meeting someone new—"

"It's much worse," he counters. "I get dizzy when I look at her. She tries to stand too close to me. And talk to me. And I have no idea what she's thinking. With you and Mom I can sometimes guess. But I don't have any idea about her."

I can't help smiling at this. "Everyone feels like that around someone they like."

"But I *don't* like her!" he bursts out, his voice echoing harshly around the small shop. "I like you and Mom. I know what you expect from me. When Hope comes over she changes everything. She makes me feel sick. How can you like someone who makes you feel like you can't breathe?"

His fair skin is flushed to the roots of his hair, and he's drumming his fingers in agitation. My instinct is to say something calming and move on to another topic, but I know I can't. I feel like a scientist on the verge of a breakthrough. Ethan talks to me a lot, but never about his feelings. Maybe that's why I was so disappointed earlier. I didn't want them to get together. I was just hoping for a glimpse of my brother's heart.

"But I feel like that too sometimes!" I tell him. "There's this guy at school that makes me nervous just like that—" I pause uncertainly and glance self-consciously at Ethan. Talking about Liam was definitely not part of my plan. I clear my throat and start again. "What I meant was that girls are nervous around guys too. So I know exactly what you're going through."

"I know you have a crush on Liam," he informs me. His voice is flat, emotionless. "But you don't know what I'm going through."

I blink stupidly at him and make a helpless sputtering noise before I find my words. "How—how did—how do you…"

"How did I what?"

"How do you know about Liam?"

He grunts and reaches out for his untouched drink. "I can hear Hope's voice through the walls."

I drop my head in embarrassment. I don't mind that he knows about my crush; there's nothing so terribly private about it. And it's not like he's going to tell anyone. But now I can't remember what else Hope and I had talked about in my room. I'm sure we've discussed Ethan dozens of times. What else has he heard?

I stand up abruptly and push away my milkshake. "I have to go to the bathroom," I tell him shortly. I need a moment to myself, to think about what to say to him. This afternoon's conversation is slowly coming back to me. One phrase in particular echoes in my mind: "Ethan will *never* get close to anyone..."

My guilty conscience follows me into the bathroom and pricks at me as I close the door behind me. How could I have said that about him? I'm supposed to be on Ethan's side, his only bridge to the outside world. And while we're together I've always done my best; I'm constantly encouraging him to try new things, to interact with people. But behind his back—when it really counts, I have no faith in him, and I'll blab my doubts to anyone who will listen.

And he heard me. He must have heard me.

I have to think of some way to make it up to him. *I bet if you relax you'll actually enjoy talking to her.* God, I'm such a hypocrite. No wonder he'd looked so pained. I'd just told Hope that he would never get close to anyone. And then gave him advice that directly contradicted what I'd just said to her. How could I expect Ethan to process my own contradictory feelings when I couldn't even make sense of them?

It was all going too fast, I realize. Of course I wanted him to experience new emotions and forge new friendships. But the key to progress is baby steps.

I could start by offering to take him somewhere. A token of my trust in him. A trip to the mall or a movie. We hadn't been out together in ages. I'd been too worried about Ethan dissolving into a panic attack. But I could try harder. Maybe Hope was right. Maybe he is lonely at home, even though he doesn't show it.

There's a muffled swell of voices from outside and a jingling sound of the bell on the ice cream shop door. Did Ethan actually leave without me? He used to have this tendency to wander off, but he hasn't done that in years. I quickly dry my hands, push open the door, and glance around the shop.

Ethan is still there, sitting in the same place at the counter. But he's not alone. I feel a queasy knot forming in my stomach. *Oh no*, I groan to myself. *Not again*.

A few people from our grade have just come in and are hovering by the counter, laughing and messing around. My brother hasn't moved from his stool, but he seems to have sunk deeper into his drink, his back hunched over, his shoulder blades jutting out like skinny wings. His eyes are fixed straight ahead, and he appears to be trying desperately to ignore the teeming group around him.

Just leave him alone, I pray silently. For once, just order your stupid ice cream and leave my brother alone.

But even as I start toward them I know it's too late. Ethan has always been an irresistible target for bullies and bored kids looking for a distraction. And Mike, the leader of this group, is obviously very bored right now.

Mike saunters over to him and throws a friendly arm over my brother's shoulders. Ethan flinches beneath his touch and shrinks even farther, his chin almost touching his milkshake. "Hey, how's it going?" Mike bellows inches from Ethan's ear. I cringe in sympathy and step forward automatically to intervene. But even as I move to help him, I know there's nothing I can do. This is the worst violation of rule one, the kind of overstimulation that can drive Ethan berserk. And yet—technically, Mike hasn't done anything wrong, so scolding him for patting Ethan on the back or speaking too loudly feels silly, like telling everyone my brother is a sleeping baby who mustn't be disturbed. I can't do that to him, especially after what I'd said to Hope that afternoon. I need to let him deal with this on his own. That's what I tell myself anyway as I stand by dumbly and watch Ethan's world crumble into his half-finished strawberry shake. His face is practically in the glass at this point.

"Dude, it's been forever," Mike continues, whacking him again across the back and stepping closer. "Where've you been?" He's grinning maliciously, and he winks broadly at Angel who skips over to him and snakes her arm around his waist. Ethan doesn't answer, but I see his fingers begin to twitch around his glass. *Oh no,* I tell him silently. *Please, Ethan, don't do that. Not around these people. They'll just make fun of you more.*

I'm suddenly aware of the noise they're all making around us, a pleasant roar of humor and fun to them—and a deafening screech to my sensitive brother. Jenna's popping gum, the throbbing beat from Grayson's iPhone, Nick's drumming palms smacking against the counter, and Mike and Angel, the smirking twosome, flashing too-wide smiles and reeking of bad cologne and malice.

"Guys, leave him alone," I hiss through gritted teeth. I have to say something, even if it makes no difference.

And it really doesn't. Mike barely glances in my direction; he's staring intently at my brother. Ethan's hands rise involuntarily from his glass and begin to move, vibrating subtly at first and then in hypnotic rhythm, snapping over and over in front of his face, his eyes focused on his clicking, clicking, clicking fingers as if his life depended on it. Everyone in the room has dropped whatever they were doing and turned to stare at Ethan's manic hands.

I need to get him out of here. When Ethan becomes anxious he sometimes calms himself by "stimming." It's a good coping tool when he's among people who understand. But right now, I know it will only make everything worse. And I don't want him to be in the middle of this crowd if he's heading for a meltdown. I push past Angel and whisper urgently to him, "Let's get going, okay?"

He doesn't respond, doesn't seem to be aware of me at all. Behind me there's a rumble of suppressed laughter, and I turn to see Mike flapping his wrists, his face contorted in a goofy grimace, his tongue hanging out of gaping lips. "Stop it!" I scream at him. There's no response from any of them, except that the giggling gets a little louder. I stomp my foot and shove Mike away from brother. "He can't help it, okay? You're just making him worse! He wants to be left alone!"

Manny has finally emerged from the back room. He hurries over to the counter and leans over to my brother. "You all right, buddy?"

A whining moan escapes from Ethan's lips, and he slides quickly off his stool, upsetting his glass and spilling strawberry mush all over the table. He shudders when he sees me and closes his eyes. "Rain burrito!" he groans.

*Oh, God*, I think. *Not that. No no no no no...*

Behind me there are squeals of laughter and someone shouts out, "Try Taco Bell, freak!"

I can't listen to them. I have to get him home.

"Rain burrito, Rain burrito, Rain burrito..." Ethan is muttering it over and over again. If anyone missed it the first time, they've definitely heard it now. As my brother rocks back and forth and chants the nonsensical phrase, Angel gives Ethan a sympathetic look and steps over to him. "Are you okay, honey?" she murmurs, and puts her hand out to touch his face.

It's the final straw. He lets out a sound between a yelp and a sob and bolts for the exit.

The bell dings, the door swings open, and then he's running, racing down the street as if a mob is chasing him down. I shout a vague apology at Manny and then take off, calling Ethan's name as I sprint after him.

I've never seen my brother run this fast. I've never seen anyone run this fast. He covers the entire road and half of our street before I finally manage to catch up with him. We're both panting and gasping as the cold air stings our faces, but Ethan's voice comes out clear and urgent as we round the corner to our house. "Please, Rain, please—"

"I know, I know, we're almost home," I shout. "We're almost there, I've got you."

We burst through the front door and clamber for the stairs, tripping and grabbing for the banister as we go. From the corner of my eye I register the surprised faces of my mother and Hope (who's still at my house for some reason), and then they're gone as we race past them to my brother's room.

"Lie on your side and inhale deeply," I order, but he's collapsed in a heap already, a long, quivering figure on the threadbare rug. I rush over to the closet and pull out Ethan's "heavy" blanket, the weighted fifteen-pound comforter he's used for years, ever since my weight stopped being enough to calm him. I haul it over him and lay it down over his trembling body, spreading it out carefully to cover all of him. "Please, Rain—" he gasps, again, his voice catching on my name. "Please. Rain burrito."

I nod silently and kneel down by his side, then slowly, gently wrap my arms around the blanket and push my shoulders into his back. "You're okay, now," I murmur. "I've got you now. You're okay."

It's strange and magical at the same time. Beneath the blanket, my brother's shaking quiets and then stops, and he exhales weakly into the floor. I can feel the tension and pain seeping out of him. All I have to do is hold him for a little longer. "It's okay, I've got you."

"Rain burrito," he sighs, and buries his face deeper into the rug.

"That's right. A couple more minutes of Rain burrito and you'll be as good as new."

I hear a rustling noise at the door and glance up to find my mother and Hope standing at the entrance. Mom looks tired and washed out; she's leaning against the doorpost and rubbing her forehead. Hope just looks stunned and helpless. She's never seen Ethan at his worst.

"What's a Rain burrito?" she whispers to my mother.

"It's—it's one of Ethan's coping tools," she explains quietly. "Our therapist recommended a deep pressure hold to calm his panic attacks. I used to wrap him in a bear hug when he was little. But Rain was always better at it—even though she was smaller than him. She'd take a beanbag and put it on top of him and then lie down on it. They called it a Rain burrito, because Ethan was wrapped up snugly like a—well, like a burrito." She laughs weakly. "He hasn't needed one in a while. I don't know what happened." She can't keep the disappointment from her voice.

"What do you think?" I growl at them. "*People* happened."

My mother nods and turns away. "I'll be downstairs if you need me, Rain."

Hope follows her out, and I hear her voice echoing from the first floor. "I don't get it. *What* happened?"

"He gets teased when he goes out," my mother tells her. "Sometimes he can handle it. And sometimes—"

I scramble up from the floor and shut the door to block out their conversation. He doesn't need to hear them. "Are you okay?" I ask my brother as he shifts uneasily under the blanket. "Do you want me to press on your shoulders again?"

He sits up slowly and pushes the comforter off his back. His face is still flushed and damp with sweat, but his breathing is slow and normal. "No, I'm fine. Thank you."

"No problem."

He gazes silently at his hands for a moment. "I'm fine," he repeats. "You don't need to stay."

I rise to my feet. "Okay. I'll go start dinner then?"

"I have to study my Netter's," he says, reaching out for his anatomy textbook and flipping it open.

"I'll call you when dinner is ready."

He nods and seems to focus on his book, but as I push the door open he suddenly looks up at me. "Rain, wait." His finger is still poised over his book.

"I don't have time for an anatomy lecture, Efan."

"It's not about anatomy. I want to ask you something."

"Okay. What's up?"

He hesitates and drops his head, his eyes focusing on the heavy blanket on his knees. His hair falls over to cover his face so I can't quite read his expression, but his shoulders are slumped forward. "Just now…" he stammers. "When I was on the floor—"

"Yeah?"

"With the blanket."

I step forward and kneel down in front of him. I still can't see his face; as I move toward him he ducks his head even lower. "What about the blanket, Efan?"

He lifts tortured eyes to mine. "She saw that, didn't she?"

I don't understand what he's asking for a moment. "Who?"

He brushes the hair back from his forehead. "Hope. She saw that."

I'm not surprised the last few minutes are a bit blurry for him. Ethan's meltdowns are like painful sunbursts in his head, obscuring everything.

"I guess she did," I admit. "I'm not sure why she didn't go home when we went out for our run but…yeah. I suppose she did see it."

"Oh."

He drops his head again, and his shoulders droop even lower.

"Maybe it's a good thing that she saw—" The words are out before I have a chance to reconsider. I realize even as I say it that I'm making a mistake. I was just trying to comfort him. But you can't blurt stuff out without explaining your meaning. Not with my brother. Rule number three. Be as honest, direct, and truthful as possible. No hints or subtlety. What was I thinking?

And sure enough, Ethan lifts his head and looks directly at me, his eyes widening with curiosity and hope.

"It is? Why? Why is it a good thing?"

Why did I open my big mouth? What am I supposed to say

to him now? There's no reasonable answer that will make him feel any better.

"I don't know." I falter to a stop, confused and embarrassed by the desperate question in his eyes. Damn it, the one time he remembers to make eye contact, he has to burn through me with that intense stare of his. "Well, you *said* you didn't like her—"

"So?" He doesn't break his glare. "How is it good?"

"I—I don't know." I hesitate, and glance toward the open door uneasily. I lower my voice a little before continuing. "Maybe now that she's seen a meltdown she won't want to hang around here so much and bother you—"

"Oh." He exhales sharply, as if I've smacked him. When I look back at him he pushes the blanket off his knees and scrambles to his feet, turning his back to me as he does so.

"Wait, Efan, hold on. I...I didn't mean it like that—"

"You should go make dinner. You said you were going to make dinner."

"But...I thought you *wanted* Hope to leave you alone—"

"Mom can't cook. You always make dinner."

"I was trying to help—"

"*Just go away!*"

I open my mouth to protest, to apologize, to say *something*, but I catch a glimpse of his wounded, baffled face and shut my mouth again.

When he doesn't speak, I leave the room and close the door quietly behind me.

# Cooking with Rain
## SERENITY THROUGH YOUR GUT

*Where I answer all your burning food-related questions!*

**Dear Rain:** I tried your mac 'n' cheese recipe. I couldn't find almond milk (and I was out of normal milk) so I used coffee creamer. No nutmeg so I topped it with Funyuns. It was okay.

—Wacky Mac from Missoula

**Dear Wacky:** I encourage experimentation; that's how great recipes are made! But—coffee creamer and Funyuns? Not okay. ☺

## ETHAN'S JOURNAL:

**Three Most Likely Causes for Manny's Heavy Wheezing:**

1) Severe asthma
2) Chronic obstructive pulmonary disease
   (less likely as he is not a smoker)
3) Heart failure/pulmonary edema

Need further history for a more accurate diagnosis, but can't go back to Manny's Ice Cream Shop anymore.

# Chapter 4

No matter what Hope had said about chemistry lab and natural conversation starters, I had no faith I would actually figure out how to speak to Liam when the time came. Definitely not on our first lab date, anyway. Still, if I was going to be struck dumb like the Little Mermaid when I mixed hydrocarbons with Prince Charming, I figured at least *looking* perfect would be a good start. Then maybe he wouldn't notice I couldn't talk to him. After a few more consultations, Hope had decided I should just work the silent, smoldering look until I scraped up enough confidence to speak. She also suggested vanilla shampoo and cinnamon pumpkin lotion, which was my favorite part of the plan. (Hope's compromise: I could smell like food, but I couldn't talk about it.)

In addition to smelling like a bakery, I'd also planned my outfit the night before. I sent pictures of half my wardrobe to Hope and got her vote (white top because it brings out my olive skin, skinny jeans, high-heeled ankle boots and black opal earrings to match my eyes). Her makeup tips were to go heavy on the mascara, light on lip gloss. Then hair—straightened and pulled back to bring out my cheekbones and eyebrows. According to her I'm all about the eyebrows—whatever that means.

So when I walk into school the next morning I feel polished and ready—but, just in case, I stop by Hope's locker to get a final touch up. She's talking to Kathy and Marcus—or "the octopus" as we call them in private—and they wave me over as I approach. Kathy has her hands in Marcus's pockets and Marcus's fingers are lost somewhere in her sweater. Those two are *that* couple, the one you can't look at for longer than ten seconds before their PDA hits you in the face. They've been together since the fourth grade, first as best friends and then eventually as a couple, inseparable and adorable in a way that's a little gross. They've even begun to look alike—slim and small with large, dark eyes and straight black hair cut in matching styles. Nobody can picture them as anything but the octopus, two heads merged into one and eight limbs wrapped around their common body. Hope thinks that if they ever fought there would be an awful rending sound like a giant piece of Velcro being ripped in half.

"Well, don't you look nice!" Marcus exclaims, grinning broadly at me.

"Thank you," I reply. "It's all Hope's work."

Kathy cocks her head over to the side and studies me thoughtfully. "I'd lose the pink scarf," she muses. "It looks like you're trying too hard."

Marcus appears scandalized. "Then the entire outfit is just black and white! The scarf brings it all together, baby."

She turns to her boyfriend and gives him an adoring smile.

"You're right. I didn't even think of that. Rainey, you should keep the scarf. Definitely."

They gaze lovingly into each other's eyes, and I concentrate on some invisible dirt under my fingernails. When I look up again they're still at it.

"God, you two," I mutter. "It's like eight in the morning. Take a breather already."

Kathy breaks the passionate stare and fakes an embarrassed pout. "Sorry. We can't help it... We're just—"

"Yeah. I know. I get it."

"You can laugh at us all you want," Marcus says, smiling, "but you'll act the same way if things work out with you and Liam."

"Work out?" I protest. "I'm not asking him on a date! We're doing a few chemistry experiments together. He never even noticed me before yesterday."

Marcus shrugs, and he and Kathy exchange a knowing smirk. "We'll see." Their arms intertwine, their heads come together, and they walk away as one, whispering about me before they're even out of earshot. "You know," he says, "sometimes I think Rain just needs to take some risks. Put her feelings out there."

"I know. She's so careful, about everything—"

"Except with food. Remember the Chia Pet pudding?"

"I can still hear you!" I shout after them. "And it was chia seed!"

One of them giggles, but they don't break their stride.

I turn back to Hope who's laughing quietly, her face hidden by her locker door.

"I warned them that it wasn't ready yet," I tell her mournfully. "But they grabbed it out of my lunch bag. I can't believe that Marcus posted it on Instagram. And titled it 'Rain's famous sperm pudding.'"

"Yeah, I saw that pic."

"*Everyone* saw that pic. I'm pretty sure that's where my twenty blog followers came from in the first place."

She wrinkles her nose. "Oh. I was hoping you wouldn't make the connection."

"I didn't really mind at first. And one guy has started writing in now. I think I'm really helping him!"

"Someone you know?"

"Total stranger. He hasn't mentioned the sperm pudding—yet. I'm hoping he hasn't seen it. Everyone who's seen it is either grossed out or thinks it's hilarious. Last week Grayson stopped me in the hall and told me he'd like to donate some ingredients."

"Ugh, what a douche." She sniffs at her ex-boyfriend, who's standing with his friend at the end of the hall. She always refers to Grayson by that name (though sometimes she substitutes "turd") even though she's never really explained what happened between the two of them. There was some awful fight on Valentine's Day (the Octopus called it the Valentine's Day Massacre), and then they stopped speaking to each other. But whenever I asked her why they broke up, she'd always change the subject. "I heard what happened at Manny's yesterday," she says abruptly. "I'm really sorry they gave you and Ethan a hard time."

I shrug. "Yeah, well. That kind of thing used to happen all the time when Ethan was in school. But he's been out of Clarkson High for two years now. And there are still some jerks who go out of their way to hurt him."

"It's high school. What do you expect? There's not much we can do."

"I guess."

I hoist my bag over my shoulder and glare silently at the bullies, who cheerfully ignore me, though I see Grayson shift slightly away from me as I pass him. *It isn't fair*, I think, bitterly. Why do people like that always get away with being mean? Why didn't anyone ever do anything to stop them? I throw one last dirty look at them.

*(Blog idea: Revenge Milkshake [or Rain Uses Her Powers for Evil]: 2 cups of ice cream, 3 tablespoons of chocolate syrup, and half a cup of breast milk. Blend well and serve topped with whipped cream, if desired. Serve to the asshole in your life, then after he/she eats, reveal the secret ingredient and run.)*

As I turn away, I see Mike lift his hands and flap them in front of Grayson's face. Their laughter echoes through the halls as I freeze in place. They're *still* making fun of him. I feel my pulse rise and my skin grow hot as I swallow against a tightening throat. I'm watching them mock my brother, and I'm standing there doing nothing about it. My helpless twin, who's now at home alone because of these—

"Assholes!"

The word is out of my mouth before I have a chance to think. The two guys turn around at once and stare at me open-mouthed.

"*What* did you say?"

For a moment, I'm just as shocked as they are. I'm not particularly shy or anything, but calling out two guys in the middle of the school hallway? That isn't my style. It's one of my personal rules: avoid confrontation and never pick fights because Ethan might get caught in the crossfire.

But this time my brother isn't here to get hurt. So I might as well finish it.

"I said that you're an asshole, Mike," I repeat, louder, so that the growing crowd behind me can hear. "You're the big macho guy who's such a pussy that he'll pick on a guy who can't defend himself."

I sense Hope materialize beside me. She leans over and gently lays a restraining hand over my shoulder. "Come on now, Rain. Let's go," she murmurs, but I shake her off and turn to face my new enemies.

"No, that's fine," Mike growls, advancing toward us. "Your brother's bigger than me. He's welcome to stand up for himself if he wants." I feel Hope moving backward, but I don't budge. I won't give him the satisfaction of watching me cower. He slowly raises his clenched fists in front of me and then with a dramatic flourish loosens them and deliberately begins to flap them inches from my face. "So where is he, then? Why is his sister here instead of him?"

I grab his hand and push it away. "He isn't here because of people like you."

He pulls his arm out of my grip and laughs. "Good. We don't need retards like him in this school." His voice echoes around the hall, and I hear a rumble of agreement from some of the students in the growing crowd around us.

"*Don't* call him that! Don't you *dare* use that word—" I'm choking on my own frustration. There's no way to explain why I'm so angry now. Words don't mean anything to them. I just want to launch myself at Mike here and now, to punch and tear at him until the rage in me is satisfied.

But the school bell rings, shattering the tense silence. Mr. Travers, the principal, emerges from around the corner and hovers ominously behind Hope. "What's going on here, guys?" he grumbles. The crowd around us shrinks back under his glare. Some of the kids begin to melt away through the open classroom doors, and Mike crosses his arms and mutters something under his breath to Grayson.

But I'm not ready to leave it yet. "My brother is brilliant, and he's going to do great things," I tell him proudly. "And you're going to spend the rest of your sad existence burning shit to the ground."

There's a ripple of laughter, and some of the kids near me applaud and hoot their approval. I turn away from them with a triumphant smile and link my arm through Hope's. *Now* I've finished it, I think grimly. And I was pretty eloquent too, while I was at it. Poetic, even. I should tell people off more often.

"That's enough, now," growls the principal. "Get to class, all of you."

As I walk down the hall, I glance back at Mike and see him fluttering his wrists in a last, futile attempt to imitate my brother. "Better tie him down, or he'll fly away on his gigantic flapping arms," he hoots after me, but no one is listening to him, and I don't care anymore. I've won this match for Ethan. God knows it was a long time in coming. I can't wait to tell him all about it after school.

I'm so pleased with myself that at first I don't notice that Hope is nudging me. "What?" I finally ask.

She whispers in my ear, "Don't look now," she says, "but I think Mr. Perfect has been watching you from the corner there."

My smile fades, and I turn involuntarily in the direction she indicated. Liam is standing in a corner by the water fountain, flipping absently through his phone. He seems to sense my eyes on him and glances up at me. He nods and possibly begins to smile, but just then half of the Octopus breaks off and blocks my view of him.

"Oh, my God, Rain! I heard every word you said!" Kathy says, panting heavily into my face. "Good for you! We were all cheering for you."

"That's great, thank you," I mutter absently and crane my neck to look around her. But the spot where Liam was standing is empty now, and my heart sinks. Oh well. *That* was the closest I've gotten to speaking to him. Kathy notices my disappointed expression and waves her boyfriend over. "You were standing next to Liam," she hisses at Marcus in a whisper that carries down the hallway. "Didn't he say something about Rain? Come on, tell her what he said!"

He shoots her a "shut up" look, puts his arm out, and in a quick, practiced motion pulls her deftly to his side. "You were fantastic, Rain!" he crows, dodging his girlfriend's question. "Really, I was *so* proud of you—"

"Marcus," I interrupt. "What did Liam say about me?"

"He didn't... I couldn't really hear..." He trails off and gives a forced cough, then clears his throat and stares down at his feet. "I don't remember him saying anything, actually."

I tap my foot impatiently. "Come on, Marcus, you are the worst liar I've ever met. Just tell me what he said."

He gives Kathy a "see-what-you've-done-now" look and then grants me a "I'm-so-sorry-to-be-the-one-to-tell-you" smile before finally giving it up. "Well, it was right after you said that bit about Ethan doing great things—"

"Yes?"

"I heard him kind of...laugh."

"Okay...?"

"And so I turned to him."

"Right. And?"

"Well, he kind of... He kind of rolled his eyes at me."

I actually feel my heart slow down. For a second, everything slows down, and I want him to stop talking. I want to live in the space before he tells me what he's getting ready to say.

He pauses (Marcus is nothing if not dramatic, especially when he's getting ready to dump cold water on someone) and then breathes, "So after you say that thing about Ethan doing something amazing, Liam says, 'Oh, *please*. He'll never change. Why is she wasting so much energy on a retard?'"

Dear God, I hate the Octopus in that moment. I know I should be focusing my hatred on the guilty party. But Liam isn't there in front of me, and they are, and right now I feel like killing the messenger with my mind. They wrap their arms around each other even tighter, as if to warm themselves against the sudden iciness of my glare.

"I'm so sorry, Rain," they say in unison.

"Maybe…maybe you didn't hear him right," Hope suggests desperately.

But he can't even give me that.

"Oh no," he declares. "Those were his actual words. I'm repeating them, *verbatim*."

"Ladies! And Marcus." Principal Travers has materialized again. "There better be a good reason you're hanging out in the hallway after homeroom has started."

"We're going!" Hope assures him, flashing her sweetest smile. "Rain just had female trouble. We were all helping her with it."

It's a ridiculous excuse, but she could have as easily claimed that I had become momentarily deranged and begun climbing the walls like Spider-Man. Travers never does anything to punish any of the students. His bark is far worse than his bite. He is friends with most of our parents—he can't exactly suspend us and then invite the whole family to his summer barbecue. So we cheerfully take advantage of his weakness. It's one of the few perks of living in a small town.

Hope gives me a shove, and a minute later I'm in my homeroom seat. My mind is still reeling from Marcus's revelation, and for a few minutes I'm deaf to everything around me—the monotone voice of the teacher, the scratching of pencils, and even Hope's pathetic whispers to get my attention. I can't believe it. How could I have been so blind and stupid? How could I have liked that *jerk*? He was my first real crush. I'd started liking him because he seemed so good, so different from every other guy I'd known. He'd met all my criteria, every last rule.

While my friends fell for the sexy bad boys—the Mikes, the Graysons—I went for the quiet, bookish one who most of the others passed over. Because he seemed so sensible and safe to me and therefore just about...perfect.

"Maybe Liam didn't mean it like it sounded," Hope murmurs, placing a consoling hand over my drumming fingers. "He's never really met Ethan—"

"No, no, Liam's met him," I tell her. "Last year my mom enrolled Ethan in swim team, and Liam was the lifeguard. They've definitely met."

"Okay, but maybe they never really talked—"

"He called my brother a retard, Hope. There's nothing more to say about this, all right? But thanks for trying to make me feel better."

She keeps patting my arm. "Oh, Rain... What are you going to do?" she says with a sigh. "You have to talk to him in chemistry next period."

"So?" I practically bite down on the word. "What about it?"

"Well, you were so nervous before. Doesn't this make it even worse?"

"No," I tell her shortly. The first period bell rings and there's a crash of moving desks and scraping chairs. "I'm not nervous anymore."

She looks confused and leans over to pick her bag off the floor. "Okay. Well, good luck, I guess."

"Thank you," I tell her. "But I don't think I'll need it."

# Chapter 5

**Turns out I do need it.**

A little. I mean, I'd like to say that I'm the kind of girl who can shut down a year's worth of feelings in the space of fifteen minutes. That would make me strong and independent, right? And I feel ready to do just that. I'm so hurt by Liam's nastiness that, for a few seconds, I *do* write him off completely. So I truly am a loyal sister for those hazy, brief moments in homeroom.

But then I walk into chemistry. And Liam is standing by his lab bench (our lab bench!) with his back to me, and all it takes is one glimpse of the familiar curve of his long neck and the mane of dark brown curls around his ears, and suddenly my anger goes from flaming crimson to a dull red. And then he turns around (and waves at me! And smiles!) and that anger fades even more until it's just a pleasant pinkish shimmer, barely obscuring the boy I like. I'm still offended and disappointed, but I'm also desperate to explain it all away. Maybe Ethan did something awful to Liam, I reason, and Liam was just hitting back. No, that couldn't be it. I shake the disloyal thought from my head. Ethan has never intentionally hurt anyone.

Perhaps Liam simply didn't understand the history of that

word and how much it hurt. Still, if that was the excuse, could I continue to like someone who was so clueless?

I advance slowly toward the lab bench. As I draw closer to him, my anger pales to gray; it's barely a shadow between us. I should forgive him, I tell myself. Forgiveness is a sign of maturity. But am I just being charitable because he's cute? I stop walking and briefly close my eyes. Repeat Marcus's words in my mind. *Oh, please. He'll never change. Why is she wasting so much energy on a—*

The anger flares to life, red-hot and roaring again. Damn.

I open my eyes.

There is only one possible explanation. Marcus had hallucinated. Clearly. The sweet boy in front of me couldn't possibly have said that. As I approach, Liam looks over at me and smiles shyly, then ducks his head over his syllabus.

How can Hope not see how cute he is? Sure, his brows are a bit thick, and he's surprisingly pale and skinny for a lifeguard. But how could she miss his large, brown eyes—made even larger by those heavy frames? The quiet, smart kid that no one dislikes but everyone ignores. I'm not sure why I'm attracted to him, but I don't want to give him up. A year is a long time to like the same guy. That's a lot of history in my head. We're talking about countless hours of daydreaming and planning. All that anticipation, waiting for him to appear from around a corner, stealing glances over my book in class, every movement and expression tinged with the hope that maybe, maybe this would be the moment that he finally sees me. So much useless, wasted hope!

In my dreams, I've heard him tell me that he loves me hundreds of times, each declaration a little different and more beautiful than the last. And now I can't believe that the boy who whispered those perfect things could be so hateful. It seems impossible.

I slowly lay my bag down on the table and turn to him. His first words to me will tell me everything, I promise myself. He will redeem himself. He has to. I will wait for him to speak. It's the moment of truth.

He says nothing. The smile is all he's going to offer, it seems. He's flipping through our chemistry syllabus now.

Okay, fine. I'll start.

"Hello, Liam." There. That's all he deserves. It's up to him now. *Impress me*, I will him silently. *Make me like you again. Prove to me that you're worth the time I've spent fantasizing about you.*

"We're making elephant toothpaste," he says.

That's not even close to what I expected.

"What?"

"Elephant toothpaste," he repeats, pointing to the syllabus. "Our first experiment."

"Oh."

*You called my brother a retard*, I think. How can you be standing there with no idea that I need you to make this better? And why are you talking about elephants?

"I didn't know elephants brush their teeth," I say nonsensically. "I mean, tusks. Their tusks. They don't have teeth, of course. Ha." Crap, I'm babbling.

"Elephants have teeth."

"They do?"

He takes his hand off the page and regards me with a vague smile. "How else would they chew their food?"

This is so stupid. Of course they have teeth. The point is that I don't *care* about elephant teeth right now. The moment of truth has come and gone, and he hasn't redeemed himself even a tiny bit. In fact, I have a sneaking suspicion he's making fun of me and my ignorance of elephantine dentistry. "I guess *I'm* a retard too," I blurt out, a touch maliciously.

And then I stare at him meaningfully. *You know what you did*, I tell him with my eyes. *I know what you're thinking now.*

"*What?*" There's a volume of innocent confusion in his voice.

"All I'm saying is that it must be genetic," I continue doggedly. "The entire Rosenblatt family is a bit *retarded!*"

"Okay…" He's looking a little frightened of me. "Which Rosenblatt family are you talking about?"

"Me! My family! I'm talking about my family, Liam."

"Oh. Your last name is Rosenblatt?"

"Yes! How do you not *know* that?" *How can you not know my last name?* I think. *When I know everything about you?*

He glances desperately around the classroom as if looking for some way to escape the crazy that is his new lab partner. There's a faint sheen of sweat glistening on his forehead. "I'm sorry," he says quietly. "I'm not so good with names."

"That's okay," I respond automatically. There's something

sweet and vulnerable about his meek apology and the vague look of terror in his eyes. I'm suddenly not so furious anymore. It's hard to be mad at someone who looks so scared.

As my head clears and my heart rate slows, I quickly review our jumbled conversation. He obviously has no idea why I'm upset. And I've been operating under the assumption that he remembers his comment to Marcus. Even worse, my righteous outrage has totally screwed with my judgment. In trying to make my point, I'd just used the word I've loathed since I first heard it in kindergarten, hissed maliciously at my brother behind the jungle gym.

I have to fix this. Say something that actually makes sense to him, for a change. I need a simple fact, something easy and obvious.

"My name is Rain Serenity Rosenblatt." I declare. For no reason, of course. It's the first thing that pops into my brain. Oh, yeah, I think. He will never forget my name now.

And of course *now* he's laughing at me.

Well, not laughing exactly, but his lips twitch in the corners, and his dark eyes have a suppressed dancing light lurking in their depths. Why did I tell him my middle name? Rain Rosenblatt is bad enough, but when you throw Serenity in there—that just screams offspring of stoned Jewish hippies, right?

"Everyone makes fun of my name," I admit sullenly.

He nods seriously, as if absorbing the information without judgment, but his eyes are still dancing. "So your parents are just— free spirits or whatever?"

I shake my head. "One of them. My mom and dad could

never agree on anything. So my big city corporate lawyer father got to name one kid and my organic granola, environmentalist mom named the other. They came up with Ethan David and Rain Serenity. Take a guess which parent named me."

He gives a nervous laugh and readjusts his glasses. "How did they ever get together in the first place?"

"They met in law school. My mother is a lawyer too, but since we moved out here to Montana she mostly does consulting work for environmental causes. People who are convinced that the nearby factory caused their kid's asthma or their grandmother's kidney stones. Stuff like that."

"Like Erin Brockovich."

I smile. "Yeah, exactly. It's my mother's favorite movie."

"There's work for your dad out here in the middle of nowhere?"

"My dad has a new family in DC. My parents split when my brother and I were little."

"Oh. Sorry." He fiddles absently with his shirtsleeve. "Didn't mean to bring up a sensitive topic."

I wave away his apology. "It's fine. I was okay with it, even then. I still remember their fights. I was really young, but I remember."

"Yeah, it's not the kind of thing that you forget, I guess."

It's weird how we've gone from awkwardly talking about elephants to the personal history of my parents' divorce—all in the space of five minutes. Mr. Green, our teacher, has finally appeared and is shuffling through his papers at the front of the class, while the rest of the students chat and arrange their stuff. I'm still a little uneasy about talking to Liam; I'm supposed to be furious with him. But I can't muster the will to scorn him. I want to learn more about him, to really understand the only boy in school who's ever fascinated me. And then maybe I can scorn him. A little bit later.

I'm not the only uneasy one though. As he stares at me, Liam's hands drift up toward the countertop, then hover over his syllabus, finally coming to rest in his pockets. He shifts back and forth in place, and the glimmer of sweat over his brow seems even shinier than before.

I decide to put away my hostility for a moment and make some attempt at normal conversation. "You're new to Clarkson," I remark. "Besides my friend Hope, pretty much everyone at our school has grown up here."

"I know." He clears his throat and glances at the teacher.

This is going to be harder than I thought. Pulling words out of him is like pulling teeth, except that it seems to be painful for both of us. I'm about to abandon the whole thing and concentrate on our assignment when he turns back to me. "I lived with my grandmother in Missoula until ninth grade," he says abruptly. "Now I live here with my father."

"Oh. I don't think I've ever met him." That's unusual for this little town. I know all my classmates' parents, and they can give a pretty thorough summary of my family history as well.

"He's a trucker. So he's away a lot."

"And your mom?"

"No idea where she is," he replies shortly. "Haven't seen her since I was three."

"Oh. Sorry."

"It's fine. Can you hand me that beaker?"

I pass it over and edge a little closer to him. He seems absorbed in arranging the materials for the experiment, but I can't help noticing that his fingers tremble a little as he reaches for the flask.

Mr. Green has begun addressing the class and droning on about lab goggles and safety.

"Respect the chemicals…" he commands. "Always wear your protective gear…"

It seems like pretty common sense stuff, and I tune out five seconds after he starts. We're at the back of the classroom anyway, so he can't see that I'm not listening. On the other side of the room, Mike has already started to mess with the lighter for his Bunsen burner, so if anyone is going to get a lecture on safety today, it isn't me.

"I wonder why they call it elephant toothpaste," Liam muses under his breath. "I wish Mr. Green had given out the syllabus before class. I would have looked it up."

"I have my phone," I suggest, pulling it out.

"There's no reception in the lab," he responds, slowly pouring out a beaker full of hydrogen peroxide. "Not on my phone, anyhow."

I check my screen and then slip it back into my pocket. No signal on mine either. "Do you really research your science experiments before you do them?"

He glances up at me, his hand still poised over the flask. "Yeah, don't you?"

"No. Why would I?"

He shrugs and concentrates on his collection of measuring spoons. "Two tablespoons of yeast, dissolve in water, add two drops of green food coloring," he reads. "I like to be prepared, that's all."

"You're already top of the class," I point out.

He shakes his head. "So far. But you haven't exactly made it easy."

I smile broadly and inch even closer to him. Hope was right. He had noticed me—or at least my GPA. "That's pretty impressive."

He turns back to me and holds out a bottle of yellow dish soap. "What's impressive?"

"You are. You've got all these other obligations—lifeguarding, volunteer work—"

"And tutoring," he puts in. "Five days a week after school."

"And yet you're still beating me. My friends are always joking that I plan too much. I have papers done two weeks before they're due, that kind of thing. But you still leave me in the dust. And I don't have all your extracurriculars." I take the container from him and place it next to the beaker on the table. The teacher is babbling on about careful titration and keeping a safe distance, but I don't need to hear him. The other students around us are still fumbling with their measuring equipment.

"So why do you do that?" He's stopped concentrating on the assignment too, and I feel the full force of his dark eyes on my face.

It's a little intoxicating. *I'm mad at him*, I remind myself sternly. He may be acting all interested and caring now, but just half an hour ago, he was an insensitive jerk. I can't let myself forget that.

"Why do I do what? Plan stuff?" I can't help smiling at the question. I'm the one who overanalyzes everybody. It's weird to suddenly turn the magnifying glass onto myself.

"Is it just about the grades?" he asks. "Or are you naturally super organized?"

I know the answer, of course. I plan because I can't afford not to. Because without my planning, without my constant attention to details, Ethan couldn't have made it through our childhood. So when my father basically abandoned us and my mother began to unravel beneath the stress of her failed marriage, I was the one who protected my brother from the world. And I would never stop protecting him. Ever. Wherever I go, Ethan is coming with me. I plan because whatever life I build for myself must always have a cozy glass bubble for my twin brother.

That's why I'm like this, Liam.

Of course I don't say any of that. That's the sort of thing you tell a therapist or maybe a best friend. But you don't say that to a boy you barely know, a boy who may or may not be flirting with you. *Is he?* I wonder. *Is that what that smile on his face means?* I push away the pleasant hope. It doesn't matter if he is. I can't flirt with a guy that would hurt Ethan. It would be like violating all the rules, all at once.

"I have to think about my family," I say vaguely. "People… count on me."

"What do you mean?"

I'm a little uncomfortable now, and I'm starting to feel strangely defensive. This is exactly the topic I was trying to avoid. "It means that I'm not just taking care of myself. I have to think about my family too."

"Yeah, okay, but so do most people."

Why is he challenging me? We've only just met. What is up with this guy?

"*Most* people don't have a brother with autism," I say, a little louder than I intended. I regret it before the words are even out of my mouth. Ethan was the last person I wanted to discuss with Liam. Especially after what he'd called him that morning. Had he really forgotten about that? Or was it so common for him to say nasty things about people that the event hadn't even registered? My anger is up again, and the expression on Liam's face isn't helping. He looks baffled—skeptical, even.

Out of the corner of my eye, I see Mr. Green advancing toward us, and I suddenly realize I've forgotten all about the experiment on the table. I grab the container of soap off the counter and invert it over the mixture into the funnel. "And another thing," I continue heatedly, squeezing out the contents of the bottle in vicious pumps. "Maybe it wouldn't be so hard on us, if *some* people didn't say awful things behind our backs—"

*There*, I think. *Now he has to know why I'm upset. What did he expect anyway? That Marcus wouldn't tell me what he said? Everyone knows that we're friends.* Yet he doesn't seem embarrassed or ashamed at all. If anything, he's just a bit distracted; he's glancing back and forth between our teacher and me. "Rain, I think you need to stop—"

But I've already picked up the yeast water, and with a quick, deliberate motion I dump the contents into the dish soap solution. "No, I think you need to—"

"Rain, get away from there!" From somewhere behind me there's a shout, and I see Liam's eyes grow wide. I turn around too late; he barrels toward me, pushes me to the ground and throws his arms up to shield my face as the rumbling sound behind us swells. And then suddenly there's hot foam everywhere, pouring from the ceiling, spilling out over countertops and floors, bubbling and spurting like green lava from a volcano. Some of it hits us as it comes down, and I hear Liam swear under his breath and swat at the soapy green mess landing on his neck.

I still have no idea what's happened, but the expression on Liam's face, and on Mr. Green's face—who's now hovering over us and shouting—makes it pretty obvious that I'm the one responsible for blowing up the class's first chemistry experiment. "Did…I add the wrong ingredient?" I gasp, sitting up shakily and brushing off the warm fizz on my shirt.

"Too *much*, Ms. Rosenblatt," our teacher bellows. "I gave *specific* instructions—"

"What…what happened?" I stammer, before catching a glimpse of our work station. It looks like an elephant took a green bubble bath in the chemistry lab. "Are you okay?" I ask Liam.

He's sitting cross-legged next to me on the floor and surveying the damage. "Well, I know what we'll be doing after class today."

"I'm so sorry," I say. I really am. I have an uneasy feeling that the foam explosion was strangely connected to my out-of-control emotions. I'd squeezed the soap too hard; I'd vented my frustration on the bottle; the flask had responded by spitting up all over us—and the entire lab.

Mr. Green kneels beside Liam and anxiously scans his foamy clothes. "The product can get pretty hot," he says, laying a hand on his shoulder. "You sure you're all right?"

"I'm fine," he replies. "Sorry about the mess. We'll clean it up."

The teacher shoots me an exasperated look and scrambles to his feet. "You weren't even wearing your safety goggles, young lady. If your lab partner hadn't jumped in front of you, that explosion might have hit you in the face."

"I—I'm sorry," I repeat. God, this is so embarrassing. The entire class has gathered to stare at the foam disaster around us. Mike is nudging Grayson and laughing under his breath at me. And our teacher isn't planning on making me feel any better about myself.

"Well, this was *barely* an experiment, people," he announces. "But one student has already demonstrated what happens when you don't follow instructions. *Thank you*, Rain."

I hang my head and mouth a silent "sorry" to the class, hoping to coax a smile from Mr. Green and maybe a brief nod of forgiveness, but he turns his back to me and marches to the front of the room without another word. As the rest of the class slowly drifts over to their stations, I get up off the floor and walk over to Liam, who's pulling paper towels from the dispenser on the wall.

"Thank you," I say to him bashfully.

He stops what he's doing and turns to stare at me. "For what?"

"Jumping in front of me," I explain. "I would have been hurt if you hadn't done that."

He shrugs and goes back to gathering napkins. "That was just instinct. You were right in front of the flask. And you were too busy yelling at me to notice that it was erupting."

"Yeah, I know. I'm really sorry about that too."

My earlier anger feels pretty pale now, especially since he may have just saved me from a trip to the hospital. "Can we just forget about it and start again?"

"Forget about *what*? I have no idea why you were angry at me in the first place. What did I do?"

"Just leave it, okay? It feels kind of stupid."

"Maybe to you. But I want to know what I did."

It's a chore carrying around this grudge already, and I've only had it for an hour. I try vainly to revive my feelings from the morning, try to refresh the righteous outrage I'd felt. But when I finally say the words, they come out like an apology, rather than an accusation. "In the hallway this morning, Marcus told me that you said—"

"Yeah?" He still looks blank.

"You don't remember? You called Ethan—"

"I didn't say anything about your brother," he protests. "I

actually thought the way you told off Mike was pretty awesome…
if a little pointless."

"Pointless?"

"Well, you're never going to get people like Mike to change."

His meaning hits me like a lightning bolt. "Oh, god. You
called *Mike* a retard, not—"

"Yeah. What did you think?" His face falls suddenly, and he
shakes his head. "Oh. *Oh.*"

"Yeah, I'm an idiot." I want to hide my face; my cheeks feel
like they're on fire. Why hadn't I guessed that earlier?

He laughs at my remorseful expression. "No, it's fine. I
probably shouldn't have used that word, even to describe Mike. I
get why you were upset."

"Well, I should have at least given you the benefit of the doubt."

He brushes the last puffs of foam from his shoulders. "It's okay.
It's not like you know me or anything."

I feel an unexpected surge of boldness. "Maybe not, but I'd
like to."

His expression is an adorable mix of surprise and embarrassment. "You would?"

I shrug to dilute the eagerness of my last statement. I don't
want to completely give myself away. "Yeah, I like getting to know
people. And I'm sorry I got so crazy just now."

It's not until I see the tension draining from his face that I
understand how nervous he'd been. His blush is a little boost of
confidence. For better or worse, at least he'd cared what I thought.

I make a mental note to thank the Octopus later. It may have been a complete accident, but Marcus's mistake had actually loosened my tongue at the right moment. Just enough to let me make a complete fool of myself, but at least I'd managed to break the ice.

And, for once, despite everyone's predictions, I'd been completely unpredictable and gotten an unexpected, quiet blush as a reward. Also a loud explosion of hot green foam—but still. Totally worth it.

# Cooking with Rain
## SERENITY THROUGH YOUR GUT

*Where I answer all your burning food-related questions!*

**Dear Rain:** There's this girl I've liked for a while. I want to make her something, but I'm short on cash and time. Do you have a quick recipe that won't cost me a fortune?

—Wacky Mac

**Dear Wacky:** Glad to help! You can't get cheaper and quicker than my Nutella Lava Bomb mug cake! Nothing says love like volcanic chocolate.

## ETHAN'S JOURNAL:

Many scientists believe that kissing evolved from the practice of mothers feeding their young mouth-to-mouth. Based on the idea that "the way to a person's heart is through his stomach," pressing lips eventually became synonymous with love.

### My observation:

Many humans (such as my sister) still associate the act of feeding with an expression of love. I showed this article to Rain (with the relevant parts highlighted), but she just asked me why I'm studying the biology of kissing. She tells me that I often misread social cues. I don't know how to tell her that she frequently misreads me too.

# Chapter 6

I'm two minutes from home when my phone rings.

"*How* did you not call me after chem lab?"

It's more of a demand than a question, and I'm too exhausted (it took two hours to clean up that lab) to defend myself. "It's your own fault for pushing off chemistry until next year, Hope," I mutter into my phone. "If you were in our class you'd have seen the show for yourself."

"What *happened*?"

"Well, I got Liam to notice me," I point out.

"I heard that they had to call the fire department."

"They exaggerated."

"I'm calling the Octopus right now."

"*Why?*"

"So Marcus can talk to Liam. Maybe he can turn this around. Tell him how awesome you are or something."

"Hope, leave it alone."

"I'm going to fix this for you."

"Hope, it's actually okay—"

But she's already hung up. I sigh and push open the kitchen door.

Ethan is sitting at the counter when I come home. I'd expected to find him studying with his online tutor, but it looks like he is already done. Ethan has five different tutors to help him with basic subjects. After school, we finish our math homework together, but his formidable knowledge of biology is too intimidating, so he does that on his own. And then he's basically free to memorize his anatomy slides. His afternoons used to be packed with therapy sessions. Until last year, each day was dedicated to a different treatment or therapy—speech, occupational, physical— plus a monthly meeting with his developmental pediatrician. But that part of Ethan's life is just a memory now. Halfway through high school, my mother decided he didn't need the specialists anymore and proceeded to cut them out of his schedule. The weaning process was so gradual that even Ethan didn't notice at first. One cancellation, weeks in advance. Then another. By the beginning of junior year, the calendar was empty, for the first time since our childhood. Now it's basically the tutor and me. My mom pitches in a little here and there when I'm not around. The reality is she handed the chief responsibilities over to me a long time ago. I want to believe it's her vote of confidence in my abilities and my patience with Ethan. Maybe, though, it's simply a result of her exhaustion, and no compliment is intended. My mother isn't overly generous with compliments, overt or implied.

Ethan looks up as I come in and ducks his head to hide the cell phone in his hand. "I have to go now," he says and hangs up, dropping the phone hastily into his pocket like he's afraid I might run up and snatch it from him.

"Oh, please, Efan," I tell him, shaking my head. "Do you really think I don't know that you talk to Dad almost every day? I do live here."

"You said I shouldn't talk to him," he points out. "I didn't want to make you mad."

"I'm beginning to feel like the cranky old lady that everybody tiptoes around," I say. "You can do whatever you want. And I never said that you shouldn't speak to Dad."

"Yes, you did. You said, 'Just because he sends us money for your lessons doesn't mean that you should talk to him.' That was last month, on the Sunday before school started. And then eight days ago on Monday, you said it again. Only that time you said—"

"Yeah, okay, I get it. I didn't mean it literally, all right? Speak to him all you want. Just don't tell Mom."

He frowns. "Why? She knows I talk to him."

"She *does*?"

"Yes. When I told her, she said that she didn't care. Then she said, 'Stupid bastard gets to be the good guy from five hundred miles away.' And then she kicked the refrigerator. It started making noise after that."

I can't help smiling to myself. "She may have *said* that she didn't care, Efan," I prompt him gently. "But then she said some other stuff and started kicking things. Now what do you think that Mom is really feeling when she does that?"

He looks up suddenly and focuses on my face, his light eyes

fix on me as if he's trying to see right through me. It always freaks me out when he does that. Most of the time he's staring at the floor or at the wall when he's talking to me. But then, without warning, he'll suddenly pierce me with those intense eyes until I find myself wishing he'd just look back at the wall already.

"What is Mom feeling?" he echoes.

"Yes," I urge him. "What does it mean when she does that?"

His brows come together and his jaw tenses. For a moment I think he's concentrating on the question, but then I realize that isn't it at all. I thought I could read Ethan like a book. But this look— this expression, I've never seen him glare at me like this before. "I *know* what it means," he snaps at me, his voice sinking into a harsh whisper. "I'm not stupid, Rain."

"I...I didn't say you were—"

"Mom doesn't like it that I talk to Dad," he continues heatedly. "But she knows I will anyway, and that makes her upset."

"That's it. That's exactly right!" I offer him a proud grin, but he doesn't appear to notice. He doesn't seem at all pleased that he's guessed correctly. His eyes narrow with frank resentment, and he leans closer to me, so close that I pull back a little.

"I also know what it means when you tell Hope that I will never get close to anyone."

He lets the statement hang there like a bitter accusation. I sit stunned and silent before him, momentarily speechless at the ring of naked hostility in his voice. He had heard me say it after all, and he hasn't forgotten it. Of course he hasn't forgotten.

I open my mouth to defend myself but I can't think of anything to say.

"It means," he continues, his tone patient and deliberate, like a teacher explaining a difficult problem, "that you're telling her to give up on me."

"*What?*" I feel a painful lump rising in my throat.

"Just like the school," he persists. "And just like *you* did. You gave up on me too."

"I never—" I begin to protest, but I can't bring myself to finish the thought. My eyes sting and blur with tears. He's never spoken to me this way before. I brush my hand over my wet cheeks and start to back away from him.

"I also know what it means when Dad tells me that he wants me to visit him in DC over spring break," he adds, triumphantly. "It means that he misses me."

"He wants you to fly to Washington—?" I shake my head in disbelief. Has our father lost his mind? I want to tell Ethan the idea is completely crazy. But I'm afraid to speak. I'm scared to be honest with my brother.

He's not listening to me anyway. "And I know what it means when you start to cry," he finishes in a quieter voice. He drops his head and the fire in his expression flickers out. "It means that you're sad that I screwed up again."

"I'm not sad," I insist automatically, but my flushed cheeks and streaming eyes belie my words. Even Ethan can see that.

"But you're crying," he states. There's no sarcasm or irony

in his statement; he's just pointing out the obvious—just in case I haven't noticed.

"I know I'm crying. But it's not your fault."

He looks genuinely relieved. "Oh. I thought it was because of me. Why are you crying? Did something happen at school today?"

*Oh, for God's sake, Ethan.*

But, on second thought, I'm actually thankful he's so literal-minded. For once it's helpful to me because I really, really want to change the subject. His accusation is still ringing in my ears. *You gave up on me...*

And worse than his words was his expression in that moment. He'd glared at me as if he resented me. Not even during his worst meltdowns had I seen that look in his eyes. No matter how miserable he felt, I was always his comfort, his rock. When we were little, he refused to go to sleep unless I was curled up near him, like a human security blanket. At thirteen, I finally insisted on separate bedrooms, but every night before I went to sleep, I let him know I was near by knocking five times on the wall between us. The one time I forgot, he stayed up all night waiting for it.

*You gave up on me...* Had my one careless comment destroyed sixteen years of trust? It's too much for me to absorb at the moment.

"I had a rough day," I tell him, forcing a bright smile.

"What happened?"

"I yelled at Liam for no reason and then I blew up the chemistry lab."

"Oh. I know that already."

"You—you *do*? *How* exactly?"

"Hope told me."

"She *did*?" Damn it, I need to stop sounding so surprised by everything. It's just so unusual for him to be getting messages from a girl!

"Here's her text," he states and pulls out his phone to show me.

I blink at the screen. "She's coming over this afternoon?"

"Yes. At three. She's fifteen minutes late."

"But—" I pull out my own phone and tap on it. There are no new messages. "She didn't tell me she was coming."

"She's coming over to see me," he states. No inflection in his voice at all. No triumph, no satisfaction. Just the fact. A clarification, for my benefit.

And meanwhile I'm struggling. I struggle not to stare and raise my eyebrows. I struggle not to be critical or amused. I struggle to be okay with it.

But I am so, so *not*.

There are so many reasons to freak out. How could Hope not tell me she was coming by to see my brother? That was not okay. I could spurt out an entire list of things to worry about. My brain is screaming doomsday warnings.

I swallow all of it. Something has changed between Ethan and me, something I just don't understand yet. But I know to keep my mouth shut until I figure it out. So I do.

I shut it tight. And I keep it that way even after Hope bounces in and wraps me in a cheery embrace. My hug is a little bit stony, and my smile is fake. I know she's reading me loud and clear, even if Ethan is not.

"We'll be in Ethan's room, okay?" she calls out as they leave the kitchen together. Like it's routine for them. Like everything's totally normal.

Like I'm not left in the kitchen mouthing, *What the hell?*

Thank God my mother walks in five minutes after they leave. The inner turmoil might have split me in half if she hadn't come in then.

"Hope is in Ethan's room!" I tell her. "*Alone!*"

"Okay." She digests it as I did, without comment. Without verbal comment, that is. Her face is commenting all over this news.

"Ethan and Hope are alone. In his room. Together," I rephrase. Just in case my first statement wasn't clear.

"I know, Rain. I got it," she says wearily and slumps down at the kitchen counter. "Good for them."

I'm momentarily distracted from my meltdown. My mother is looking more than usually pale and worn. There are dark shadows under her large blue eyes, and her cheekbones seem even more prominent against the pallor of her skin. "Are you all right?" I ask her.

She nods half-heartedly and gestures toward the tea pot. "My stomach's been off for a little while. Make me a glass of tea will you?"

"What kind?" I ask, opening up the cupboard. It isn't a simple question. We have about fifty different types of tea. My mother belongs to the school of medicine that believes all illnesses can be cured by some combination of plant or tree root. I remember my dad yelling at her that I would have gone deaf from ear infections if he hadn't finally taken me to the doctor. She'd insisted the garlic clove in my ear was more than enough to draw out the infection. To this day I still associate the smell of garlic with pain, shaking chills, and the sound of my parents fighting.

"Hawthorn berry," she instructs. "Put in a pinch of ginger, a teaspoon of apple cider vinegar, and two tablespoons of honey."

It's only a simple pot of tea, but I feel a calm settle over me as I add the ingredients. Though my mom limits herself to creating healing hot beverages, she's always encouraging me to take my food cures obsession to the next level. We have bins full of weird and exotic spices, cabinets stuffed with grains from unlikely sources (arrowroot, chickpea) and a fridge packed with vegetables no one's ever heard of.

I bring the steaming mug back to my mother, and she downs it like a tonic. "Thanks," she says with a sigh, settling back against the counter. "That's so much better."

Truth is, she doesn't look much better. I'd been noticing that she was a bit worn out over the last few weeks, but today I'm actually worried about her.

"Your clothes look loose on you," I point out, reaching out and pinching her sleeve. "This shirt used to fit you well."

"I'm fine," she mutters irritably and pulls her arm away.

"I've been a little stressed, and I haven't been eating right. I'll get it together after we settle on the Stenson case." She's helping a group of farmers sue their former employer for health damages from a strawberry pesticide.

"Okay," I say, unconvinced. "I was about to make dinner. We have some gluten-free pasta."

None of us are gluten sensitive—not if you believe the doctors anyway, which my mother doesn't. She suspects there might be a link between gluten and autism—so we haven't had a soft piece of bread in the house in years. *(Notes for the blog: Flaxseed challah—it tastes better than it sounds!)* During elementary school, she had the same theory about casein and autism, so we were practically vegan for a while. Twelve years ago, she decided that air pollution in the big city was the cause of Ethan's issues. And so we moved out to Montana, leaving the smog and my father behind.

When I was little, I'd complained about her beet noodles and fennel cupcakes. It's hard to be the only kid at the lunch table with snacks that no one wants to trade. But over time I'd learned to embrace weird food combos and substitutions. The day I took over the family kitchen was a turning point. I was going to find the perfect recipe for Ethan, and for all of us. Five years later, I was still searching. And we'd eaten *a lot* of seeds in the process.

"Pasta sounds good," she says. "Do you think Hope will stay for dinner?" Her face still looks tired, but her voice is smiling. Oh, right. *Hope*. How did I forget?

"Honestly, what are they *doing* in there?" I mutter. I'm

seriously considering tiptoeing up to his bedroom and listening at the door. I don't care how wrong and invasive it is. It's only because I'm worried about him, I swear. Mom seems to read my mind; she puts a gentle, restraining hand on my arm. "Rain, concentrate on the pasta, and leave them alone."

"How are you not nervous for him?" I demand loudly. "How can you just sit there calmly doing nothing?"

"What would you want me to do? Barge in there and stare at them? Send Ethan the message that I don't trust him at all?"

"Trust? What are you talking about? This has nothing to do with trust!"

"Okay, so what is it then?" she inquires patiently.

How am I the only person seeing it? It's so obvious. "I'm scared he's going to get hurt. I'm scared she'll hurt him, and he won't know how to deal with it."

She stares at me for a while in silence and taps her fingers lightly on her clay mug. I can't stand it when she gets this way. Whenever I'm upset, that's what she does. She studies me. Silently. Like I'm a strange beetle in a glass jar, bumping around, clueless about the real world outside. And she's the scientist with all the answers.

"Hope is your friend," she remarks quietly after a moment. "You seem to have a pretty poor opinion of your friend if you can't even trust her around your brother for a few minutes."

"No, that isn't it at all. I love Hope," I say quickly.

"So do I. She's a good girl. She's thoughtful. Responsible. Somewhat naive." My mom has a way of passing swift judgment on everyone and boiling them down to three adjectives. Hope has come out of her evaluation with fantastic marks. Most people don't fare so well. (Marcus was pronounced self-absorbed, finicky, and melodramatic. Kathy was vain, talkative, and immature. I'm glad she hasn't met Liam yet; I'm not ready for that verdict.)

"It's just… Hope has lots of other options," I begin slowly, testing out my thoughts. "She can date anyone. She dated Grayson for six months, and he's the hottest guy in school. But Ethan— Ethan is *so alone*. What if he falls for her? And then screws it up? You know he's going to screw it up. Or what if Hope just gets tired of the novelty and stops coming around? For her it's just another adventure. But for him it might become everything. And when it ends it will just crush him."

She nods solemnly and seems to consider what I've said. I wonder how I would fare in her three-adjective evaluation. If I asked her, how would she describe me? Reliable, stable, loyal? That's what I hope she'd say. But I have no idea what she thinks. It's not the kind of thing you ask.

"What makes you so sure that they will ever date in the first place?" she inquires after a moment. "They could be just friends."

I can't tell her, of course. I can't reveal what Hope has told me in confidence. Even pointing out that Hope's face lights up like a cherries jubilee flambé every time my brother enters the room seems like a betrayal. So I just shrug. "I'm scared he's going to get hurt," I repeat mournfully.

"Well, if he does, he'll be just like other sixteen-year-old boys," she remarks. "It's a rite of passage, isn't it? Getting your heart stomped on by a girl. No reason that Ethan shouldn't experience that part of life just like everybody else."

Well, that is the stupidest thing I have ever heard. My mother is inviting her own son to get his heart broken—and she's saying I should stand by and let it happen. I was pretty sure a cure for Ethan's heartbreak didn't exist in the natural world.

"You need a distraction, Rain," she says after a moment. I get the bug-in-a-jar feeling again as her eyes focus on me. "Maybe leave Ethan alone a bit and concentrate on yourself."

"What do you mean?"

"I mean, what are your plans for college? This is the year to strengthen your resume, you know. I'm not sure you're doing enough to stand out."

*This again?* I think irritably. Like I haven't already told her my plan for managing college while caring for Ethan. "What are you talking about? I'm getting good grades. And I'm memorizing the psychology book just like you recommended. I'm even trying to apply what I've learned! My friends are actually pretty sick of my attempts at psychoanalysis."

"You probably don't want to put that on an application."

"And there's my cooking blog—"

She dismisses me with a wave. "Nobody cares about your experiments with lemongrass and kale. You need extracurriculars that will look good on your resume. What about volunteering at MCC? Take your experience with Ethan and use it to help others.

They have a program that teaches high school students how to interact and work with kids with autism—"

"That sounds great, Mom. But I don't need extra experience. And we've already talked about this. I'm going to U of M so that I can be close to home. For Ethan."

She sighs and takes another drag of tea. "Of course you'll have to stay close to home. But that doesn't mean you can skate through high school—"

We're interrupted by the sound of a door slamming on the second floor and the hurried dash of feet on stairs. A moment later Hope appears in the kitchen and waves hastily to my mother and me. Her face is flushed and her lips widen into a large fake smile. "I gotta go now, guys. See you later. Bye," she calls out and is gone before I can stop her.

I blink at the closing porch door and turn to gape at my mom.

"What *happened*?" Her face wears the same blank question as the one I ask.

I head to Ethan's room, my mother trailing behind me. The door is open, and I knock gently and peer inside. My brother is sitting on the floor, his anatomy textbook open across his knees; the carpet around him is littered with drawings of body parts. He's clicking away on his laptop and staring at a large projection in front of him. The television and the computer screen are facing him, so I can't see what he's looking at, but based on the intensity of his concentration, I guess that he's absorbed in his favorite subject again.

"Hello, Rain," he says. "Hello, Mom."

Nothing seems wrong here; everything is just like it always is. Why was Hope in such a frantic hurry to go then? She'd seemed eager enough to hang out with him just a few minutes earlier.

"Is everything okay?" I ask him tentatively. He frowns in my direction, then turns back to his computer.

"No, it isn't," he grumbles. "I got everything wrong."

I advance slowly into the room and settle down on the rug next to him. "I'm sorry it didn't go well," I tell him earnestly. I really am sorry for him. As much as I'd been against the two of them becoming a couple, a part of me had hoped it would miraculously work out—at least for a little while. I certainly didn't want him to fail on the very first try.

He focuses on my face and his eyes widen hopefully. "Secret Rule?" he inquires.

"Really?"

"Yes. I need it."

"Okay," I answer automatically. "What can I do?"

"Would you talk to Hope for me?"

"Of course. What do you want me to say?"

"I need you to tell her to come back. I made a mistake."

"What mistake?"

"The fetus can implant on the cervix in rare cases," he replies. "Not just in the fallopian tube."

"Excuse me?" Next to me I hear my mother make a choking noise, and I glance back to find her gesturing mutely at the television screen. I turn to look at the still projection and freeze, openmouthed, and all thoughts of calling Hope evaporate as quickly as they came.

"Efan, was *that* picture up when Hope was here earlier?" I ask.

He shakes his head and taps quickly on the mouse. "No, this one was. And this."

"Oh my God!" my mother and I exclaim in unison.

It's a series of dissection slides, and the photos are close-ups of a cut-up uterus. With everything—*everything*—clearly labeled. And on one of them there's a bloody bit of—well, let's just say I won't be able to get that image out of my head for a long, long time.

"*Why* would you show those to Hope?"

He seems perplexed by the question. "Why not?" he asks innocently. "She said she wanted to talk about what I was interested in. So I said I'd show her."

"Why didn't you just show her a picture of a *lung* or something then? Why did you choose that...that..."

"Ectopic fetus," he finishes helpfully.

"*Why?*"

"Hope's a female," he replies simply. "I was trying to show her things that might affect her. She may need this one day."

My mother gives him a tight and patient smile. "Ethan, do you think that Hope enjoyed going through those slides with you?" she asks him in a voice that's straining to be gentle.

"She said she did," he responds, clicking through his slide show again. "But I got some of the facts wrong when I explained them to her. It's not my fault, though. This lecture was incomplete."

"I'm sure she'll forgive you," I murmur without conviction.

"Just call her and explain, okay? She left before I realized my mistake."

*She sure did*, I think, as we turn to leave the room. It seems cruel to tell him he really *had* gotten everything wrong but not at all in the way he thought. Better let him think his error was anatomy-related.

My mother shakes her head. "I'm going to let you cover this one, Rain," she says. "Maybe go over the basic rules of dating with him? And do it before he scares anyone else."

There's a subtle sting of criticism beneath her mild suggestion, and I hang my head. She's right, of course. I should have given Ethan rules for talking to girls. We had rules for everything else. But somehow, showing graphic anatomy slides had never come up before. How could I have anticipated that? My mother takes one last look at the screen, shudders, and then quickly crosses the hall, shutting her bedroom door behind her. It's up to me now. But isn't it too late to speak to him? Hope has already fled the scene, probably forever. If I tell him why she left, won't it just make him feel bad? I'm considering the question when my phone buzzes in my pocket.

"I'm coming back," Hope declares before I have a chance to say hello. "I'm so, so sorry."

I slip out of Ethan's room and shut the door. "You don't have to apologize," I assure her. "I saw what he showed you—"

"No, there's no excuse. I can't believe I ran off like that. I have to come back and explain—"

"You really don't have to—"

"I'm on my way—"

"It's seriously not a big deal—"

"I'm outside."

"Oh."

I hang up.

I come downstairs to find her standing by the kitchen door, jiggling back and forth like a kid waiting to use the bathroom. The blushing confidence of her first visit has vanished; she's a portrait of indecision and embarrassment now. "God, I'm so ashamed of myself," she blurts out when she sees me.

"Hope, I just talked to Ethan—"

"He must hate me—"

"Not even close."

She pauses and glances anxiously toward the stairs. "Are you sure?"

I walk up to her and place a hand over hers. "You're freezing cold. Doesn't your car have heat?"

She hesitates, and a little color creeps back into her face. "I didn't make it to the car. I've been walking in circles around your house for the last few minutes."

I can't help smiling at her anxiety. "You know Ethan has no idea that he offended you, right?"

Her eyes grow large, and she squeezes my fingers eagerly. "He doesn't?"

"Nope. But he is *very* worried that he made a medical mistake when he was telling you all about—"

She waves her hand to stop me. "I *wasn't* offended," she insists. "I was just freaked out for a second. But then when I got outside I realized that he hadn't meant to shock me or anything. He really believed that he was making interesting conversation, didn't he? And then I felt just awful."

I'm not sure what to say to her. I knew this would happen sooner or later. But I'm also sorry for her—for both of them. It's like watching two people who don't speak the same language try to communicate. Still, I can't tell her that. I've already hurt my brother by suggesting their relationship wasn't going to work. The only decent thing to do is step aside and let her figure this out for herself.

"You didn't hurt him," I say. "Ethan generally believes whatever you tell him as long as it's reasonable. So he probably bought whatever excuse you blurted out."

She shakes her head and covers her face with her hands. "I'm a little out of my depth here," she admits after a brief silence. "I think I need a guidebook."

There's something so lost and vulnerable about her; I reach out and wrap my arms around her. She falls against my shoulder and buries her face in my sweater. "I should have warned you that I was coming over to hang out with him," she admits. "But I knew what you would say if I told you. So I figured I'd just show you that there was nothing to worry about. Now I just proved the opposite, didn't I?"

"Not at all," I say. "But if you'd told me, I could have written you a little guidebook. Just to get you started."

I don't know why I suggest it. It's the last thing I wanted to do, really. But Hope is my best friend. She's going down this path whether I like it or not. Even if I'm sure she's making a mistake, I can at least try to be supportive. And writing rules for her is way easier than the detailed dos and don'ts of dating I'll have to submit to my brother. I have no idea how to even begin that task. Instead, I can start by helping Hope understand Ethan. And while she learns, I'll have to watch over Ethan even more carefully than I already do. Maybe if I get involved, instead of just shouting warnings from the sidelines, I can minimize the damage.

"I'll do it now, if you want."

She pulls back and gives me a funny look. "I was just joking, Rain."

I head over to the counter and open one of the drawers. "Well, I'm serious." I grab a notebook and tear out a page. "This may actually be helpful to you," I add as I start to scribble.

"I've been watching YouTube videos," she muses as I write. "But they haven't been so useful, really. Each person is so different—"

"Trying to understand autism by watching videos is like trying to understand boys by reading *Cosmo* quizzes on dating," I point out.

"Yeah, I'm beginning to realize that. I watched a couple of movies too—"

"Let me guess. *Rain Man.*"

She nods, grinning. "Oh my god, that is so *not* Ethan."

I scrawl down her instructions and push the paper toward her. "No, but this is."

"*The Rules of Ethan*," she reads out loud.

"It's just the basics that I've learned over the years," I tell her as she scans the page. "Every time Ethan tries to interact with others he has to stick to rules that are hard for him—that make him feel different. It's only fair that we should get a set of rules too."

"Which one of these is the Secret Rule?" she inquires.

"The Secret Rule's not on there," I reply, shortly. "That rule isn't relevant to you."

"Oh. Okay." She looks down, disappointed.

"I can give you more details if you need," I continue. "There are plenty more minor ones—" But she's not listening to me. Her eyes have frozen at the bottom, on the last rule. *Ethan doesn't like to be touched, especially without warning.*

She looks back at me, her brow furrowing. "I was wondering about the touching thing," she says, hesitantly. "Are you sure?"

"Yes." I knew it would be painful for her to read, but I wrote it down anyway. She needs to hear the truth.

"Not at all?" she inquires in a small voice.

I suppose I should give her some kind of encouragement. But wouldn't that be lying?

"Sorry," I reply.

She nods and takes a deep breath. "Okay."

I wonder if she's questioning their future together already. Or does she think she'll become the exception to Ethan's rules? She doesn't look nearly as dismayed as I thought she might. In fact, if I have to be completely honest, she actually seems a bit…relieved. My theories about her motives are looking doubtful. The whole Sleeping Beauty adventure idea doesn't make sense to me anymore. I have no idea what to make of that quiet smile on her face.

Well, whatever her motivation, as long as she sticks to the rules I've written out, I can't exactly object to her trying to get closer to him.

"You told Ethan you were leaving," I point out, indicating rule number five with my finger. "He'll be upset if he finds you hanging out in the kitchen."

"I know, I was about to go. But I wanted to tell you something first."

My phone buzzes while she's speaking, and I frown at the unfamiliar number on the screen. "I don't know who this is." I begin to push it back into my pocket, but she puts out her hand to stop me.

"Answer it," she commands. Her face is beaming with suppressed excitement. "Answer it, answer it."

I'm suddenly extremely wary of her abrupt change in mood. "What are you up to, Hope? What's going on?"

"Answer it!" she squeals, banging her hand on the counter.

"Who's on the phone?" I demand. We're on the fourth ring already, and she looks like she's going to explode.

"Oh, for God's sake," she huffs and grabs it from my hand. "Hello?"

"What are you doing?" I ask quietly.

"No, this is Hope," she purrs into the phone, ignoring me. "Can I take a message?"

"Who are you talking to?" But she's not even looking at me now.

"Hi, Liam," she murmurs pleasantly. "No, that's fine. I'll go get her." And she shoves the phone back into my hand. "Speak," she growls in a menacing whisper. "Now."

I stare at the cell in my hand for a moment and then slowly bring it up to my ear.

Thirty seconds and about five hundred heartbeats later, I hang up and hold my phone out in front of me. "He wants to get together after school tomorrow."

"You're welcome," she trills and waves at me as she heads toward the door. "My work here is done."

"Hope, what did you *do*?"

"Wear your green sweater," she calls out over her shoulder. "And don't forget to call me after!"

I still have a thousand questions to ask her, but she disappears into her car and begins to back out of the driveway before I'm even on the lawn. "It's only a study date," I shout after her. "Maybe it doesn't mean anything—"

"Just don't overanalyze this too, and you'll be fine!" She throws the suggestion out of the window and flees before I can protest.

Not overanalyze it? What is she talking about? What am I supposed to do until tomorrow evening? Turn my head off?

## Cooking with Rain
### SERENITY THROUGH YOUR GUT

*Where I answer all your burning food-related questions!*

**Dear Wacky Mac:** I haven't heard from you in a while. What did your crush say when you gave her the cake in a mug?

**Dear Rain:** It exploded. Three times. I decided to take it as a sign. Or a metaphor for my love life.

## ETHAN'S JOURNAL:

A glance over her shoulder emphasizes a woman's figure and contours of her face. This signals a release of pheromones and the desire to attract a mate. Women instinctively do this when trying to flirt.

### My Observation:

Hope performed this movement when I showed her the anatomy slides. But then she left the room immediately. Is she sending "mixed signals?" Mom told Rain that nice girls don't send mixed signals and don't play games. Is Hope not a nice girl?

# Chapter 7

The good news is that Liam says hello to me the next morning and we make plans to meet at my house after school for a study date.

The bad news is that my friends seem to be united in some sort of massive conspiracy which is apparently hilarious and top secret. Marcus purses his lips and shakes his head when I ask him point-blank what he said to Liam. Kathy just giggles and simpers. Hope intentionally avoids me all day.

The worse news—I really would have preferred Liam's house to mine, for obvious reasons, but when I suggest it, he brushes me off with a simple "no, sorry." Not a brooding, mysterious, I've-got-sexy-secrets "no," either. And not a bitchy one. Just no, sorry, could we go to your house? And then a shy smile which almost knocks me over.

Why not his, though? This town has all of 1,500 people in it. I could find his house in no time if I wanted to. So why not? Is he trying to hide something?

I swear I'm not overthinking this.

I've formed ten theories before I leave the school though. To prevent more theories from entering my brain, I plug my earbuds in and concentrate on Katy Perry as I walk home. Her roaring distracts me from my obsessive thoughts. I'm a clean slate before I reach my neighborhood—relaxed, confident, and singing (mostly silently) to the rhythm in my head. Hope would be so proud of me.

As I approach my house, I glance up and see Liam standing on my front porch. And he's talking to Ethan.

My earbuds are out, my confidence is gone, and I'm suddenly walking a lot faster.

"Hi, guys!" I call out a bit too brightly. How long have they been standing there? How did Liam get here before me? What are they talking about?

"I'll ask him tonight," I hear Liam say. "And I'll let you know."

"Thank you." Ethan turns to me as I walk up to the porch. "Hello, Rain. Don't forget our run today."

"You don't have to remind me every time. I never forget. But can we push it off by an hour, maybe? Liam and I are studying chemistry."

He's never going to say yes. I know that. There's going to be some resistance, at least. We always run at four, Rain. Every day. Always at four.

"Okay."

*Wait, what?*

"We can run at five," he states. He looks uncomfortable— *really* uncomfortable—but he says it. Just like that. Then he glances at Liam.

What's going on here? How much could I have missed?

"Great. Thanks." I look to Liam for a clue, but his face is blank too. "Should we go inside then?"

We settle at the kitchen counter, and Ethan immediately heads off to his room. Part of me is a little relieved that he goes so quickly, but part of me is frustratingly curious. And although I had texted him earlier to let him know that Liam was coming by, I'd hardly expected that he'd leave his room and try to start a conversation. Ethan doesn't do small talk with strangers, or with anyone for that matter. Still, I can't ask Liam what they were talking about without seeming totally nosy and inappropriate. So I swallow my questions and pleasantly offer him a snack.

"Sure, thanks. What've you got?" Liam looks up from unpacking his books and peers into the open fridge.

"I made a batch of Tums muffins."

He blinks at me. "What's a Tums muffin?"

"It's one of my gluten-free experiments for Ethan. If you crush an antacid in the dough, it makes it fluffier and less rocklike. Ethan calls them Tums muffins. Except for him, I haven't been able to get anyone to try them."

"Yeah, you might want to rethink that name. You got some cold cuts or something? That's what I usually have after school."

I laugh and shake my head. "You mean like salami? God, no. My mom is terrified of processed meats."

"Really?"

I nod. "I think hot dogs may have caused my parents' divorce."

"That would make a great title for a talk show or something." He grins at me. "How did that happen?"

I pull some organic cheddar and portobello mushrooms from

the crisper and close the fridge. "My last memory of them together has to do with hot dogs. My mom was holding a pack of frozen Oscar Mayers in her hands, and my dad was scowling at her in the corner. And she was yelling, 'This is what did it! This is why he's like that. Because you keep feeding them this poison!' And then she threw the package at him, and it hit him on the head."

"Oh, wow."

"Yup."

"Sorry I asked."

"No worries. If you want, I can make you some algae flour pizza."

"Algae *what*?"

Hope's warning pops into my head, and I shake it away. Isn't the best advice to "be yourself?" Well, this is the way I flirt (I think), with the coolest, top-secret food tips I've gathered from years of research. "I have a small packet of algae flour I got at a trade show a while back. It's pretty new—and kind of scandalous."

My offer is the foodie equivalent of front row tickets to the Super Bowl. Seriously. No one has this stuff yet, and those who do certainly aren't sharing. Probably because the company that was using it had to recall some of its products last year. But I've tested it in my own recipes with no problems at all. Still, I'm not surprised he doesn't seem impressed.

"I'm sorry… *Algae?*"

"Yeah, I know it sounds weird, but you wouldn't even know it's there. And the dough comes out amazing! Algae is basically a substitute for *everything*—eggs, wheat, dairy…"

His lips twitch, and his brows come down. "You want me to try your pond scum pizza."

I shut the refrigerator. "Oh, no, please don't call it that. Just forget I mentioned it."

"But I don't want to forget." He seems to be choking on suppressed laughter. "No one has ever offered me algae before. This is a special moment."

"Never mind. Offer withdrawn."

"I'm not making fun! I swear. I'll eat the entire pizza. And no matter what it looks like, I promise I won't post it on Instagram."

I sink down on the kitchen stool and toss the package of mushrooms on the counter. "You saw the sperm pudding pic."

"Everyone saw the sperm pudding pic."

"That thing has ruined my reputation," I mutter. "I was trying to find a way to make it look less…gross. Marcus just caught it in the sperm stage. I've made improvements to the recipe since then. Like anyone cares."

He smiles and clears his throat. "Well, I basically live on pasta and bologna sandwiches. So I'll be happy to try your sperm pudding." He chuckles quietly. "Hah. There's a phrase I never thought I'd say."

I get up from the stool and fetch a covered bowl from the counter. "You're the first person to taste this since I've fixed it. It looks kind of like tapioca now."

He lifts the spoon and sniffs, his eyes wary. "Holy crap," he says after the first swallow. "Rain, this is actually…*good*."

"Just good? Could you be more specific? Since that photo went viral I don't get very many volunteers to taste my recipes."

His shocked expression is the best compliment I've ever gotten. "It's *fantastic*. Like a cross between butterscotch and—"

"Cashew cream. Yeah. And that's raspberry syrup in the topping."

"You should put *this* picture up," he insists, scooping a giant spoonful into his mouth. "Like a 'before and after' piece. Show how far you've come."

I feel my face getting warm. "I can post it to my blog. With the title 'How You Like Me Now, Haters?'"

And there goes Hope's last piece of advice. I'm discussing my blog with my crush. And he hasn't run away. (Take *that*, traditional flirters.) I can't tell if his smile is in response to my blog comment or the sugar rush from the raspberry syrup drizzle, but I'm clearly doing something right.

"Well, algae or not, I think you've got a career here," he remarks as he scrapes the bottom of the glass. "For what it's worth. Like I said, I live on sandwiches and pasta so I'm not the most discerning critic."

"That doesn't sound like living to me. Your dad doesn't cook?"

"My dad is almost never home," he replies. His smile fades. He studies his empty glass and runs his finger over the last traces of pudding.

"So it's just you? No brothers or sisters?"

"Just me."

"Oh. That's…"

That just seems *wrong,* I want to say to him. He comes home to nobody, goes to bed in an empty house, wakes up to…silence. I can't imagine it. For all my brother's quirks and my mother's nuttiness, I wouldn't be able to live without their warmth and energy around me. "That must be…quiet," I finish lamely.

"It is what it is," he replies. "Hopefully I won't be there much longer."

"You won't? Where are you going?"

He sets his spoon down and glances up at me. His quiet statement upset me a little, and I'm doing my best to hide my confusion and disappointment. It doesn't sound like he's talking about postgraduation. His tone clearly implied that he's got one foot out the door already.

"I'm sorry," he says sincerely. "I just thought that you should know."

Know *what*? And why does he think I have a right to know, anyway? It's not like we're dating. He doesn't owe me anything. "What do you mean?"

He sighs and rubs his hands over his forehead. "I'm trying to graduate early. I'm applying to the Global Gap program with Projects Abroad."

"Projects Abroad?"

"Yeah, they have six-month training courses in Ghana, Peru, South Africa, and a couple of other places. Before college. Mostly volunteering in day cares, medical internships, irrigation and clean water projects—"

"Wow. That sounds amazing."

"Yeah, but it's not cheap. So that's why I've got the after-school tutoring jobs and the lifeguarding. My grandmother says she can help with some of the cost, but I feel guilty asking her for that much. So I'm trying to raise most of it myself."

"No wonder you're never around. Doesn't leave a whole lot of time for hanging out with friends."

"No, I guess not." He doesn't sound regretful or bitter when he says it. Just quiet. And a little tired.

"I'm sorry." I really am too. Not only because I realize we can never truly become close if he's so focused on leaving. I'm also sorry for him—for the picture he's just painted. His life seems so lonely as he's described it. I wonder if he'll look back one day and wonder where his teenage years went.

"Anyway, I figured you should know," he murmurs almost guiltily.

There it is again. What does he mean by that?

"*Why?*"

He glances up again, and I see a flicker of indecision pass over his face. He opens his mouth to answer, hesitates for minute, clears his throat, and then seems to reconsider. "Never mind. I just meant… You know, if you were looking for a long-term study partner or whatever."

I'm not sure what he's hinting at. What had he meant by "long-term study partner?" *He* had asked *me* for a study date, not the other way around. Where had he gotten the idea that I was interested in more? Hope's strange behavior had already roused my suspicions. I'd guessed that my friends had been conspiring to set us up somehow. But had they flat-out *told* Liam how I felt about him? They wouldn't do that… Would they?

"Speaking of studying," I say, flipping open my book. "Should we start with the section on acids and bases? We can take turns answering the chapter questions."

"Sure." He pulls his textbook out of his bag.

I begin reading out loud, but my mind is nowhere near pH balances. Is it so bad if he knows that I like him? Girls ask guys out all the time. Whatever happened to taking chances?

But he'd just *said* that he wasn't interested in a long-term study partner. Was that code for something? Was it a preemptive brush off? I definitely need to think about this more. Later after he goes home, I'll go over every word and expression and then plan for our next conversation. I'm way too confused to sort through this while he's sitting next to me. *Enough*, I tell myself. *I'm going to concentrate on the book in front of me like it was the only important thing in the room.*

For the next half hour, I'm the most dedicated student in Montana. I don't even sneak a peek at my study partner, who seems to be getting quieter and more hesitant as the minutes tick by. When I finally do look up, I see that he's staring at me, his finger still poised over the page, his brows pulled low over his dark eyes. He starts when I glance at him and quickly drops his gaze, but I've clearly flustered him, and he has to go back over the last paragraph from the beginning.

I watch him as he reads, and a familiar ache forms somewhere in my throat. I need to stop caring about this guy. He's almost gone, he's leaving, he was *never* a part of my life, and he never will be. I know that. So why can't I stop wondering how those brown curls would feel against my fingers? Why can't I stop picturing my hands running over his shoulders and down his back? I want to know everything about him, want to talk to him until our mouths are dry and our eyes heavy, want to be the person that bursts into his solitary, quiet life and makes him happy. I don't even know why I want it so badly. I just know that the last half hour of fake indifference is all that I can handle.

Marcus and Kathy had teased me for being too careful, never taking chances. If my mother had to evaluate me in three words I bet that one of them would be "guarded." And for once, that's not who I want to be. My friends are all waiting for me to call them, to break the news that the guy I'd had a crush on had finally asked me out. But that wasn't going to happen, that much was obvious. He wasn't looking for "long-term" anything.

Well, that's okay, I think. Neither am I. I'm looking for now, this moment. And I'm tired of waiting.

"Liam…"

I have no idea what I'm going to say before I say his name, but I know whatever comes out of my mouth will be a fantastic, rule-breaking revelation. Hey, I'd talked about my blog and pond scum pizza, and he was still there, wasn't he? I'd even made the chia seed sperm fiasco work for me. I could do anything. And right now, I was going to bring down walls.

"Liam..." He stops reading, his eyes are focused on me—waiting, expectant. My trembling voice promises a great confession.

"I just wanted to tell you—"

"Yeah?"

Oh God, where did all the words go?

"Liam. I like your..."Crap, I can't remember English! How do I finish that sentence? How do guys do this? How does *anyone* do this? Can I say eyes? No, too cliché. Body? Ew, no. Personality? No, don't know him well enough. "Liam," I gasp out in breathless desperation. "I really like your face."

Oh, God. *Did I just interrupt our chemistry lesson to tell him that I liked his face?*

He doesn't laugh. Thank all the stars in heaven, he doesn't laugh, not even with his eyes. All he says is, "My face?" as if looking for clarification on something he'd misunderstood. I feel like I've swallowed a mountain of rocks.

"No. Not face—not—no."

I am not a leader of women, after all. I am just an embarrassing weirdo.

"Not your face," I splutter helplessly. "I mean, your face is fine. What I meant was—"

Oh, God, I hate *everything*.

"I like *you*," I finish miserably. "I was just trying to ask you out."

Is that better? Is that closer to normal? I can't tell anymore. All language and sense has abandoned me.

His expression doesn't change. He eyes me skeptically and

slowly closes his chemistry book. "Rain, if this is a joke, I'm not going to give you any more material. Our exploding lab experiment should get you enough views on YouTube without the fake date proposal." He starts to rise, but the pained look on my face makes him pause, and he sinks slowly back into his chair.

"What are you talking about?" My voice comes out strangled, somewhere between a wheeze and a squeak. "How could have I posted it to YouTube?"

"Hope told me to call you because you needed help with chemistry," he replies. "I didn't believe her." He sighs. "And yet I'm here anyway. For some reason."

Well, that explains Hope's behavior. Still, as annoyed as I am with her, I'm going to have to deal with that later. Right now though, I'm totally pissed at Liam. He's not following any kind of reasonable script. But then, neither am I.

"You didn't believe her?" I retort. I'm breathing more normally, and I even manage to add a touch of vinegar to the question. "Or you didn't *want* to believe her?"

"I thought she was making fun of me," he replies quickly. "And after what happened in lab, I was sure you two were in on some kind of a joke and that one of your friends had filmed the whole thing."

I shake my head. "Hold on. You thought I was asking you out as a joke?"

He shrugs and slides his glasses off his nose. "It happened at my last school. Look, I'm not exactly homecoming king." God, those eyes are even more potent without the frames. I'm finding it hard to concentrate on what he's saying.

"But why would you think I was trying to prank you? Who does that? Who would find that funny?"

He blinks at me in surprise. "Thousands of people, apparently." He hesitates and slides his glasses back into place. "You have no idea what I'm talking about, do you?"

"No. Not a clue!"

"Wait. So you haven't seen—" He hesitates again, and the doubt in his eyes flickers out. "Oh. *Oh, man.* I just assumed you'd seen that clip…and you were trying for the sequel."

I pick up my phone. "What clip?"

He reaches out to block my hand. "Please don't. I know I can't stop you from looking after I go. But at least don't do it in front of me."

"Internet bullies?"

"Yeah. At my last school. They said it served me right for thinking that the prettiest girl in the grade actually liked me. Apparently I had it coming."

"Then why did you ask me for a study date? If you thought I was like those people?"

"Honestly, I wasn't sure what to think. Hope texted me after the lab explosion and told me to give you a call. She said you were having trouble with chemistry and needed my help. That's what made me suspicious. People ask me for free tutoring all the time. I know that girls notice my grades, not me. But *you* don't need my help. Then I started wondering if you made that experiment explode on purpose. That all of this was part of some elaborate joke. I hoped that I was wrong. But I didn't want to make a fool of myself again."

His honesty disarms me and my frustration melts in a moment. "You mean more than I just did?" I ask, smiling. "I don't think that's possible."

He grins at me. "Well, just now I was thinking that my only hope of acing chemistry is if I suddenly discover I'm gay."

"*What?*"

"Because it's distracting."

"What is?"

"*Your* face."

I can't think of a response to that. Our conversation is so broken that I'm not sure where to begin. And Liam's blush is so deep that it just adds to my embarrassment.

"What I meant was," he concludes meekly. "It's hard to concentrate on chemistry when you're sitting there."

"Oh."

"Yeah. You're basically the chemistry antitutor. You make me stupid."

It's the strangest compliment I've ever gotten. But it makes me smile anyway. His expression visibly relaxes. "I've always thought you were pretty, Rain," he admits after a moment.

"But…" I protest weakly, "but you didn't even know my last name."

"I lied. Of course I knew your name. I was freaking out

yesterday that you were going to be my lab partner. But then you started acting so…uh—"

"Batshit crazy?"

He chuckles. "Well…yeah. So I thought baffled ignorance was my best bet. At that moment."

"I get that. But why didn't you say anything before? I mean—if you liked me—" I pause, uncertain. That's what he'd just admitted, right? I hadn't imagined it?

He nods heavily, and the old tired look settles over his features. "I don't know how to explain this to you."

"Just try," I urge him. "I'm not going to judge."

"It's just that I've never really asked a girl out. After what happened at my last school I decided to play it safe—at least through high school. Ever since I got here, I've only had one goal—to get the hell out. So I wasn't going to get attached to anybody. I wasn't going to care."

"Yet you still came over here today."

He shrugs and glances back at me. "Yeah. First time I didn't follow my own advice. Couldn't help myself. Anyway, I was ninety-five percent sure you weren't interested. So there wasn't any real danger."

"Danger? Liam, that's an awful way to look at people."

He looks surprised and a little hurt. "It isn't personal," he says defensively. "I haven't gotten close to anyone here."

"I know. That's awful too."

"I thought you weren't going to judge."

"I'm not judging you. I just can't imagine living like that."

"Well, you don't live in my house."

That shuts me up. I feel my face get hot, and I drop my eyes. He's right, I think. I don't know his story.

"Look, I'm not expecting forever either," I say after a moment. "We're only sixteen."

He shoots me a doubtful smile. "I thought you prefer to plan everything, to play it safe. Like me."

"Yeah, I also believe in trying new things. Like algae." I'm all cool confidence now, which is a nice improvement from wheezing and sweating. I throw him a flirtatious wink, but he just stares at me. "And I'm trying to be spontaneous for a change."

"Spontaneous?"

"Sure. That's why I told you how much I like your face."

He grins. "Yeah. Right after you tried to blow me up in chemistry lab."

"Oh, that was just me playing hard to get."

We're both laughing now, and I try to freeze this perfect snapshot in my mind. I want to remember it. I inch a little closer to him and gently nudge the pudding cup out of the way.

And then Ethan appears behind us. "It's five o'clock," he says.

The moment's over.

"Right. I better go." Liam sweeps his books off the table and stuffs them into his bag.

"Rain, it's getting late," Ethan urges. "You don't even have your tennis shoes on."

"One more minute," I tell him. "I'll just say goodbye to my friend, okay?"

We walk out onto the porch, and I shut the door behind us. "I want you to know, I'm not going to look," I tell him as he turns to leave.

"What?"

"I'm not going to watch the YouTube clip. I promise."

"Thank you." He hesitates for a moment. "It got three thousand views," he says. "I can't believe no one at Clarkson High has seen it."

"It was more than a year ago, right? And three thousand views is hardly viral."

"Everything feels viral in high school."

I can hear the shame in his voice; the memory still stings him like a new wound. It's no wonder he wants to play it safe. I know a small part of him still doesn't believe I like him, even after I told him. He's holding his breath, waiting for the "gotcha" moment and for it to all come crashing down around him. And I realize he's never going to reach through the wall he's built, not unless I pull some bricks out for him first.

He slides his glasses off his nose and rubs the lenses with his sleeve. If there's ever a moment to be spontaneous, it's now. I want to blot out any doubt in his mind. I want him to go home happy tonight. But I have less than a minute to act; my brother is inside literally counting the seconds.

I can't think or analyze or plan. Just this once, I have to grab the moment. So I do. Rather, I grab Liam.

I step forward and wrap my hands around his neck. He

startles so hard that he drops his glasses. As they hit the ground, I lean up and kiss him. I miss his lips by a little and have to go in again. Then there's a little awkwardness due to a miscalculation of nose angles and some embarrassed laughter as they knock together. We get it right by the third try.

"There," I say after I catch my breath. "Do you believe me now?"

I take his speechlessness as a yes. He runs a shaky hand through my hair. The tremble of his fingers is the hottest thing I can imagine.

"There's a Halloween party next Saturday at Kathy's house," I whisper.

"Okay." He's still staring at my lips.

"Her parents are out of town."

"Mmm-hmm."

I smile. "I'm asking if you want to come with me."

"Next Saturday? Sure. Okay." I get the feeling he would have agreed to lion taming lessons on the moon right now.

"Rain!" Ethan throws the door open and drums his foot against the mat.

Liam jumps away from me and picks up his glasses. "Okay. Bye, then," he calls and stumbles down the porch stairs.

As he disappears around the corner, I do a little dance of joy around the porch. A party with Liam! The super serious guy with the weight of the world on his shoulders is coming with me to a party. Our first real (no parents) party. It seems too good to be true.

And then Ethan speaks again.

"So what are you going to tell Mom?"

I hadn't considered Mom at all. I know exactly what she'd say. She wouldn't need three adjectives either. No "responsible" daughter of hers would ever—*ever*—

"I won't say there's a party. I'll tell her I'm going to Kathy's house."

He considers for a moment. "Why can't we tell her about the party?"

*We?*

"Because," I explain patiently. "That will lead to more questions. And probably a call to Kathy's parents. And the party will be canceled."

"Why?"

"Because, Efan." I sigh as he drops my tennis shoes in front of me. "There's going to be beer and stuff. And since I've never been in trouble in my entire life, it's not that big of a deal to bend the rules a little bit. This once." I let him ponder that as I duck into the house to change into my running clothes. He doesn't say anything when I join him outside; we jog silently down the stretch to the ice cream shop and round the corner to return home before he finally speaks again. "I'll tell Mom that I'm going to Kathy's house too," he remarks calmly, as if it were the most natural thing in the world.

"*What?*" I stop suddenly in place and stare at him even as he continues past me, oblivious.

A few paces forward, he realizes I'm no longer next to him,

and he turns to face me, confused. "I said I'll tell Mom—" he begins before I cut him off.

"I *heard* you. Where do you plan on going Saturday night?"

"The party. At Kathy's." How does he manage to destroy everything while wearing such a blank and innocent expression?

"*What?*"

"The party—"

"Stop repeating yourself!" I exclaim. "I can hear. I just can't *believe* what I'm hearing."

"Okay." He doesn't look hurt at all. Considering my tone and the pissed off expression on my face, I'd say that is one of the miracles of autism. Or maybe it's just Ethan, I don't know. "What can't you believe?" he asks.

"That you want to go. To a *party*."

"Oh. Hope asked me to go with her," he responds in that infuriatingly even tone of his. "She texted me while you were studying with Liam. Here, I can show you—" He begins to pull out his phone.

"You don't have to prove it to me," I interrupt. "But Efan—"

"We have to finish our run," he mutters, looking up at the sky with growing concern. "It's going to get dark."

"Fine," I respond irritably. "Never mind. I'll just talk to Hope. I have no idea why she asked you to go to a Halloween party. She must have lost her mind." I take off down the path in a rapid sprint, and after a couple of minutes I hear Ethan behind me panting and struggling to keep up.

We're close to home by the time he finally catches up. His face is flushed, and his eyes are shining with a strange light. He's usually all pepped up after our run, but today there's something new there, something underneath the surface that I've never seen before. And that something is freaking me out.

"I think she asked me because she wants to go to the party *with me*," he states quietly, as if there hadn't been any break in our conversation. "I don't think she's lost her mind. But you can talk to her if you're not sure."

From anyone else's lips those words would have been loaded with injured pride and sarcasm. He would have spat them at me angrily before storming off to slam his door. But from Ethan, the declaration rings pure and simple, untainted by malice or double meaning. And I stand there totally speechless, shamed silent by his sincerity.

# Chapter 8

I mention the party to Mom the following day, and she barely even notices. Of course I call it a "get-together" instead of party. And I don't say that Ethan wants to go too. I'll have to reveal that part later, after I've introduced her to Liam. I've never talked about him before (there was nothing to talk about), but if he's going to be hanging out at my house, I should at least get her used to the idea. So I start with that.

"Liam?" she says, her eyes suddenly alive with interest. "Is he one of your friends?"

"Yeah. I guess." Friend is as much as I can call him, despite the bumpy kiss.

"Wait. Do you mean Liam Franklin?"

I give her a strange look. "How do you know his name?"

"It's a small town, Rain."

"You've met his parents?"

"No. His mom isn't in the picture as far as I can tell. But I know his dad. Most people do." I'm suddenly scared of what she's about to reveal.

"What's wrong with his dad?"

She shakes her head. "He's one of those guys who's probably a social worker's knock away from losing his kid. He works for a trucking company, and as far as I know he's barely home."

I stare at her quietly. So far so good. All familiar information. But what else did she know?

"There was a custody question some years ago," she continues. "His grandmother consulted me, actually. But I had to tell her that it wasn't my area of expertise. I have no idea why someone who's always on the road insisted on taking back his son after all those years. The boy was obviously better off with his grandma in Missoula, even if she was too old to look after him. Anyway, in the end, Liam came to live with his dad in that old trailer park behind the strip mall."

*The trailer park?* How did I not know that? A few of the other students in my class lived there, but somehow I'd never associated that place with Liam. There were decent, respectable trailer parks in our county. But that area was definitely not one of them.

"I didn't realize he lived there."

"Well, I can't imagine it's something he would advertise. I assume he hasn't invited you over."

"No."

She crosses her arms and puts on her stern parenting face. "You know you're not allowed to go over there, right?"

I roll my eyes. "Okay."

"Good." The Mom face melts. "Because that man is not someone I want around my daughter."

Despite never having met the guy, I'm suddenly pissed on his behalf. "Mom, you don't even know him."

She raises her eyebrows. "I know that he's a drunk. And mean. And a gambler. I think that's enough to go on, don't you?"

Well, I'd gotten my three adjectives. Or two nouns and an adjective, anyhow. "So what? You can't judge a kid by his father!"

"I'm not. I just don't want you hanging out there, that's all."

"Why? Because his dad abandoned him? You could say the same thing about me and Ethan!"

Her face hardens. She has way more than three adjectives to describe my dad. And not one of them is complimentary. "Yeah, well, you have a mother who stuck around."

*Yeah, and you never stop reminding me*, I think.

"Speaking of fathers, did you know that your brother speaks to that man almost every day?" she says.

"Yeah, Ethan told me."

She shrugs and runs her fingers through her fair hair. It's funny how much my brother resembles her on the outside but is so different on the inside. But then, Ethan is unlike most people.

"Well, I guess I shouldn't take it personally," she mutters, waving a dismissive hand. "I suppose they don't teach loyalty in all those therapy sessions."

"Mom!"

"Oh, I know Ethan's not trying to hurt me."

"Of course he's not! All he's doing is talking to him. It has nothing to do with you."

"Really? I've spent every free hour of my life tending to Ethan's needs, and he turns to the man whose only contribution is a monthly check?"

*A pretty large monthly check*, I think. We could easily live on what my father sends, even without my mother's income. But still, I see her point. "I can try to talk to Ethan, if you want."

"No, he's made his choice. We all make choices, Rain. And then we have to live with them. I'm just glad one of you understands."

She smiles at me fondly and draws me into her arms for a warm hug. I return her embrace, but my heart isn't in it. Am I supposed to feel proud of myself because I chose her over my father? Is that what she's saying? I imagine she's telling me that one of my adjectives is "loyal." And I try to appreciate the compliment behind her hug. But in that moment, I have a surge of strong emotion, like a bitter aftertaste, and it feels like the exact opposite of loyalty.

## *Cooking with Rain*
### SERENITY THROUGH YOUR GUT

Heartburn and indigestion? Stressful conversation with parents? Try Rain's soy milk ice cream topped with olive oil and sea salt!

# Chapter 9

There's some sort of stomach flu outbreak at school a couple of days later, and I show up to find that half the class and most of our teachers are out sick. Early that morning I'd gotten a dramatic text from Hope declaring, "Dying from puke. Pray for me." And later Kathy sends me a message begging me to pick up that day's assignments for her. Marcus is also ill (he and Kathy share a bloodstream, after all), so I make a mental note to stop by both their houses and then go to Hope's.

There are only a handful of students in chemistry lab that morning. After a few lame attempts mixing acids and bases and waiting for the phenolphthalein in the solution to turn red, Liam and I give up when Mr. Green suddenly turns green and rushes out of the classroom.

We're supposed to stay in school until after lunch, but havoc has broken loose, and halfway through second period, there's a mass exodus. Those of us who are lucky enough to have escaped the puke virus hang around in cheerful solidarity until the principal announces that school is closing for the day, and we head out, selfishly thrilled at the unexpected day of vacation.

"Can I pick you up in an hour?" Liam asks me as we gather our books.

"Sure! Where are we going?"

He smiles enigmatically and takes off, and I rush home to change into something more date-worthy.

There aren't a lot of choices for romantic venues in Clarkson. We've got Manny's Ice Cream Shop, which is the popular pick for a quick and cheap afternoon date. There's Milly's Diner, where you can take someone you don't like in the hopes of getting rid of them with a case of salmonella. And there's Bob's Burger N' Chips, but that's just a more expensive salmonella sandwich. So I'm a little relieved when Liam shows up at my door with an oversized picnic basket and suggests driving out to Trout Creek Campground. "I'm taking care of the food this time," he says.

I eye the basket suspiciously and sweep a container of Rain's peanut butter and date cookies into my bag. Better safe than hungry.

What Clarkson lacks in fine dining it makes up for in nature. It's all on display as we pull off the interstate onto Diamond Road. We're so far from the car horns and big city congestion, it's as if we're in the Garden of Eden.

Liam chooses a secluded bench and spreads out the food. He's done well for someone who can't cook. There are crackers and slices of cheddar cheese, melon cubes tossed with sliced grapes (which he calls fruit salad), and ingredients to make s'mores. Well, most of the ingredients.

"Where's the chocolate?" I break a graham cracker in half and press a marshmallow into its center.

He draws out a mug wrapped in foil. "Open it," he says.

It's filled with steaming, fudgy dough that sticks to my fingers. "What is this?"

"You don't recognize it?" He gives me a sheepish grin. "It's your recipe."

"My recipe?" I sniff the contents and poke at the mushy center. "Lava Bomb?"

"Yep. It's from your blog."

"You're kidding! You read my blog?"

He drops his head and begins to rearrange the fruit slices on the platter. "It exploded the first few times I tried it."

I stare at him. "Wait a second... That was you? You're Wacky Mac from Missoula?"

He's focusing on the fruit as if his life depended on it.

"Why didn't you say something?"

He shrugs, head still bowed over the plate. "It went on too long. I found it weeks ago, through that link on your Instagram, and I thought the blog would be a good way to break the ice. I was going to bring in one of your recipes, sweep you off your feet..."

"Why didn't you?"

"I kept wrecking the recipes. Also I don't own an oven, and everything I tried microwaving either burned or exploded. So I decided to wait until you posted something simple. By then it felt too creepy to bring up. So I asked you to be my lab partner instead. And then things got really weird anyway."

I slide over next to him. "You know what's even weirder? Wacky Mac is the only subscriber who's ever written to me."

He looks up for the first time since his confession. "But you've had tons of other letters—"

"Nope. Just yours. I wrote the others myself. I was really excited that someone was writing to me."

"And you're not mad that it was just me?"

"I'm glad that it was you."

The relief in his eyes is so sweet that I can't help myself; I lean forward and kiss him. He doesn't startle this time. We find each other easily, effortlessly. His lips move just as they're supposed to, softly over mine, then down my cheek, behind my ear. He takes his time—entire minutes seem to pass between each kiss; his hands hover by my waist, frozen at the safe spot just above my belt line. I love how new I am to him; I love how careful he is when he touches me. But I don't want to be careful anymore. I want to startle him again, like I did with our first kiss.

I slide my hands over his and move them beneath my shirt, then listen eagerly for the sharp intake of breath as his fingers brush my skin. But instead he falls back and stares at me, mouth open, eyes wide with surprise. His hands are trembling against my back. I want to push past his shyness, calm his shaky touch. So I kiss him again, hard. I lick his lips. I'm waiting for that look of sudden wakening again. I'm addicted to that look; I could live on his shock forever.

"It's okay," I whisper. "I'm nervous too."

He drops his head before I can kiss him again. "Rain, I think I need to wait a bit."

"It's all right. I don't want to go any further either."

He swallows hard, and the color rises to his cheeks. "No, I mean, I just need a breather. Give me a second, okay?"

"Did I do something wrong?"

He cuts me off with a look and pulls me back into his arms so fast I lose my breath beneath the crush of his kiss.

His glasses fall off. So does my hair clip. My elbow ends up in the cake mug. The fruit scatters, and the graham crackers crumble to dust.

Not that I have anyone to compare him to, but *holy hell.*

I think he realizes that now *I* need a breather, because he pulls back and surveys the red-faced, heavy-breathing mess he's just created. I take a deep breath, smooth down my hair, and give him a drunken grin. "Well, that was…really good."

His phone buzzes, and he fumbles to shut it off. "Sorry, you were saying? Just good? Could you be more specific?"

I'm not sure how to answer that so I just lift my elbow and peel off a chunk of chocolate cake.

"Well, there goes your Lava Bomb."

He grins. "It's okay. It did its job."

"Haha, very funny." I flick it at him. "Are you going to answer your phone?"

"It's one of the students I tutor," he says, glancing at the screen. "Four missed calls."

"You should see what he wants."

I regret my suggestion a minute later. He has to go, of course. Some PSAT emergency. I can hear the whining and begging from where I'm sitting.

"It's okay. We'll finish our date another time," I assure him as we gather up our crushed lunch and load the basket into his truck.

He drops me off at home and waves sadly as he drives away. So I'm left alone, nursing the memory of the greatest kiss of all time. I'm not sure where Ethan is, but I want to replay my first date in my head without chance of interruption. I change out of my chocolate-stained shirt and head out the door toward the shopping plaza. It's a good thing the streets are quiet because I probably look sort of drunk. I'm not staggering or anything, but my face is all kinds of goofy. Soon enough, I will text Hope every detail, but I'm enjoying the buzz too much to ruin it with words. I stroll happily through my neighborhood and grin at everyone I pass; every house is warm and friendly today, and I cherish each familiar landmark. I love the hardware store, the string of mom-and-pop shops, the fish and tackle stand, and even Milly's Diner. Milly's been gone for ten years, but Big Joe has never taken down her name. In the meantime, Big Joe has gotten greasier and hairier, and his hash brown patties have gotten greasier and hairier too. Still, Joe somehow stays in business, probably because his diner is visible from the interstate and is a trap for unsuspecting truckers too hungry to worry about hygiene and health department notices.

It's close to noon when I pass Milly's, and Big Joe has just put up the open sign. I glance inside dreamily and prepare to move on when I suddenly notice that the diner is not empty, as it usually is at that hour. There are two customers sitting at a corner table, and the one facing me is Ethan. I'm so shocked to see my brother in a diner that for a moment I don't even think about the man sitting with him.

I push open the door, wave at Big Joe, and walk quickly up to my brother's table. Ethan is talking animatedly as I approach, and I hear the words "maybe an appendectomy if I'm lucky" before he sees me and freezes midsentence. I'm not upset, just curious and confused, but the terrified expression on Ethan's face implies that he's just been caught red-handed. And then I glance over at his companion and understand.

"Rainey," the man murmurs, his voice catching on my name.

"Dad." The word escapes my lips, and suddenly I can't move or speak; it's painful to breathe. *Dad*, I think numbly.

Ethan is shooting frantic looks at both of us, his head whipping back and forth like a cornered mouse. "You didn't ask," he says. "Rain, you didn't ask."

*Ask what?*

My father struggles out of the narrow booth and takes a step toward me, then stops, arms out uncertainly. "Rainey."

*It's been two years. Two years. Does he really expect me to hug him?*

I do though. Mostly to buy time because my stunned brain hasn't quite caught up yet. I give him a stiff, arms-only embrace and then quickly back away. He smells like after-dinner mints and expensive cologne, the same Dad combo I remember from when we were little. I shake the thought away and try to focus on the present.

"Does Mom know you're here?" I ask him. He shouldn't forget where my loyalties lie.

"I have visiting rights," he declares. My father looks like a thicker version of Jeff Goldblum, with bigger eyebrows and less hair. When he gets angry, those eyebrows meet in the middle to form an intimidating 'V.' "I am legally entitled to see my children every weekend if I choose."

"If you choose," I retort. I really don't want to get into an argument here. Big Joe is eyeing us with growing suspicion from behind his counter, and my brother seems so miserable that I want to spare him any further drama. What's the point, anyway? My father lives a thousand miles away, and we never see him. He has a pretty fiancée and a replacement stepson named Timothy. Why does he need us?

"Well, I didn't choose *this*," he protests in a softer voice. "I didn't choose for the two of you to live halfway across the country. I could have fought it. I could have insisted that your mother not leave the state. That was my legal right."

I know all of this. Why is he telling me again? "Why are you here *now*?" I ask him. I want this meeting to be over. There's a part of me that's never felt comfortable with our estrangement, and seeing him again is bringing back all kinds of warm memories that I tried very hard to forget. It doesn't seem fair to our mother, that, as she puts it, he can just send money and be the good guy without any of the hard work. After everything she's done for Ethan and me, she deserves somebody on her team.

"I've been here more often than you realize," he replies grimly. And then we both look at Ethan.

"You didn't ask," my brother repeats doggedly. His face has lost whatever color it had.

"Ask *what*?"

"I've been coming to visit your brother every couple of months for the last two years," my father replies. "I take the connecting flight from DC through Salt Lake and stay for a couple nights in a hotel outside Missoula. Ethan and I meet at this diner when you're at school."

I don't know which portion of this statement shocks me more, that my father has been in town at least twenty times and I didn't know, or that my brother has kept a secret from me for two years. No, never mind, I know which one is more upsetting.

"You never told me!" I yell at Ethan. "All this time. You never told me!"

"You never asked!" he retorts, as if relieved that his prepared reply finally makes sense.

"*Why would I have asked?*" I wail at him. He cowers visibly before me, and from the corner of my eye I see Big Joe puff up and lumber toward us.

"Enough." Dad puts a restraining hand on my shoulder. "Don't yell at your brother. You were the one who decided to stop answering my calls, Rain. What did you expect him to do?"

"I expect him to be honest with me!" I can't believe my brother would hide something like this from me. My father is here with me, with us, after almost two years. I should be focusing on that. That should be the only thing on my mind. Instead, all I can think about is that Ethan has let me down in the most unbelievable way. My compulsively honest brother has done the impossible; he's actually lied to me. For *years*.

"How *could* you?" I demand. I take a step closer to him, but he falls back and slumps in the booth seat. His head is down, his eyes fixed on some point beneath the table. "The one thing I was always sure of, the only thing I could count on is that you would *never* lie to me."

"I didn't lie," he insists stubbornly. "You never *asked* me if Dad was visiting me."

"Oh, for God's sake," I growl at him. "You're going to try to slip through a loophole? Seriously?"

He doesn't understand the expression I've just used. Even as I say it, I know he won't understand. But I don't care. I'm done here.

As I storm out of the diner, I'm absolutely certain I'll regret what I've just done. But my reaction feels predetermined, inevitable, even though I hate myself for it. Instead of making things right, I run. A voice inside my head scolds me for it, insists I turn around and leave my father with some sort of decent impression. But right now, all I can think about is how much Ethan hurt me.

I'd already come to terms with losing my father years ago. What I can't handle is the thought of losing Ethan. He's all I have.

# Chapter 10

When my mom gets home from work, I borrow her car to drop off Kathy's homework and a pint of Rain's Antiqueasy Lemon Ginger Gelato. She seems surprised that I made her a batch of ice cream, but the color comes back to her face after she takes a few licks. "Thank you," she says gratefully. "This is the first thing I've been able to keep down."

"Lemon and ginger are natural antinausea remedies," I tell her. She doesn't seem interested in the recipe details, but her progress through the container is impressive. Between swallows she tells me about her recent woes. (Marcus has seemed kind of distant recently, and the new cafeteria menu is making her bloat.) After an hour, she drifts to sleep (still clutching the spoon), and I drive over to Marcus's house with a second pint of magic gelato. Then I listen to his problems. (Kathy's been kind of needy lately, and he's considering trying out for community theater without telling her.)

Normally, these seismic shifts in my friends' lives would have occupied my imagination all day.

But I can't concentrate on their issues now. The truth is, I'm lingering at my friends' houses because I don't want to go home.

For the first time in my life, I have no idea how to act around Ethan. What am I supposed to say to him? How can I explain feelings to him that even I don't understand?

It's way after our running time when I finally get back. I expect him to be standing on the porch waiting for me, bouncing in his tennis shoes. But the kitchen is empty when I enter the house. There are voices coming from the second floor, and I hurry upstairs.

The door is open, and I step into the room. I'd been picturing a bunch of possible scenarios: Ethan upset and sulking, Ethan ignoring me, Ethan pretending nothing happened. But the last thing I could have imagined was what I see when I enter his bedroom: Liam and Ethan sitting on the floor and staring intently at the laptop in front of them.

"*Liam?*" They turn to look at me. "What are you doing here? Didn't you have a tutoring crisis?"

He shrugs and jerks his head in Ethan's direction. "He texted me that there was an emergency with his sister. I was just wrapping up with my student when I got the message. I'm still trying to figure out the emergency. But in the meantime he's explaining aortic dissections to me." He waves his hand toward a diagram of a large blood vessel. "You should join us. It's really interesting."

"I don't want to talk about arteries," I say to my brother. "Why did you call Liam?"

He refuses to meet my eye. "Hello, Rain. I'm not finished with this diagram. We haven't gone over Stanford B type—"

"What is the emergency?"

"—also called DeBakey Three dissections—"

"Efan, answer my question!"

"—which are distal and can usually be managed medically but require surgery if there are complications."

"That isn't important right now!" I'm almost shouting at this point, even though I know Ethan reacts poorly to shouting.

"It's important to him." Liam's comment is so quiet that at first I don't hear it.

"What?"

"Nothing, never mind."

I exhale slowly and turn back to my brother. "Would you please explain why you texted Liam?"

It's Ethan's turn to look impatient. "It's our running time," he says. As if that answers all of my questions.

"*Okay*. And?"

"Dad said you were upset with me before," he adds, a little reluctantly.

"Dad was right. But can you please tell me what that has to do with Liam?"

"Last time you were upset with me was March third."

I don't remember what he's talking about but I'm sure he will eventually explain himself. It's making the connections in his rather bizarre patterns of reasoning that's the difficult part. "I was?"

"When you were upset with me you came home really late. And when I complained, you said that I should have gone by myself."

"Fine. Whatever. Please get to the point."

"I *am*. I don't like running by myself."

"Okay. So you called Liam?"

"Yes." He looks relieved that I've finally gotten it. But I'm actually nowhere close to understanding.

"Wait a minute. You want to go running with *Liam*?!"

"No!" He's beginning to rock back and forth. He closes his eyes tight and turns his head away from me. "I only run with you. I want to run with you!"

I know I'm seeing signs of the beginning of a meltdown, but I'm so frustrated that I don't care.

"Then *why* did you call my friend?" I demand furiously. "Why not just call me?"

"Because Dad said you were upset with me. And I should do something to make you feel better before I ask you for anything."

Things are beginning to connect now, in a hazy, kooky kind of way. I'm finally on stable ground. "You wanted to make me feel better?" I ask softly.

He nods vigorously and opens his eyes again. "But I didn't know how. So I looked it up. On the internet."

Liam is laughing softly to himself, and I can't help smothering a smile. "You found Liam on the internet?" I tease him. It isn't a fair joke, but it's too funny to resist. How could I have been mad at him? How could anyone stay mad at him?

"No." He's completely serious. "But wikiHow said 'If all else fails, get her a small present, something she likes.' I didn't know what 'all else' was, so I decided to start with the present idea. And Liam is something you like."

I can't believe this. I don't know whether to laugh or hide my face in embarrassment. "So Liam is your apology."

He looks confused again. "No. Liam is a person."

"But you were trying to apologize to me. That's what you're saying."

"No. I didn't do anything wrong," he persists. "You apologize when you do something wrong."

I sigh. Sometimes I have to pick my battles. "Okay, okay. But you wanted to make me feel better anyway."

"Yes."

"Thank you."

"You're welcome."

"Did it work?" The question comes from Liam, but beside him Ethan is asking the same thing with his anxious rocking. "Do you feel better?"

"Yeah, it worked," I tell him. And now I like Liam even more. Despite the tacit laughter, I know that unlike most people, he understands me and Ethan after just a few minutes with us. It's such a relief to not have to explain it all to him. *Thank you*, I mouth to him.

*Anytime*, he answers with his eyes.

"It's time for our run," Ethan says.

# Chapter 11

School is canceled for the remainder of the week due to the puke bug that sickens half the students and most of the staff. The disaster even makes the local news. Turns out it was actually food poisoning from some iffy turkey salad in the cafeteria. Since I make all my own lunches, I'm not affected by the epidemic. Liam is also spared because he can't afford the cafeteria food. (I couldn't help noticing his homemade lunches were sparse—bread and individually wrapped orange cheese slices, mostly. So I'd started doubling my lunch portions and slipping him stuff I "couldn't finish.")

I text Liam and invite him to hang out after breakfast, but he's tutoring and can't do anything until the next day. So I decide to spend the morning with Ethan.

He wants to teach me about mitral valve prolapse. I want to watch TV. We compromise by watching a documentary on open heart surgery advancements. It isn't much of a compromise, but arguing with him just delays the inevitable, so I don't bother. At least I'm spared Ethan's postshow commentary and lecture when Hope shows up.

I'm surprised to see her, but Ethan doesn't bat an eye. "Hello, Hope," he says and rises to his feet.

"See? I'm on time." She points at the clock.

"You are?" I ask her. "On time for what?"

"I told Ethan that I was coming at one o'clock to chat with you," she explains. "It's one o'clock."

She's referring to the Rules of Ethan, I realize. Number five: always be on time. I guess she didn't think it was necessary to warn me too. She probably assumed (incorrectly) that he would inform me.

"Are you feeling better?" I inquire as she settles next to me on the sofa. "I figured you'd still be in bed."

She looks the same as always, really. Maybe a little paler, but her eyes have a strange light in them that balances out the pallor. For her sake, I hope her glow is not due to Ethan's presence, even though I can't imagine any other explanation. It's not the first time she's looked at him like that. But here's the thing—shouldn't it be both of them all radiant and lovely together? Because Ethan hasn't sparked up at all. In fact, he's already getting up to leave us.

"I'm doing okay now," she says absently, her bright eyes still fixed on Ethan. "You don't have to leave. I'm not contagious or anything."

"I know food poisoning isn't contagious," he replies, sitting back down. "But Rain wanted to speak to you about the Halloween party because she thinks that you lost your mind when you invited me. I can stay if you want me to listen."

I'm embarrassed by his frankness. It's hardly the first time he's blurted out an inconvenient fact without realizing it, but I don't think he's ever managed to sound this sweet before. And *innocent*.

All without trying at all, and with no idea he's just made me sound like a cranky baby. I shift uncomfortably in my seat and shoot him an embarrassed look, which he doesn't see.

"I didn't mean it that way," I mutter, mostly to myself. "I just don't think it's a good idea."

"Ethan, maybe you can give us a minute alone?" Hope suggests.

He gets up immediately. "Goodbye, Hope."

"Bye, sweetie."

I cringe. *He doesn't like nicknames.* "It will probably be more than a minute, Efan," I tell him. Otherwise I know he'll be back in sixty seconds exactly.

"Okay. How long will it be?"

"Give us ten?"

Ethan glances at his watch and nods. "Okay."

"Well?" Hope says after he leaves. "You're worried I've lost my mind?"

I cross my arms. "No, I'm worried about Ethan," I tell her sharply. "And the party you're dragging him to."

"I'm not dragging him," she protests. "He said he wanted to go. Why won't you let him try at least?"

"You don't understand," I say, in a softer voice. "Ethan can be hard to read sometimes. He might have told you he was okay with the party, but I'm sure he doesn't really want to go. He realizes that big crowds overwhelm him and that he needs to avoid them. That's why it's one of the rules."

"Yeah, it's rule number one. Rule number two is about

hand-scrubbing before touching his food. Should I recite the rest? Rule number three is—"

"Okay, I get it," I interrupt, holding up my hands. "I'm glad you've memorized the list. But it doesn't matter if you don't actually follow them."

She nods quietly and glances at the staircase before turning back to me. There's no sound coming from the second floor except the faraway echo of Ethan's computer. "It's okay. We have an escape plan."

"A what?"

"I've thought this through. And I've spoken to Kathy about it. There's a little side patio behind the kitchen. She told me Ethan and I could sit there. We'd be far enough from the crowd and music that it shouldn't bother him too much. And if he wants to go inside for a bit, we can try it."

"If he *wants* to go in? Why would he ever want to?"

"Well, he said he'd think about it." She shrugs. "Why don't you ask *him* how he feels?"

"I *know* how he feels. I've known since I was born."

"But I thought you said he was hard to read!"

"For you!" I retort. "For other people. Not for me! Nothing he does ever surprises me."

"Really? Are you sure about that?"

And yet even as she asks, I know she's right. I used to think I knew everything about Ethan. But he shocked me just a few days ago. And there was his whole new friendship with Hope. And even the brief bond he seemed to form with Liam when I wasn't around.

But the worst of it was seeing him with our father and realizing he'd kept a whole part of his life secret from me.

"Did he tell you that I saw him at Milly's Diner?" I ask her after a pause.

She shakes her head. "He was with your dad?"

"So he *did* tell you."

"No. But I know he meets him there every couple of months."

"You *do*? How?"

"I asked him if he ever sees his dad. And he told me that his father flies here to visit. You didn't know?"

"I had no idea. Until a few days ago when I saw them together."

"I'm so sorry. Maybe I should have said something to you. But I thought it was probably a sensitive subject. The one time I asked you about your dad you said you never saw him."

"*I* didn't!"

"Oh." She slips my hand between her palms and gives me a compassionate squeeze. "You must be furious with him. With your dad, I mean."

"I guess so. I mean, the truth is that I was the one who stopped talking to him. It's complicated. I didn't do it all at once or anything. But I felt bad for my mom. She did all the hard work of raising us, and he did phone calls and Christmas presents. It just didn't seem fair to her. So I felt guilty when he called, and eventually I cut the conversations shorter and shorter. And then one day while Ethan was talking to him on the phone I found my mother crying quietly in her bedroom. And she finally told me why they'd split up. I knew they'd never gotten along. But I never knew about the girlfriend. His girlfriend."

"He cheated?"

I nod. "For years, apparently. When she found out about it she left him. She told us it was to get away from the "poisonous factory fumes" that were hurting Ethan. But I think she was just trying to get as far away from Dad as possible. Make it as hard as she could on him. Hence…Montana."

"Oh, wow," she murmurs. "But, you know, I don't think Ethan has any idea about that part."

"He doesn't." I laugh shortly. "And I still tell people that they split up over hot dogs. When we were kids, that's actually what we thought. That was our last memory of them—fighting over hot dogs. After I learned the truth, I decided Ethan didn't need to know. What good would it do? Honestly, I don't know how he would react if I told him."

She nods thoughtfully and glances in the direction of the second floor. "I don't know either. We've been talking quite a bit lately but—"

"You have?" I interrupt. "When? *How?*"

She gives me an offended look and crosses her arms over her chest. "What's that supposed to mean?"

I need to get better at hiding my doubt, especially when I'm talking to someone who can pick up on it. "I just haven't seen you guys together much," I amend quickly. "So I was wondering when all this communication was happening—"

"We talk on the phone a lot," she retorts defensively. "I think he likes that better than my coming over. It's more comfortable for both of us."

"For *both* of you?" Damn it, there's that doubt again. I should try to be more positive. She was supportive of my crush on Liam. She deserves a little understanding from me. It's just so strange, though. "Hope, what are *you* getting out of this?"

"What do you mean, what am I getting out of it?"

"Look, please don't take this the wrong way. I just can't help comparing this relationship with your last one. You and Grayson were all lovey and attached at the hip most of the time. But this is all so…different. And I can't figure out what's going on here—"

"Yeah, well, maybe different is a good thing," she responds heatedly. "And maybe instead of trying to analyze my motives like you always do, you can just smile when you see me happy and stop wrinkling your face like you're smelling something bad when I'm with Ethan."

"I'm not… I don't—"

"And another thing," she continues without stopping for a breath. "Don't *ever* compare Ethan to Grayson again, okay? I don't even know how you can say their names in the same sentence. Grayson is basically a self-centered pig, and Ethan… Well, Ethan is a gentle sweetheart. He'd never hurt a soul even if he tried. You of all people should know that. Maybe he's not Mr. Perfect like Liam or whatever, but he's what *I* want and—"

"Hope, please. I'm sorry," I interrupt. "I really, really am. You don't have to explain anymore."

She stops her tirade midsentence and swallows. It's not my apology that quiets her, I think, but the raw sincerity in my voice. I do mean it, with all of my heart. In this moment, I'm honestly sorry for everything I've thought and said about the two of them. I've been more of a bully than a friend, an overprotective nut from the first second I saw Hope blush near my brother. "I didn't realize," I tell her quietly. "I didn't know you felt this way."

She nods and her frown disappears. "You could have asked."

"I was just trying to protect him."

"You don't have to do that," she assures me. "I promise I won't hurt him."

*You can't promise that,* I want to tell her. *You aren't in control of Ethan's happiness. I know him better than anyone, and even I don't understand what makes him happy.*

But I don't say any of that out loud. I'm done with the "bad smell" face. She wants to be good to him, so she deserves my wholehearted support. "If you think he'll like the party then you should totally go together," I tell her in a burst of optimism.

The guarded look fades from her eyes. "Hey, who knows?" she says with a laugh. "Maybe he'll actually surprise you."

I sigh and give her my brightest smile. *Maybe he will. Maybe he'll blow all our expectations away.*

I know I'm supposed to be rooting for him. My greatest joys have been Ethan's successes. So why am I so afraid she may be right?

## Cooking with Rain
### SERENITY THROUGH YOUR GUT

Thank you to EpiPen from Nebraska who wrote in asking about substitutes for chocolate. Try carob instead of cocoa! Half of the people I polled couldn't tell the difference.

# Chapter 12

"Are you hungry?" I ask Liam the next afternoon at my house. "I've been experimenting with carob brownies."

"I know you have. You forget that I'm a faithful reader."

I open the oven and peer inside. "So you saw that my blog got ten new followers over the weekend? And real people have started writing in."

He raises his eyebrows. "I'm not real?"

I shoot him a mischievous look. "*You* weren't actually interested in my brownies. Speaking of which, where are they?"

"Oh, right. Ethan stole them while you were in the bathroom. He said, 'This is lunch?' and then took the entire pan up to his room. Don't worry about it; I ate at home. We should probably get some work done."

We'd agreed to study for our chemistry exam that weekend, but after ten minutes of partial pressures my attention drifts. Liam doesn't put up much of a fight. He seems too tired to care about school today. There are dark circles beneath his eyes, and his thick hair is matted and limp. I offer him some organic coffee and a plate of the kale and goat cheese patties I've been working on. He stares at the greenish brown lumps and reaches out with a brave smile.

"They're good for your eyesight," I say, pointing to his glasses. "Not the prettiest of recipes but they're actually—"

"Delicious!" he finishes. He tosses a second one into his mouth. "It's too bad they're...green."

I shrug. "Ethan calls them yummy goat turds."

He chokes. "Is that the official name?"

"No, just Ethan's. He comes up with colorful names for some of my beta tests. Promise you won't tell anyone."

He nods and takes the plate from me. "So all these wild ideas, the chia seeds and dough made out of mold—"

"Algae."

"—all this is for your brother? I thought that people with autism are pretty picky about what they eat."

"He's very picky in his own way. When he was six, he watched a program about hygiene and food workers. It was a disaster. He refused to eat anything but fruit at first. Nothing processed. Forget about takeout. Finally, he downloaded a tutorial on operating room scrubbing techniques and made me learn it. Since then, he won't touch anything unless I've prepared it. Manny's the exception because he agreed to do the scrub thing."

"Wow. Why don't you just teach him to cook? Take some of the responsibility off your shoulders?"

"Because I like doing it. For a while, my meals felt like the only thing that helped Ethan. My meals and our daily run. I know some people would say that it was the therapy—or just time. But I feel like I'm making a difference with my own hands. I love that."

"It's definitely making a difference for me," he says, handing back the empty plate. "You should consider marketing these."

"Seriously? Holistic healthy eating in Clarkson? I wouldn't want to cut in on the burger joints and diner business."

"You don't have to stay in Clarkson forever."

I ignore his comment. I do have to stay in Clarkson. "I offered to cater Kathy's party," I tell him. "She was just going to order pizza. But after tasting my ginger ice cream she was really excited about my menu suggestions."

"So Ethan will agree to eat. That was a good idea."

"I didn't do it for Ethan," I say shortly. "I still don't think Hope should have invited him."

"Why not?"

"She's pushing him too hard and is way out of her depth. And I still don't understand what she's getting out of the relationship."

I shove our books aside, and we move over to the sofa with our coffee mugs. "I mean, I'm trying to be happy for them. I really want to be supportive," I continue. "But I just don't get it."

"Well, maybe you don't have to get it."

I laugh shortly. "You don't know me very well, do you?"

"Look, Ethan seems like a great guy to me. He's intelligent and quiet. Maybe that's what Hope wants right now."

I shake my head. "I thought at first that she was like that Pygmalion guy. That Ethan is like this diamond in the rough for her."

"Really?"

"Okay fine, that's stupid. But I don't know what to think! It's like she's completely changed her type. She dated Grayson for most of last year. The truth is, none of us really liked him that much. But at least that relationship made sense to me."

"Grayson treated her like shit," he says evenly. "Or didn't you know that?"

I stare at him and place my drink down on the coffee table. "Why do you say that? Did she tell you that? Because she never told me—"

"I don't know what she told you. But guys gossip about their relationships too. Maybe even more than girls do."

"But you're not even close with Grayson and that crowd."

He shrugs. "A guy will sometimes spill his guts to someone he barely knows. If he thinks that it'll make him look good."

"Seriously?"

"It's a pissing contest, Rain. That's all it is. And between the two of us, I was the obvious loser when it came to girls. I've never had a girlfriend, right? So Grayson was more than happy to share all kinds of stuff with me. It was a while ago—back when he and Hope were still dating. He was heading to Missoula, and I offered to split gas if he gave me a ride to my grandmother's house."

"What did he say to you?"

He grunts and takes a long sip of his coffee. "Ugh, what *didn't* he say?"

"Really? Because I was pretty surprised when they broke up.

Hope seemed so happy with him. She kept telling me how in love they were."

He snorts and looks away. "Maybe *she* was. But if I had to guess, I'd say they probably broke up soon after Valentine's Day. Am I right?"

I stare at him. "The day after. How did you know that?"

"Because right before I got out of his car Grayson said, 'We'll see if she changes her mind on Valentine's. Girls always put out then.'"

I'm speechless for a moment. Liam's eyes are downcast and embarrassed; he fiddles absently with his mug and sloshes the coffee around. "I guess you can figure out what happened—"

"Oh my God."

"As I said, he treated her like—"

"*Shit!* Oh, shit! I get it now."

"Yeah. So either Hope changed her mind, and Grayson got what he wanted, and then dumped her. Or she *didn't* change her mind—"

But that isn't what I'm thinking about at all. "I don't care what Grayson wanted!" I exclaim. "I mean now I understand why Hope is attracted to Ethan."

"What do you mean?"

"How did I not see this before? It's so obvious!"

He glances over my shoulder and lifts his hand. "Rain, maybe you should lower—"

"Ethan is basically like a eunuch to Hope! Like one of those castrated servants they used to guard the harems in ancient times. He won't touch her, so he can never hurt her—"

"Oh, *Jesus*, Rain, just quiet down—"

But his warning comes too late. My words have already echoed through the room before I realize what Liam is trying to tell me. I turn around to see my brother standing by the stairwell.

He doesn't speak at first. His head is down. His hair falls over his forehead to cover his eyes.

There are no words left, absolutely nothing I can say to take it back.

"Efan—" I get up and move toward him.

"That isn't my name," he says. There's no anger in his tone. But I don't understand what he means; I have no idea what he's trying to tell me.

"Efan, I'm so sorry—it came out wrong—"

"*I said that isn't my name!*" he shouts.

I step back, warm tears pricking my eyes. Beside me, I feel Liam draw closer to me, feel his hand steal slowly into mine. I'm shaking all over, and his firmness steadies me.

I swallow hard and take a deep breath. "Ethan?" The word is just a whisper on my lips. It's the first time I've called my brother by his real name.

I love the sound of it. I want to say his name again. I want him to smile when he hears it.

But he's gone before I can.

I'm shaking too hard to follow him. I start forward, stumbling toward the stairs, and then I feel Liam grasp my hand as he pulls me back.

"Give him a minute," he says. "He just needs some space."

"I have to tell him I didn't mean it! God, I'm such an idiot."

I lean against Liam's shoulder; my cheek brushes against his shirt. I want him to hide me, to comfort me, to tell me sweet lies about how my brother still loves me. I want him to make me feel a little less horrible.

He hesitates for a moment and then draws me close to him and wraps his arms around me. It feels so good, so warm and perfect. I think I must be the most selfish person in the world because I smile through my tears. I hate myself, and I adore Liam, and I didn't know happiness could be so guilty. "Thank you," I whisper.

I rest my head against his chest; he smells of spice bodywash and coffee. He bends down and touches his lips against my forehead. I feel a pull... I want so much to lift my lips to his, but I just can't. I don't deserve this boy, his warmth, his sweetness. I can't be happy with him now, not after I've just destroyed my brother. "I'm sorry," I say, more to myself than him.

"He's coming back," he tells me.

I twist around to look, and there's my brother again. His eyes are calm as always. There's no trace of my own pain in his expression. I gently break Liam's embrace and move a step away, but one of my arms still rests around his waist. I'm not ready to let him go yet.

"Hello, Liam," he says, as if he didn't just see him two

minutes before. "I forgot to ask, did you check with Dr. Peters about the surgery?"

*Surgery?* I wonder, but I know better than to say anything out loud.

"Yes," Liam answers. "Next Wednesday works for him. I'll pick you up at four thirty. I'll have my father's pickup, so I can drive you."

*What is going on?* I want to ask. What surgery are they talking about? "But we run at four—" I blurt out, and stop, embarrassed. *We run at four?* Damn, I sound exactly like my brother.

His eyes rest on me for a second, and then he turns his attention back to Liam. "We run at four," he echoes.

"I know," Liam replies. "But it's the only time he can do it. It's your choice, Ethan."

He seems to consider for a moment, but only a moment. "I have to go to the surgery," he tells me. "So we can't run on Wednesday."

*Who is this person?* Something inside me sinks, and the tears that Liam dried spring back into my eyes. I should be happy I'm getting the afternoon off, that for the first time in two years I can leave my running shoes in the closet. But I'm miserable at the thought. Is this my punishment for what I just said about him? Is this how he's getting back at me?

"Okay." It's embarrassing how weepy I'm getting over this, and I hastily brush my hand over my cheeks.

There's a flicker of concern in Ethan's eyes. "I'm sorry," he says. His brow furrows. "I made you cry."

"You didn't—"

"Because I canceled our run. I'm sorry. You can come with us to the hospital if you want. We're going to watch a cholecystectomy."

I still have no idea what he's talking about, and not just because I don't know what the word means. All that registers is that Ethan is apologizing to *me*, when it should be the other way around.

"He's only given permission for the two of us, Ethan. And I don't know if Rain wants to watch a gallbladder operation," Liam suggests.

"You're going to an operating room?"

Ethan nods happily. "Liam knows a surgeon in Missoula County Hospital. He showed him some of my anatomy sketches, and the doctor wants to meet me. He said I can watch the surgery with the medical students. We'll be behind a glass window, but I'll be able to see it all live!" He flashes us a brilliant smile. "It will be so much better than watching it on the laptop. And then afterward I can ask questions."

"But, Ethan," I falter. "You won't like the hospital. It can get pretty noisy—"

"I know that," he says. "But I don't have a choice."

"You don't?"

"Of course not. I can't do surgeries in my house."

"What?"

"Surgery has to be done in a sterile room," he explains patiently, "with anesthesia equipment and nursing staff. So that's where I have to do them."

I stare silently at my brother and then turn helplessly to Liam.

"I think what Ethan is trying to say," he tells me, "is that he wants to be a surgeon one day."

A surgeon? I'm not sure how to respond to this. There's a million things I want to ask, of course. *Have you actually thought this through, Ethan? How many years of school is that? How many new people will you have to meet and talk to, how many giant classrooms, how many bright lights, how many overwhelming sounds?*

But there's only one thing I do say: "You'll be a great surgeon, Ethan."

He nods. "I know."

*Cooking with Rain*

SERENITY THROUGH YOUR GUT

---

*Special Halloween Edition: Rain's Bloody Skulls Punch*

Peel and carve seven apples, then whittle some holes for eye sockets and a gaping mouth. Immerse them in a bowl of sweetened pomegranate juice (vodka optional). Pomegranates are like nature's Roto-Rooter. So why not unplug a few arteries while you're having a good time?

## ETHAN'S JOURNAL:

### Blood Alcohol Level and Effects of Behavior

0.02–0.03 BAC: Slight euphoria
and loss of shyness. Depressant
effects are not apparent. No loss of
coordination.

0.04–0.06 BAC: Feeling of well-being, relaxation, lower inhibitions, sensation of
warmth. Euphoria. Some minor impairment of reasoning and memory, lowering of caution. Emotions intensified.

### Desired Effect:

I wish to avoid loss of coordination, memory
impairment, and heightened emotions. I would
like to enjoy the benefits of a decreased level
of shyness, especially as relates to members of
the opposite sex. Optimal amount of alcohol
consumption for a male of my weight with
unknown tolerance would be thirteen ounces of
beer with 5 percent alcohol content.

## Proposed Experiment:

Consume slightly increasing quantities of beer every night to test response. Will begin this evening with six ounces of Michelob.

# Chapter 13

Choosing a Halloween costume for a party is way more complicated than working out a catering menu. For a girl, anyway. A guy can just stick a prop knife through his shirt and be done with it. But a girl has to take a lot into consideration. This Halloween I want to be sexy but classy, with just a dash of silly. I also recently bought the prettiest little green dress, and I want Liam to see me in it. So whatever costume I choose must somehow include that.

The idea comes to me three days before the party as I'm making breakfast. Twenty minutes later I've constructed a light-weight cardboard frying pan and pasted in two paper sunny-side-up eggs. I attach it to an elastic band and fit it around my head. Perfect. It's a little silly, and I can debut the dress without looking like I'm trying too hard.

Ethan is upstairs working on a large cutout of a lightning bolt. He and Hope have decided to do a couples themed costume. He is strangely excited by the whole thing even though the costume wasn't his idea and was responsible for their first fight—if you can call it a fight. My brother basically just rattled off pairs of organs for costume ideas: "We can be two kidneys! Two lungs! Two sides of a heart!"

But Hope said, "No. No. No. No body parts, Ethan," and Ethan eventually got pissed off and walked away. They finally settled on "struck by lightning," which featured Ethan as the lightning bolt and Hope in singed, hole-filled clothing.

I'm impressed by Hope's idea because it satisfies both of them; the holes are in strategic, sexy spots (midriff, back) allowing Hope to look awesome, but the costume also appeals to Ethan's obsession with human physiology. He spends a shocking amount of time lecturing all of us about the various consequences of electrocution. (Did you know that the capillaries in your skin explode and make a Christmas-tree-shaped burn all over your body?)

The final concern, after I've gotten the costume out of the way, is making up a white lie to tell my mom and getting her to extend my eleven o'clock curfew. I instruct Ethan to say nothing, and the day before the party I casually mention I've decided to take my brother to Kathy's house and introduce him to a couple of my friends.

My mom actually glows at me. "That is a *wonderful* idea, Rain," she says. "I'm so happy that you're including Ethan."

I sigh and shake my head. "Well, I don't know if it's going to work. Maybe we'll only stay an hour. You know how he doesn't like to have his schedule changed."

"No, no," she insists. "You should stay as long as he can handle it. The later the better. It's going to be so healthy for him."

"Do you really think so?" I say, wrinkling my nose. "Ethan's never been out past ten."

"Absolutely!" she says. "Stay out all night if he'll let you. I give you my permission."

"Well…okay." I sigh again. "I'll do my best."

Oh, *yeah*, I will.

My mom gives me a tired smile and lies back on the couch. She's gotten even thinner over the last couple of weeks, but when I ask her if she'd like some dinner she just waves her hand and tells me she's not hungry. It worries me a little. I know she's finished the case she was working on, but for some reason she hasn't picked up anything new. In fact, over the last few days she's been mostly at home, lounging on the sofa and listlessly surfing the internet. I would suggest she see a doctor, but I know she'll just say she hasn't seen a doctor for more than twenty years and she's not about to start now. Maybe it's a good thing she isn't working on a lawsuit now. She looks like she needs some time off.

I'm dying to share my curfew triumph with someone so I knock on Ethan's door and dance over to his desk. He's pushed his books off onto the floor, and his table is littered with strips of aluminum foil and cardboard. The room smells faintly of beer, which I assume is coming from the cultures he grows on his windowsill. He glances briefly at me when I come in. "Hello, Rain."

"Guess what?" I declare happily. "No curfew."

"Okay."

I was hoping for a more enthusiastic reaction. "After Kathy's party," I persist. "We can come home whenever we want. Mom said."

"Oh. That's good." He goes back to cutting the cardboard.

"Just don't say the word 'party' around Mom, okay? That's really important."

"I know," he replies quietly. "You told me three times."

"Yeah. Okay, sorry. I just wanted to make sure."

"I know."

I want him to look at me so badly, but he's barely glanced up since I entered the room. He's slicing tin foil with an intensity that's severe, even for him.

"Ethan," I venture timidly. "Secret Rule?"

He stops what he's doing and stares stonily at the silver pile in front of him. "What can I do?" he mutters resentfully.

"Would you look at me please? I need to talk to you."

He lays the scissors down and turns to me; his pale eyes fix on mine.

"You're mad at me. For what I said before."

He shakes his head. "I'm not mad about the curfew. But you need to tell me when we're going home. So that I'll know."

I smile to myself. You'd think by now I'd know not to be vague with him. "I didn't mean what I said right now. I was talking about that comment I made about Hope. About Hope and you."

I know I need to be more specific than that, but I'm finding it hard to repeat the words. It was bad enough that I said it once.

But now he appears to be replaying everything I've ever said about them back over in his mind. I'm going to need to help him out.

"The eunuch thing," I mumble finally.

"Oh. Okay."

"I didn't mean to hurt your feelings. When I said that."

"But I'm not a eunuch."

"I *know* you're not, Ethan. That isn't the point." It's weird trying to explain to my brother why he ought to be mad at me. I probably should just quit while I'm ahead.

"And Hope knows it too," he continues seriously. "I asked her."

"You did?"

"Yes. She didn't know what the word meant. So I explained it to her. And then I told her that I'm sure that I wasn't one."

"You told her that—"

"That I masturbate normally. Once or twice a week."

"*Oh my God!* Ethan!"

He flinches at my tone and shifts uncomfortably in his seat. "Please don't yell, Rain."

"You can't say that to a girl!" I exclaim, throwing my hands up in the air. "You can't say that to anyone!"

"I know," he replies evenly. "She informed me."

"She…she did?"

"She said I'm only allowed to speak about that topic if someone asks me about it first."

"If somebody *asks* you? Who's going to ask you about that?"

"People talk about it all the time on TV."

"That's different! It's funny when comedians do it." But even as I say it, I realize it's impossible to explain to him why it's comical when Seth Rogen jokes about the subject and completely horrifying when Ethan blurts out his personal habits. "Just don't talk about it again."

"I already promised Hope."

I stare at him for a moment and then sniff the air. "Is that beer smell coming from your culture plates?"

He shakes his head and taps a half-empty bottle in his trash bin. "Experiment."

"Oh. Did you *drink* the experiment?"

"Yes," he replies shortly. "Am I done with the Secret Rule for today? Can I go back to my costume now?"

"Yeah—I guess." I'm not sure I got what I'd come for, though. I got him to look me in the eye and talk to me. But I can't invoke the Secret Rule to ask for something as vague as understanding or forgiveness. Even the Secret Rule has limitations.

# Chapter 14

The juniors of Clarkson High have been planning Kathy's Halloween party for a long time. There was a sad attempt at Mike's house on the last day of tenth grade, a couple of half-parties that fizzled over Christmas, and an embarrassing spring break disaster at Angel's that ended with a host of furious neighbors, three roaring cops, and two kids in an overnight holding cell.

I wasn't involved in any of that stuff; I heard about it the next day in school. Ethan and I generally stayed clear of anything with noise, alcohol, or the possibility of arrest. I always kept away because my mom has enough to handle without me adding to her worries. Maybe I'd party when I got to college or grad school. Until then I was just treading water in the safe area of the pool. Ethan stayed away from parties because no one ever invited him. Among other reasons.

But Kathy's event would be the perfect mix of fun and safe. All the necessary stuff would be there: music, food (mine!), people, and beer. And Kathy's house was in the middle of twenty acres of quiet farmland, and her nearest neighbor was a mile away. This weekend her parents were going to be in Great Falls, and she had no little siblings to worry about. So nothing could spoil the fun.

Most importantly, I now had a reason to go to this party. A six-foot-tall, curly-haired, serious, and sweet reason whom I couldn't stop thinking about.

And of course there's also Ethan and Hope. I had to be around to make sure her plan didn't blow up in her face like my elephant toothpaste. So my countdown to Saturday's party is tinged with a strange combination of excitement and dread.

The green dress looks good though. Hope gives her enthusiastic approval after I text her a selfie. The fried eggs on my head are an adorable touch, she adds.

Still, I'm worried my mom will start to wonder about the nature of the little "get-together" if she sees us all in costume. Most people don't get dressed up to hang out with a couple of kids, even on Halloween. But Mom skips dinner that evening and by eight is already in bed with her laptop and a warm jug of tea. It doesn't occur to her to question my explanation or our plans. After all, I've never been in trouble in my life. All she wants is her son to fit in for once, and she shouts her good wishes through her bedroom door. "Have a great time, Ethan!"

The doorbell rings a couple minutes later, and I run to answer it. Liam is standing on the porch bashfully twirling a pink tail. He's wearing an overstuffed puffy hat with hanging ears, and a snout dangles lazily off one cheek.

His eyes scan my outfit. "Wow," he breathes.

"You're a pig!" I say simultaneously. And then my face gets warm. "I meant, the costume…"

He glances down at the tail in his hand. "Sorry, it was the only thing I could find. Porky Pig. It's really old."

"It's cute. And no one can accuse us of doing a cheesy couples thing."

"The fried eggs on your head are because you like to cook?"

I shoot him a flirty smile. "Sure. But mostly because I wanted to wear this dress."

His eyes skim over me again and his face goes pink. "Yeah. You look...really... I mean, *really*. You know..."

I'm already loving this party, and we haven't even left my house yet. It's intoxicating to feel him looking at me like that. I'd be happy to bask in Liam's bashful half sentences forever.

But then Ethan appears behind us. "Hello, Liam. The party starts at eight. It's eight fifteen."

"It's okay," he says, turning to my brother. "Most people come a few minutes late. I like your costume, by the way."

"Thank you. We should go."

Liam helps me load the platters of Halloween treats into his truck, and we head off to Kathy's. Ethan spends the entire trip staring out the window at the night sky and carefully readjusting the cardboard lightning cutout around his neck. I'm worried about him; I'm sure he has no idea what he's getting into. Small, calm gatherings of close friends have overwhelmed him in the past, and tonight is not going to be small or calm. The entire junior and senior class is coming, and some kids from Alberton and Missoula as well. It's comforting to think that Hope has an escape plan, but I'm not certain she'll recognize Ethan's warning signs until it's too late.

The noise and music hit us before we're halfway up the gravel path to Kathy's house. Twenty other cars and pickup trucks are parked along the road, strewn like discarded toys across the green. There are large gouge marks in the soil leading right up to the house. I have no idea how Kathy's going to explain the tire marks to her parents when they get home, but she's obviously not worrying about that tonight. She's hanging out in the front yard with two girls from Alberton High and laughing into a beer. As we get out of the truck, she hollers my name and waves at us.

"There you are! Come here!" She glances at my brother and smiles broadly. "Hope's waiting for you by the side porch, Ethan. Behind the oak tree."

He nods and swallows audibly, then turns and walks in the direction she indicated. As he nears the house there's a sound of crashing glass from inside and a high-pitched shriek of laughter. Ethan flinches and falls back a few steps. "They need to turn down the music," I mutter to Liam. Why did they have to pick Iron Maiden of all bands? I feel the sound attacking him; I hear him exhaling his fear, see him shutting his eyes. Instinctively I move toward him. I can't let him go to pieces in front of everyone. It would be better if we turned back now.

But then I feel Liam's firm hand close over my elbow. "Let him try, Rain," he whispers. "Just give him a chance." I look back at Liam and shake my head. He means well, I know he does. He's watching Ethan's slow progress across the yard with the concerned expression of a friend. But he isn't scared like I am. He isn't feeling Ethan's heartbeat in his own chest.

"Why don't I carry the food inside?" Liam suggests. "You can get us a couple of drinks before they run out."

"Oh, we won't run out," Kathy crows. She's looking a little unstable already, and the party's barely started. "Everyone's pitched in. We've got lots of cases of beer and a box of Bailey's and Mike stole a couple of bottles of Jack Daniels from his uncle. So we aren't going dry for a while. But if you're planning to drink, I'm going to need to take your car keys." She holds out a shaky hand and Liam tosses her his key ring. "Sorry, guys, but after what happened to those kids in Great Falls—" She breaks off and squints at the frying pan on my head. "Oh, I get it now!" she exclaims, clapping her hands and glancing between Liam and me. "I can't believe it took me so long!"

"Get what?"

"Your costume! You guys are green eggs and ham," she says, pointing at my dress and at Liam's tail. "That is *so* cute!"

"Oh," we say in unison, and Liam chuckles to himself. How did we not see that before? So much for avoiding cheesy. "So what are you?" he inquires, peering at Kathy's feathered headdress and wings. "A dark angel?"

Her face clouds over and she crosses her arms over her chest. A couple of black feathers flutter to the ground. "I'm a girl whose boyfriend put off picking a costume until the last minute. So I decided to come as a bird. A bird who flies solo."

There's a ring of defiance in her blurry voice. I give her a baffled look. Is the Octopus seriously in trouble?

"You should go inside and get some punch," she tells me sulkily. "Marcus won't stop talking about it. He's more interested in his stupid punch than..." She trails off and takes an angry sip of beer, then turns back toward the house and weaves her way across the lawn. Halfway there, she trips, and one of her heels gets stuck in the muddy holes by a hydrangea patch. She kicks the shoe off irritably and limps slowly up the stairs.

"I think she needs someone to talk to," I say.

Liam nods. "Yeah, but maybe I'll try talking to Marcus first and see what's going on. Let's go find him."

The full force of the party hits me as we walk in the door. I can't help loving it: the noise of people, the roar of talk and laughter, the smell of aftershave and beer, the psychedelic glow of faces in the shifting colors of the blinking strobe light. I love the way I can just float among them and lose myself in the beat of the screaming music and swaying bodies. Without Ethan by my side, I can enjoy the heat and energy of the crowd, and for just a minute I forget that I have a brother outside.

Liam lays the trays down in the kitchen, and there are delighted shouts of "Food! Finally!" and then "What the hell is that?" as I unwrap the treats. We push through the crowd and wave at Marcus, who's hovering over a giant punch bowl and ladling generous portions of bright red liquid into plastic tumblers. He's doing a very bad job; the table is soggy and dripping and some of the cups have tipped over and spilled their contents all over the floor. "Rain!" he shouts over the crowd. "Come here! You guys gotta try this!"

Liam reaches out and grabs a cup from him, then passes a second one to me. "It's my own recipe," Marcus bellows and takes a sloppy slurp of his drink. "You'll never guess what's in it."

I take a careful sip and wince at the taste. "What kind of punch is this?" It's sweet with a cherry tang and a good deep burn at the end. It takes some getting used to, but it isn't bad.

"Bloody Vampire," he burbles. "Rain inspired me."

"I take no credit for this," I mutter into my cup.

"Drink it slow," Liam cautions me. "I think it's mostly alcohol."

"Oh my God, you're a giant sperm!" Marcus squeals delightedly. "That's *awesome*!"

Liam raises his eyebrows and chuckles. "Dude, how much of this have you had?"

"Oh! You guys are egg and sperm! I love it!" He points at the frying pan on my head and giggles. "*Hysterical.*"

I glance over at Liam's costume again. Maybe if you squint at him sideways and you're really drunk, Liam's pig costume could look a little like a monster sperm. I liked it better when we were a cute line from a Dr. Seuss book.

"I'm going to grab some food," I tell Liam. "Maybe you should talk to Marcus and make him find Kathy. Or at least cut him off. He looks like he's had enough."

"Use protection!" Marcus bellows and tosses a plastic trash bag at Liam's head.

"Good luck," I say and head for the kitchen.

It's mostly empty when I get there, and the only sign of the platters I'd brought is a senior licking up the last drops of hummus. "This Vampire bean dip is awesome!" he crows. "I love how you dyed it red!"

"I never dye food," I tell him scornfully. "It's chickpea paste and beets. Completely natural."

He doesn't seem to appreciate the correction. "Ew." He glances sadly at the empty bowl. "So, wait...do you have more?"

I shake my head and pick up the last pita crumbs from the counter. As he stumbles out of the kitchen, a voice floats in through the window behind me.

It's Ethan. He's sitting outside on the side porch with Hope. The music and noise of the party is muted here, and I can hear everything he's saying. I move quietly toward the window and press myself up against the wall. From that angle, I can see them clearly, but the curtain hides me well enough so they can't see me.

"No, I'm glad I came," Ethan is saying. "Now I can tell my father that I went to a party."

Hope laughs and moves closer to him. There's enough space for another person between them on the bench but she scoots over a little to narrow the gap. "He wanted you to go?"

"Yes. It was on his list."

"What list?"

"He gave me a list of things I need to do. Last time he was here. He called it the list of Ethan's dreams."

She laughs again and reaches her hand out to touch him. He isn't looking at her so he doesn't see the movement, but I hold my breath as I wait for the moment of contact. It's not going to be pretty, and she's going to be sorry, but there's nothing I can do to stop her.

But then she pauses, her fingers an inch from the corner of his sleeve and seems to hesitate; her hand wavers, and then she slowly draws it back. I breathe again.

"Going to a party is one of your dreams?" she asks.

"No," he replies. "I don't like parties. But it's one of my dad's steps."

"His steps?"

"He says there are many steps I have to go through, if I want to become a surgeon."

"Oh, right! Well, obviously there's college, and then medical school—"

"No, he wasn't talking about that. Those are everybody's steps. But I have my own. He wrote me a list."

"What's on the list?"

He glances at her for a moment and then looks back down at his hands. "There's a lot of things that are difficult for me. Like parties. Big restaurants. Crowded malls. But I must do them, even if I don't want to. Dad said I get points for every one I do. So I'm making myself get through each one, so eventually I can get there."

She nods and stares out into the night. "You mean like a list of everyday things," she says. "You basically just want to be normal."

He shakes his head emphatically. "No. I never want to be normal."

"Oh. Okay." She bites her lip and looks away. "I'm sorry, I should have said neurotypical, right? I didn't mean that you're not—"

"I don't want to be neurotypical, either. If I were normal I wouldn't be able to see things the way I do. I wouldn't be able to visualize my diagrams, my sketches, my books; they're like pictures in my head. I'd have to memorize every detail, one by one, like everybody else. Like you have to do when you study for exams. That would be terrible. I never want to think like you."

I wonder if Hope is hurt by his bluntness. Even though his words sounded harsh and cold I know they weren't intended that way. And she seems to realize that. She swallows and turns back to him.

"So what *do* you want, Ethan?"

He's still staring at his hands, but as she speaks she reaches out and lightly touches his sleeve. He starts and turns to look at her, then sighs and shifts back slightly.

"I want to pretend," he tells her softly. "I need to learn to pretend so other people can't tell."

"I see," she murmurs. "And am I a part of that?"

He keeps staring at her but doesn't respond. He doesn't understand the question, I want to tell her. But I'm just a mute observer on the wrong side of a kitchen curtain. I have to let her figure it out on her own.

"Am I part of your plan to pretend to be normal?" she amends after a moment of silence.

"No."

"Okay. Well, that's good, I guess." She reaches her hand out to him again and holds her palm out in front of him. "So what do you think about touching people? Is that on your list of things to get through?"

"Yes."

A shade of hope flickers over her face. "Well...do you want to try that now?"

He shakes his head and shrinks back farther. "I can't. It's at the bottom. I'm not there yet."

She smiles patiently and moves a little closer. "But you told me that you hug your father when you say goodbye. And your sister does that Rain burrito thing to make you feel better. So why can't I touch your hand now?"

"That's different. The burrito hold is not skin to skin. I like firm pressure but not light touch. And I don't mind a quick hug, when my dad insists on it. He knows how to do it so my skin doesn't touch his."

"Okay. But if I touched you now... If I put my hand on yours—" She slowly brings her fingers closer to his. "What would that feel like to you?"

He flinches under the threat but doesn't move his hand away. "I can't explain it."

"Try," she urges. "I want to understand."

He swallows and clears his throat nervously. "I don't know. Bad."

*Stop!* I want to yell at her. *Just leave him alone! How can you understand something you've never felt?*

"Bad how?" she persists. "Like painful?"

He shakes his head and swallows again. "No, not painful. Maybe like slime feels to you. Or like when a bug crawls up your hand."

Her hand falls to her side and her mouth drops open. "I feel like a slimy bug?"

"I don't know. I've never touched you." There's a thin note of frustration sharpening his tone. "But when someone touches me, especially when I don't expect it, it's like they're violating my personal space. It would be like if a stranger came up and licked your cheek."

She laughs shortly. "Okay, I'll be sure to warn you before I start licking. But if you don't like physical contact, why do you even want to get close to me? If you're sure it will be awful for you?"

He sighs and for the first time lifts his eyes to look at her. "You can feel both worried and excited at the same time, right?" he replies. "Well, I can feel more than one thing too. My father said that I should think of girls like hot chocolate. The first try might burn my tongue. But eventually I'll get used to the temperature. And then I can just concentrate on the sweetness."

"Oh, I get it. That's just like—"

"Rain!"

The whisper behind me makes me jump, and I turn around to find Liam staring at me. "What are you doing?" he asks in a low voice.

I move away from the window and take a long sip of punch to buy a little time. I have no idea how to explain myself to him. What *was* I doing? Until Liam interrupted me, it hadn't occurred to me to question the decency of eavesdropping on my brother. I had a duty to be there, just in case Ethan needed me. It had seemed obvious that I was only there for his protection. But now, seeing myself through Liam's shocked eyes, I suddenly realize that my presence behind the curtain was not exactly normal.

"I was looking for food," I say evasively, and take another sip of punch. It burns on the way down, but I like the warm, deep glow it leaves behind. It's like drinking a relaxing day on the beach. "Someone ate all the hummus."

"Well, there's no food out there," he says, pointing at the window. The motion throws him off a bit, and he sways before regaining his balance.

I drop my head. "I guess I got a little carried away," I admit after a pause. "I heard them talking, and I wanted to make sure he was okay—"

"All right, I get it." His tone is far more gentle than I deserve. "You're worried for him. But still—"

"I know, I *know*." I don't want to talk about this anymore. There's no way to justify it. "I need some more of this punch," I tell him. Mostly to change the subject. And also because I truly do want more. I've had beer before, and wine—but I've never tasted anything that feels this good. "I need to ask Marcus for the recipe."

"I've had two cups already," Liam admits. "You want this one? It's mostly full."

I take the glass from him and swirl the red juice around. It's easier to concentrate on the punch than talk about what I've just done. Liam seems to feel the same way, and he shuffles off to fetch more drinks for us. We enjoy them in silence; minutes pass, maybe hours. By the end of the second cup, I'm not so embarrassed anymore. "We should get out of here."

"Okay." He reaches out to take my hand—and misses. His fingers barely graze my wrist. I giggle at the baffled expression on his face. "You're drunk," I scoff.

"I'm not drunk," he retorts. "You moved."

"I don't think so. You're *wasted*."

I'm fine though. I'm just feeling fuzzy and peaceful and a little slow. I want to explain everything to him, but I don't have as many words as I did before. But I'm nowhere close to drunk.

The third cup feels even better going down than the second one did. It slows down time. Liam is trying to walk over to me but he's moving like a turtle, shuffling one foot in front of the other like he's making his way across a rickety bridge. He doesn't look upset at me, just red and confused. Maybe he's forgotten about the spying stuff.

I feel better about it already. I feel better about everything.

Who was I looking for? I really need to find Marcus and ask him—something. And Kathy—I should tell her that someone drank all the whiskey and didn't share. There are three empty bottles on the counter next to the empty platters of food. Who stole all the whiskey?

Liam is leaning forward and gripping the edge of the table. He moans and squints up at the clock. How long have we been standing in this kitchen? An hour? Two? Did somebody turn on an oven? It's so hot in here. "I think we're missing the party." But I don't really care. It's hard to care about anything when I feel this good.

"I don't think you should be drinking more—" Liam says suddenly. The last words come out slurred. "Give it back."

"No." I sink down onto the floor. The floor is more stable than the counter. The counter feels mushy. "It's all gone now."

"Where did it go?"

I giggle and the empty cup drops out of my hand. "Oopsie." It's the funniest word in the English language. I want to say it again. "Oopsie."

"Oopsie," he echoes, and collapses on the floor next to me. "I want to go to sleep."

"It's hot in here," I say. Or maybe Liam does. It's like he's reading my thoughts now. It's good that he can do that, I think happily. Maybe I don't have to speak so much with my mouth.

"Let's go outside," we say together and then we start to laugh. It begins as a little chuckle, but soon we're doubled over, and he's holding on to me. I love the way he laughs. His cheeks get all red and shiny, and his eyes are bright with tears. I never want him to stop laughing. I love how funny he is and how funny I am when I'm with him. I love him.

"I love you too."

Did he just tell me he loved me? Of course he did! Of course he loves me. Did I tell him I loved him too? I better make sure I did.

"I love you, Liam."

"You just told me that."

"Oh."

It's the most beautiful moment in my life. We've said everything and we can be happy forever. I'm pretty sure he needs to kiss me now. Except maybe outside where it's cooler. It's so hot it's making my stomach hurt.

It takes a really long time to get out of the house. There are lots of people in the living room and they keep bumping into me when I walk near them. Liam helps me push them off. Then he pulls me up when somebody trips me and I fall down. There's a lot of really drunk teenagers at this party, and they need to be more careful. It's probably time to leave anyway.

The front yard is peaceful and cold. The grass feels like a cool blanket on my face. I could stay here for a long time. "Why are you lying down?" Liam asks me.

"Lie down with me."

"Where's my truck?"

He's moving away from me slowly, and I don't want him to go. He hasn't kissed me yet, and I don't want to be alone in the dark outside. I try to get up to follow him but my knees are heavy, and my head needs to lean against something. Then his shoulder finds me, my arms wrap around his neck, and together we walk back to his truck. He reaches through the open window and pops open the lock. It's funny that he has to try three times before he gets the door open. "Stupid handle," he mumbles. I don't care about the handle; I don't care about anything. I just want to lie down on the vinyl seats and close my eyes for a little while. But when I'm inside I suddenly remember  my brother is still back at the house and I was supposed to be watching out for him.

Except maybe he doesn't need me to do that anymore.

It's the saddest moment in the happiest moment of my life. Ethan doesn't need me anymore. He's found Hope and wandered away, the way he used to wander away when he was little and I'd have to find him before he got lost. Only this time he doesn't want me to find him. And just now Liam thought I was a weirdo for caring too much about my twin.

"I'm not a weirdo," I sob suddenly. I don't mean to start crying, but I can't help it. I might never find my brother again, and my boyfriend thinks I'm crazy. Also I can't remember if Liam ever asked me out so maybe he isn't my boyfriend after all and I'm lying pressed up against a total stranger in a pickup truck. Did I just tell a total stranger that I love him?

My face is resting on Liam's chest and he's lying back across the seat, his head pushed up against the steering wheel. He shifts over and looks down at me. "I know. Me too."

I don't know what he means, but it's very comforting. He

knows exactly what to say to make me feel better. I need to stop crying and kiss him before I fall asleep.

His face is so near mine now. I just have to reach his mouth. I try to get closer, but it's very hard to move my body over his. But then he slides down a little and pulls at me, and our lips meet, and everything is easy suddenly. He's moving under me, my chest is pressed against his ribs, I feel him breathe and groan. I inhale his smell, the spice-wash sweetness of him, and taste the sweat and whiskey on his lips, and I want more. I don't know how to tell him what I want because I can't remember how to speak, and his lips grab whatever words I have. As long as he keeps kissing me I'll never lose him. He's slipping away, everyone is slipping away from me, but maybe this is my last chance. It feels like my only chance to be okay. He loves me, he said he did. It's the only thing I know for sure. I want to tell him that I love him too; I never want him to forget, but if I say the thought out loud I'm scared he'll run away. So I have to show him.

I should show him with my body, and then he'll understand.

# Chapter 15

My stomach is kicking me. It's the first thing I feel before my eyes open, before I have any idea where I am—there's a twisting wrench of nausea and an awful searing pain beneath my ribs. For a moment I can't breathe, and my eyes snap open. I gasp loudly, my lungs contract. And then it comes, a belch of air, a retching sound, and then a gush, a stinking volume of punch and puke. It pours from me like spit up from a baby, and the only thing I feel is relief that my stomach has stopped tearing itself to pieces.

When it's over, I sit up weakly and look around me. I'm completely disoriented; the first thing I see is a steering wheel covered in reddish vomit and the glint of moonlight on the windshield. I have no idea how I've gotten there. There was a party, I remember. I was supposed to be at a party tonight. Liam was waiting for me. And Ethan—where was Ethan? I shift forward and my arm presses into something soft—someone soft that moves and groans beneath me. My breath catches as I glance down. Oh, God, I've been lying on top of Liam this whole time. I'd just elbowed him in the gut. He doesn't wake, just mutters something under his breath and then turns over with a sigh.

*Why am I here? And what is that awful smell?* I scramble off the seat, push open the car door, and look around. The house at the end of the drive has gone quiet; the night around us is completely still. The lawn, which had been crowded with cars, now only has two remaining.

A gust of wind whips my damp hair back and makes me shiver; I realize suddenly that the front of my dress is soaked through with vomit. And Liam—he's still stretched out sound asleep across the seat, his head resting against a soggy steering wheel. It's hard to see clearly by the light of the moon, but I can tell his clothes are wet and rumpled. I'm disgusted at myself. There's no way I can clean this up. When he wakes up he'll realize I threw up all over him. I don't remember much about our night; I can't remember if it was fun or crazy or romantic. But none of that matters now. I puked all over him and his car. I don't know how I'm going to face him.

And Ethan. What am I going to tell Ethan? Where did he go? Hope's car is parked near the porch. Maybe they're still here together.

I stumble across the lawn and toward the house. My head is swimming, my stomach is empty and churning, my throat is raw, my tongue like gritty sandpaper. I don't remember eating anything at the party. I have no idea what could have made me so sick. I hadn't drunk that much, had I? Could party punch make you this nauseated? There's a weird soreness between my legs too, a twinge that makes me wince as I climb the stairs. It feels like a cross between a period and the beginnings of a UTI. Am I getting my period early? There's no way I can blame the punch for that. I need to figure out what's going on.

There's a gust of wind from the porch as I open the door and the cold bites at my naked legs. I look down and groan. My dress, my sexy green dress, is completely ruined. I'm never going to get that stain out. I smooth it down; it had bunched up around my hips while I was sleeping. I have to clean myself up before anyone sees me.

I find an empty bathroom on the main level and close the door behind me. As the light comes on, I moan and put my hand up to cover my eyes. My entire body hurts, but that million-watt light bulb over the sink feels like it's burning a hole into my brain. I squint at my ruined outfit and dab some water over the cloth. It's hopeless. The best I can do is pat down my matted hair and wash the streaks of mascara off my face.

That burning feeling is worse now too; it feels like I haven't peed in days. I hike up my skirt to take a look. My underwear is crumpled and stained, and my legs are all streaked with blood. I can't believe this; my period's not due for another two weeks! And I'm *never* early. There's no way this night can get any worse.

Luckily there are a few pads beneath the sink, so I grab one while I clean myself up with some wet toilet paper and hand soap. Maybe the stress of vomiting made my period come prematurely. Is that even possible? But why am I so sore? That doesn't make sense. My period never makes me feel like this.

Why can't I remember how I got to the truck? How long was I asleep? I stick the pad into place and straighten my clothes. There's something important I need to remember. A memory that feels like vinyl and smells like spice and sour whiskey. *"Are you sure, Rain? Are you sure?" His glasses gone, his brown eyes large, confused.* What had we been talking about? I need to wake Liam up and ask him.

"Rainey? Are you in there?" It's Hope's voice on the other side of the door.

"One minute!" I splash some cold water on my face, comb my wet fingers through my hair.

She's blinking and rubbing her eyes when I step into the hall. "We fell asleep on the living room sofa," she says with a weak smile. "I heard you come in. Were you waiting for us?"

I shake my head. "I fell asleep too. Where is everybody?"

"Marcus passed out next to the punch bowl. Kathy threw up in the sink and then went up to her room—"

"Where's Ethan?"

"He's asleep on the sofa," she says softly. Her face is glowing. "He did really well tonight, Rain. You should be proud of him."

"That's great," I say. "But I really need to get him home." I don't mean to be short with her; normally I'd want to know every detail about Ethan's success, but right now every word hurts me. My head feels like a band of iron is wrapped around my temples. I'm praying I don't vomit again.

"I can take you," she says. "I only had one beer, and that was hours ago."

"Thanks."

"What happened to Liam? Did he go home already?"

"He's still asleep in his truck."

She hesitates and glances at my soiled dress. "Is everything okay with you two?"

"No, not really," I tell her. "I just threw up all over him. He's still asleep. I just need someone to take me home." My voice breaks and I clutch my forehead. "Look, Hope, I know I'll have to deal with this in the morning, but I just *can't* right now—"

"Okay, okay," she says, reaching out and patting my arm. "Relax. I'll go get Ethan."

He appears behind her as she says his name. "Hello, Rain. What happened to your dress?"

I have no energy to answer him or anyone else. "Let's just go."

The drive home is silent and tense. Hope keeps glancing at me and opening her mouth, then closing it again. Ethan busily messages someone on his phone. After a few minutes, the tick-tick-tick of his typing starts getting on my nerves. "It's four in the morning," I finally snap. "Who are you writing to?"

"It's six a.m. in DC," he responds. "Dad is up. He wanted to know how the party went."

"Oh. What are you telling him?"

"It was noisy, and I didn't like that. But other parts were good."

Hope glances over her shoulder and throws him a beaming smile that he doesn't see. I get the feeling I'm missing something.

"Did Dad ask about me?" I inquire, in spite of myself.

"No."

"Oh. Okay."

I lean my head against the window and close my eyes.

*Cooking with Rain*

SERENITY THROUGH YOUR GUT

*Rain's Hangover Cure: Vegan Frito Chip Chili*

Who feels like trekking to the grocery store with a splitting headache? Throw the leftovers from the party into a pot and simmer for the perfect hangover remedy. (See next week's blog for recipe. I'm too sick to write at the moment.)

# Chapter 16

I sleep through my phone the next afternoon—through a bunch of texts from Hope, Kathy, and Marcus and three calls from Liam. When I finally wake up, the sun has started to set, and the rays of light between my curtains have softened to an evening glow. I bury my head deeper into my pillow and squint at the blinking messages on my cell.

Hope: Are you feeling better? Want me to come over?

Marcus: I made everybody sick. I'm really sorry. I read the recipe wrong. It was supposed to be a third of a bottle of whiskey. Not three bottles.

Kathy: I have to talk to someone.

And finally, a desperate text from Liam after the missed calls: Please call me. We need to talk about last night.

The thing is, I don't want to talk about last night. I never want to talk about it. My memory of the party is blurred and patchy, but I remember enough to be absolutely mortified. I remember spying on my brother, I remember Liam's shocked face, I remember falling on top of him in the truck, I remember kissing him, and then—what happened then?

I remember the word *Please*. Whispered over and over. *Please, Liam, I want you.* How could I have said that? It didn't sound like something I would say. Not yet. We just started dating.

But I definitely remember *I love you*. Did Liam say that? Did I? Who says I love you to someone they've just started dating?

I should have stayed and waited until he woke up. But I'd run off and left him there lying in my vomit. He was probably freaking out. There was nothing I could say now to excuse myself, except possibly plead temporary drunken insanity. But we'd all had too much to drink, and I was the only one who'd acted like an idiot. I know I should call him, but I need a little more time to figure this out. It's obvious we went too far; but I need to remember what exactly happened before I can decide what to say.

He deserves a reply though. Even if it's just a stall until I get my thoughts together. I stare at my phone for a long time before finally touching the screen. I'm writing Liam a carefully worded answer when I hear a sudden shout outside my door and the soft thud of something hitting the landing.

"Rain! Wake up! Come quick!" It's Ethan's voice, but it rings out so loudly that I jump up from my bed. I've never heard him call out like that.

I drop my phone and rush out into the hall. Ethan is crouched over the prostrate form of our mother who's fallen in the doorway of the bathroom. I stand frozen for a moment, and then I spring to action. "What happened?" I ask him as I turn her over. "What's going on?"

He reaches out and shakes her roughly. "Are you all right, are you okay?" He glances up at me. "You call 911," he orders flatly and hands me his phone. His tone and movements are robotic, like someone going through a rehearsed protocol. Then his hands are on her neck and his ear is by her mouth. I start to dial.

"Do you know CPR?" I ask him shakily. I learned the basics a while ago but my mind is a total blank now. I'm praying he remembers.

"I know CPR," he replies calmly. "But she doesn't need it. Her pulse is good, and she's breathing. We have to put her in recovery position."

I watch him quietly as he turns her on her side and gently smooths her hair back from her face. She's breathing normally, but her closed eyes are sunk deep into their hollows, and her face is pale as a corpse.

"What's the nature of your emergency?" the voice on the phone demands.

"I don't know," I gasp out. "Something's happened to my mom. Just come quickly please."

# Chapter 17

Ethan seems to be enjoying himself in the ER. That alone distracts me from the terror of the evening. He's practically bouncing in his seat, eyes darting all over the triage area, curious fingers touching everything in his path—the oxygen nozzle on the wall, the multicolored test tubes on the nurse's trolley, the buttons on the beeping monitor attached to our sleeping mother.

I calm down a little after the paramedic assures me that she only fainted and wasn't in immediate danger, but Ethan's frenetic curiosity still chafes a bit. Our nurse is amused by his interest at first, but he eventually begins to fray her nerves too.

"The blood pressure cuff you're using is too big," he tells her. "My mom's gotten very thin and she needs a smaller size. Your reading will be falsely low."

She nods grimly and makes the adjustment.

"My mom's dehydrated," he declares after a moment.

The nurse grunts and points at the clear bag on a pole. "That's why we're giving her the IV, hon," she explains patiently.

"I know," he retorts. "But shouldn't you be measuring her urine output as well? That way you can calculate how much fluid she's losing."

She turns to stare at him for the first time. "How old are you, sweetheart?" There's a frustrated edge to her voice.

"I'm sixteen. And you haven't answered my question."

"He means well," I say apologetically. "My brother has autism. So sometimes he can cross some boundaries—"

She nods and gives him a doubtful look. "My cousin's kid has that. But he doesn't talk."

"I have excellent verbal skills," Ethan says.

"Yes," she remarks acidly. "You sure do, sweetie."

"My name is Ethan," he tells her. Then he turns to me. "And if I crossed boundaries you should tell me, not the nurse."

That shuts me up. But Ethan doesn't stop buzzing around the room until our mother begins to stir.

When she opens her eyes, I sit down by her side.

"What happened?" she asks me weakly.

"You fainted. The doctors are trying to figure out why."

"The doctors haven't been in to see you yet," Ethan puts in. "And the nurse doesn't know what she's doing."

I'm thankful she'd just left the room and didn't hear that. "They're taking good care of you," I say, throwing Ethan a warning look that goes right over his head.

Mom doesn't seem convinced. "What are they doing to me?" she complains. "I don't want to be here. I hate hospitals."

"People say they hate hospitals," Ethan declares. "But a hospital is just a building. What they really hate is the feeling of helplessness that comes with being sick."

"I want to go home," my mother insists. "I'm taking this needle out of me."

"Mom!" I put my hand out to stop her. She's already started peeling the tape from her arm and plucking at the tube. "Stop! Let them check you and find out what's wrong. It was awful to see you passed out like that. What are we supposed to do if you get sick again?"

The ring of fear in my voice seems to give her pause, and she stops messing with her IV. But the rest of the evening doesn't go by easily. She challenges the nurses at every step. "If I'm dehydrated why are you taking more blood?" she demands. "No, I don't want a CAT scan. I won't be irradiated for no reason. I'm sorry, I can't eat this food; it's full of preservatives."

I plead with her every time the nurses come in, and I fight with her until she agrees to the doctor's orders. It's obvious they've found something wrong with her, because they refuse to let her go, but no one will speak to any of us to explain what's happening. Hours after she's admitted, Dr. Handel, the attending physician, finally comes in to speak with us. As he settles down in front of her, Ethan turns to me and holds up his phone. "Liam just texted me. He says that he's been calling you and you aren't picking up."

"I left my phone at home," I whisper to him. "Just tell him that I'm speaking with a doctor. And I'll call him as soon as I can."

All talk and thought about the party will have to wait. There's no way to message Liam through my brother while my mom is listening. I don't want her to suspect I'd lied to her and gotten drunk. She has enough to worry her now. I'm scared the doctor has come in to tell us some awful diagnosis. His face looks grim. Ethan types out my response quickly and then turns to listen.

"Your blood count was very low," the doctor explains. "We don't know why yet, but we're running a few tests and hopefully we'll have more answers for you soon. I understand that you've been feeling sick for quite a while."

"Not that long," she says defensively. "It's probably stress."

"Well, it might have been triggered by stress, but there's definitely something else going on. Can you tell me how long you've been bleeding?"

She glances at Ethan and then shakes her head at the doctor. "I don't want to talk about this in front of them."

"Mom!"

The doctor shrugs at us and motions toward the door. "Maybe you two should wait outside."

"But I want to know what's going on!" I protest. "What kind of bleeding? What is he talking about?"

"Rain, please!" Her eyes narrow, and the faintest flush of color darkens her white cheeks.

"He's obviously talking about intestinal bleeding," Ethan remarks. "And the most likely causes are either colitis or Crohn's, which are inflammatory diseases affecting the large intestine—"

"No more anatomy lectures, Ethan!" I snap. "I want to hear what the doctor has to say."

But the physician is staring quietly at my brother. His

expression is serious, but his eyes wrinkle at the corners. "Actually, he's right. How old are you, young man?"

"Sixteen. Why does everyone keep asking me that?"

"Well, most of my medical students wouldn't have gotten that diagnosis." He smiles. "But that's not the point right now. Your mother has asked that you two leave the room. And a doctor has to respect the wishes of his patient."

It's like Dr. Handel has just given Ethan one of the ten commandments. My brother rises immediately and gestures to me. "Come on, Rain. I have to respect the wishes of the patient."

"She's not your patient, she's our mother! And I want to know what's going on—"

"It's okay," she murmurs, holding up a hand to calm me. "You guys can stay. Ethan clearly knows more about this than I do."

We settle back down into our chairs, and Dr. Handel begins his "differential diagnosis," as he calls it. (Which basically means "we don't know what's wrong but here's a list we've come up with.") The next hour is a blur of words I can't understand. The doctor talks and gestures with his hands, my mother sits stone faced and tight lipped, Ethan nods sagely and throws out random questions that make me crazy. In the end, though, I only want to know one thing. "She's going to be okay, right?" I ask him finally. "It isn't something…something really bad…like—"

"Like cancer?" I'm terrified and relieved that the doctor has anticipated my fear. How did he know that's what I was afraid of? "No, Rain. There aren't any signs of that on the CAT scan. But there is a long road ahead. And there are still more tests to run."

"What if I refuse the tests?" We all turn to stare at her. It's the first time she's spoken since the doctor began talking. "I want to consult a friend of mine," she continues. "She's an alternative healer, and I'd prefer to try that route first. So I'd like to check out of here now." Doctor Handel clears his throat and rubs a hand over his eyes.

"Well, you always have that option, of course. We can't force you to stay. But I strongly recommend—"

"I *know* what you recommend," she interrupts. "But I'm feeling a lot better. So what will happen if I leave now?"

"You could die," Ethan states flatly. "And then Rain and I would have to move to DC to live with Dad."

"Ethan!" I exclaim. "Tell her you don't mean that!"

"But I do mean it. One of the complications of untreated colitis is cancer. Or worse, a perforated bowel. If that happens, she could be dead by next week—"

"Okay, okay!" the doctor interjects. "I think your mother gets the picture."

She definitely seems to. I don't know if it's the threat of imminent death or the prospect of her children moving in with their father that changes her mind. But it does the trick. She sits back against her pillow and gives the doctor a resentful look. "All right, fine. I'll give it a couple of days."

I let out an audible sigh of relief. Ethan stares at the IV pole.

"Can we stay with you?" I ask.

"No," she says. "You have school tomorrow. And I don't want you breathing this hospital air."

We go back and forth for a while, but eventually we reach a compromise. Ethan and I can stay during visiting hours for the next two days. But we must sleep at home, and we have to promise to keep up with our schoolwork.

And since visiting hours are over, it's time for us to leave. "Tomorrow I can borrow the car to get us here," I tell Ethan after I kiss Mom goodbye. "But how are we getting back tonight?"

"I texted Hope," he says as I close the door behind us. "But it'll be an hour before she can get here."

I settle back on one of the waiting room sofas and watch him as he types away on his phone. "You know," I say after a moment. "That thing you said back there about Mom dying and us going to live with Dad. That wasn't right, Ethan."

He sits down next to me and slowly puts down his phone. "Yes, it was. That's what would happen."

"No, I mean, the *facts* may have been right. But it was wrong to say that. It made it sound like you didn't care."

"It did?"

I sigh. "Yes. It sounded like it didn't matter to you if Mom died. Because then you'd just go off and live with Dad."

His eyes widen. "Does Mom think that's what I meant? She thinks that I wouldn't care?" He inhales sharply and springs up from the sofa. "I'll tell her she's wrong—"

"No, no, sit down! Mom *knows* you, Ethan. She knows you care about her. But other people... They might take it the wrong way. So if you want to deal with people—with patients, for example—then you have to be careful when you talk about dying."

He digests the information for a moment. "I still have to tell the truth."

"Yes, you do. But a doctor also should be compassionate. And you want to be a doctor, right?"

"Yes."

"Then you'll have to get used to talking to patients who are scared and vulnerable."

"What should I have said?"

"Well, you should have said, 'The complications can be very dangerous.' Leave out the part about dying. People can figure that out themselves."

"Oh." He glances at me and smiles. "Thank you."

It feels like years since he's smiled at me like that. The spontaneous, unexpected warmth, our twin connection, the understanding we'd once shared—I've been missing that so much. But now that simple smile, that feeling of being needed is so precious, that for a moment I'm at a loss for words. Without thinking, I reach out and touch him lightly on the shoulder. He doesn't flinch or pull away. "That's what I'm here for, Ethan."

If it wasn't too sinister, I'd say Ethan is more pleased to hear that his diagnosis turns out to be correct than concerned with the fact that our mother has a lifelong illness. The giant cardboard hologram of a human intestine which Mom had relegated to the shed now makes a reappearance in the living room. Over the next two days my brother spends hours covering it with Post-it notes and lists of various medication names.

I pass most of the following days in the hospital with Ethan and evenings doing the homework Hope drops off for me. During dinner Ethan regales us both with excruciating details about the digestive system. I learn to eat through it. Hope seems weirdly fascinated by his lectures, or maybe she's just better at faking interest than I am.

It's not that I don't care about my mother's illness. But I only want to know what I need to know, namely, what I can do to make her better quickly. And so far, all I can understand is that she needs to take some pills (which she doesn't want to do) and that her children need to stop stressing her out (which is very hard to do while I'm yelling at her to take her pills).

It's a fine balance.

But I try my best to reason with her calmly, even as I tell myself she's being completely unreasonable. And frankly, Ethan doesn't help much at first. Now that he's realized that telling people they're going to die imminently is unacceptable behavior, he's a bit tongue-tied. By the second day of mom's hospitalization we still haven't convinced her to take her meds. So I take Ethan aside.

"Secret Rule?"

"What can I do?" he responds immediately.

"Tell Mom that you're going to ask Dad to come stay with us. Tell her that you're scared to be home at night without a parent."

"But I'm not scared. Are you?"

I'm not, of course. But if I tell him that, the lie will stick in his throat when he talks to Mom. So I nod. "Yeah. I'm terrified."

"But I'll protect you."

"I know you will, Ethan. But three is way safer than two."

"So why don't you tell Mom you're scared?"

"Because you're the one who talks to Dad. She won't believe it if I say I'm planning to call him."

"Wait, so do you want me to ask Dad to come stay with us?"

"No! But if Mom *thinks* you will, then maybe she'll take the pills and get better."

"Oh! Oh, I get it."

"Exactly."

And just like that, we're coconspirators again, the way we used to be when we were little, and I had to be his voice. Only this time, it's Ethan who's speaking for me.

And he does it perfectly, with merciless and relentless precision. He texts Dad in front of her. He gets into animated discussions with him right outside her door. He even mentions buying the hot dogs dad likes from the grocery store. Mom turns a little green after the last one. So maybe he tilts the scales too far in the "stress" direction, but it finally works. She swallows her medicine.

And Ethan and I go home.

# Chapter 18

It's been three days since the party, and I still don't know how to face Liam. My mother's hospitalization has been a good excuse so far, but I cringe when Mom insists that I'm going back to school on Wednesday. I can't avoid him anymore. But I have no idea what to say to him, how to act now that our relationship has progressed to the next level. Worse, I can still only remember bits and pieces of that night. But those snapshots are enough. I know that Liam and I went way too far—about as far as two people can go. And I'm actually thankful there's still a black fog over most of it and that my mom's illness is distracting me from dwelling on it too much.

Still, maybe Liam was too drunk to remember what happened between us. Or maybe he's upset I yakked all over him while he slept. And maybe he's hurt that I haven't communicated with him at all since then.

The mother excuse can only go so far, after all. I've had time to call. During lunchtime. Or before I went to bed. But I haven't because I'm too afraid to start that conversation.

So on Wednesday morning, I'm not exactly racing for the door. I drag my feet as I walk to school and arrive a little late for homeroom. Then I concentrate very hard on the empty notebook in front of me. Out of the corner of my eye I see Liam looking at me, but I'm stubbornly spellbound by the blank paper on my desk. When the bell rings, I sprint for the bathroom and wait there until chemistry lab starts, then I slip in after the bell, meekly hand a late pass to Mr. Green, and quietly place my books beside Liam as if it's just a regular day.

It should be less awkward when other people are around, right? I can be pleasant while pretending to be a diligent student. And then maybe after a little while things might go back to normal.

But Liam won't stop trying to meet my eye, no matter how stubbornly I avoid him. Finally, he places his hand over mine and blocks my view of the page in front of me. I have no choice but to look up.

His eyes are wide and scared, searching mine. "How's your mom?" he whispers. But his expression is asking something else.

"She's better. Now that she's taking her medicine, they're talking about discharging her from the hospital. Maybe even tonight."

"That's good. I was worried about you."

"Oh." I push my lips up into a cheery smile. "I'm fine."

He hesitates and glances around the room before turning back to me. "When I woke up," he says, lowering his voice so I can barely hear him, "you were gone. And I couldn't believe what… what had happened—"

"I'm so sorry about that," I cut in. "I can pay for the truck cleaning. I brought some money with me." I dig into my pocket. "Will this be enough?"

He stares at the crumpled bills I've pushed into his palm. "I wasn't even thinking about the car. I was worried about you."

"I'm fine. And it isn't fair that you should have to pay to clean up the puke."

He shakes his head. "I thought *I* did that. I threw up after I woke up. So did most of the people who drank Marcus's punch, apparently. But I never thought to blame you. I was worried that you weren't answering my calls because you were upset about—"

"Why would I be upset?" I interrupt. "We both screwed up, that's all. Honestly, I just want to forget that night completely—"

"I'd *really* like that," he says. "We can just start over, okay?"

"Okay." He doesn't look convinced, though. There seems to be a follow-up question struggling to get out, but I want to put an end to this conversation now. So I decide to lighten the mood a little. "I came up with an awesome hangover cure. Want to hear?"

"I'm not hungover anymore."

"Whatever. For next time."

He makes a face. "There isn't going to be a next time. I never want to lose my judgment like that again—"

I *don't* want to talk about this. "I've been reading that the Namibians drink buffalo milk after a night of partying," I tell him quickly. "It's not *actually* from a buffalo. Basically, they make this ice cream float with spiced rum and clotted cream. So I thought if you add a bit of licorice root, which decreases stomach inflammation, it could make the ultimate hangover—"

"Rain, are you *sure* you're okay?"

I make a frustrated, noisy clatter with the stirring rod. "I don't want to talk about it right now," I say shortly. "We're in the middle of lab."

"Okay." He shifts uncomfortably and seems about to speak again, but a look from the teacher silences him. We work quietly for the rest of the period. When the bell rings, he turns to me and touches my sleeve.

"Can we talk after school? I promised to take your brother on that surgery observation this evening," he says. "But I'm free before that."

"Sure," I say with a shrug.

I can feel Liam's eyes watching me as I gather my books and shove them into my bag. I want to tell him again that I'm fine, that we'd both made a stupid mistake I'm just desperate to forget. I don't care about being healthy or responsible or right. Pretending to move on is what I need now. Between my mother being hospitalized, my dad waiting on the sidelines, my brother diagnosing the hell out of everything, I just need our relationship to be simple.

But I don't know how to say any of that. So I just say, "Hey, did you know that the Sicilians used dried bull penis as a hangover cure? Seriously. Dried. Bull. Penis."

For a moment, his smile washes away the worry in his eyes, and I feel happy for the first time in days. *We're going to be just fine,* I tell myself. *I'm not going to let one mistake ruin us.*

# Chapter 19

After school, Liam takes me on a walk around Green Pines Overlook. We're silent most of the way. "It's a beautiful day," he finally says.

He wants to talk about the weather? "Yeah, this is one of my favorite spots."

"It's my first time here. I haven't explored much since I moved."

"Well, you should give this town a chance," I tell him. "On days like this I actually understand why my mom chose to move out here."

He nods and gazes at the white-topped mountains. "I see what you mean, I guess. I understand why people come out here to breathe this air and drink in all this green nature. But honestly, it doesn't do anything for me. I look out over the farmland, or the mountains, or those clumps of quiet, perfect little houses, and I feel myself just...falling asleep. Not a good, peaceful sleep, either. It feels like someone's injected some powerful anesthetic into my blood, and if I don't fight it, if I don't tear it out of me, I just might never wake up. And I can't think of anything worse."

"So you don't see yourself ever coming back?"

"Oh God, no. What for? I'll come by to visit my grand-mother as often as I can. But you're going to leave too eventually. So who else would I come back for?"

I'm not sure what to make of that. It's nice that he's acknowl-edged that my future whereabouts are important to him—that he's considered where I'd be living one day. At least, I'm pretty sure that's what he just implied. Yet I don't know how to follow that thought. We've been together such a short time.

"Where do you want to end up?" I ask him finally. "I mean, after you've done the international doctor stuff."

"I don't know, exactly. Somewhere big. Huge, impersonal. Someplace where no one cares who you are, nobody gossips about your family or your business. Somewhere you can lose yourself in the energy of a million other busy people. That's what I want."

"Like New York? Or DC?" I can't help thinking about my old home and my father. Is he there now? Is he planning yet another visit that only Ethan knows about?

"Yeah. Someplace where no one will notice that a person's missing until his neighbors comment on the odd smell coming from his apartment."

I laugh and smack him playfully on the shoulder. "That's just morbid."

He grins and tosses a pebble over the cliff. "Not more morbid than the housewives of Mineral County pecking at their neighbors like a bunch of bored and hungry vultures."

I remember what my mom told me about Liam's father. "I

know what you mean. Just another year and a half though. And then we can go anywhere we want."

He shrugs. "This town is good for some people, I guess. Like your brother, for example. Big cities might not be right for him."

I shake my head. "I don't know about that. He's being homeschooled because we ran out of options here. But it might have been different if we'd been somewhere with more resources."

"Well, he seems to be doing okay."

"I'm not sure. I have no idea how he's doing anymore. He doesn't really talk to me. Not that he was ever much of a talker. But lately, it's like he's deliberately trying to shut me out."

He studies me for a moment. "You're kind of the same way, Rain," he says, softly.

"What do you mean?"

"Well, you don't talk much about your own feelings either. I mean, I keep asking you how you're doing, and all you want to do is pretend nothing happened between us. And then you change the subject to weird food. Which is fine, I guess. But it's still kind of confusing."

I take a deep breath. "You want to talk about it, don't you?"

He gives me a baffled look. "You don't?"

"Look, I realize we went too far—*way* too far. And I just want to roll things back to how we were three days ago. I know I said I wanted to be spontaneous and free, but I think I should go back to being me for a little bit. Responsible Rain. Not Halloween-party Rain."

He blushes and glances down at his hands. "That wasn't me either. Not that it wasn't great," he adds hastily.

"My bloodstream was, like, ninety percent whiskey," I point out. "So was yours. You could make the argument that it was the alcohol that did…all that."

I don't know why I suddenly can't say it.

"You're the first girl I've kissed," he tells me. "Hell, until a few days ago I just assumed that I'd graduate high school—maybe even college—a lonely virgin."

It's my turn to blush. I'm not squeamish about the idea of sex. Half of my class has already done it, and I figured it would happen someday for me too. It's just that I've always associated losing my virginity with finding true love. Not with being wasted in the back of a truck with a boy I barely knew. I'd never understood the race to lose it, never felt the need to tear the scarlet V off my chest. I *liked* being sort of old-fashioned. Liam was a great guy, but I wasn't ready to have sex with him—or with anyone. I was having a hard time just coming to terms with the realization that for us, that blurry night in his truck was *it*. The earthshaking stuff they write poems and songs about.

I felt like we'd been sold a fancy, brightly wrapped box. We'd torn the paper open, thrown caution to the wind, and now I was staring over an empty carton at a boy whose eyes were begging me for something I couldn't give him. I wanted to feel like a woman now, like I'd checked off this big, important milestone, but instead I was just disappointed. Not with him. I was disappointed with *it*.

He was patiently waiting for my response, and I couldn't say what I was thinking.

"You're my first everything too," I admit. "And I'm totally not ready for everything."

He nods slowly, his eyes fixed anxiously on my face. "We're supposed to be the super cautious kids that everyone trusts." He clears his throat. "And we didn't even use—"

"It's fine," I interrupt. I don't want to talk about protection or our lack of it that night. "I still can't believe we were that stupid. But I got my period. Don't worry about it."

His look of relief embarrasses me, and I realize he's been trying to ask me about that since it happened. And I've been avoiding him and that question for the last three days.

It's almost true, the period thing. I thought I was on my period the night of the party. I was so confused and foggy from the alcohol that I didn't think it through. And then when my mom got sick I sort of forgot about it. The truth is, I'm not exactly sure anymore. And now it's been more than three days since the party, and it's too late to take a pill or do anything but wait and hope for the best.

*It's going to be okay*, I tell myself. *I'll be super responsible from now on. We both will.*

We walk around for a few more minutes, and then I ask Liam to drop me off at Hope's before he takes Ethan to watch the surgery. I need to talk to somebody about this, someone who isn't Liam. As I get out of the truck, I give him a fake, confident smile and an uncomfortable peck on the lips. For all our brave talk about turning back the clock and taking things slow, I think we're both going to need a little time to figure this out.

# Chapter 20

When I arrive at her house, Hope asks me about Liam, and I answer, "We're great! He's great! I'm great!" and then cheerily ignore her doubtful look. I'm going to have to ease into this conversation slowly, it seems.

"There's something I want to show you," she says after a pause. "I wasn't going to tell you at first but I was worried that you'd just see it somewhere else. My cousin in Missoula sent me this old video of a prank her classmates played on Liam back in the ninth grade—"

"Yeah, I know all about that," I interrupt. I place my hand over the screen on her phone. "And I'm not watching it. I promised him."

She seems relieved. "Oh, good. It's pretty embarrassing. If it makes you feel better, I don't think anyone else at our school has seen it. I just thought you should be prepared. They made Liam cry at the end—"

"I don't want to watch it, and I don't want to hear about it," I tell her. "Every view that video gets is an extra point for bullies."

"You're right. You're right. I'm deleting the message right

now. I shouldn't have brought it up. And I'm really glad you guys are doing so well."

"We are. Liam and I are doing great."

I'm surprised at my own lie. I'd been planning to be honest with her. That was why I'd come, to share my worries with her. Normally I would tell her everything, and we'd dissect it all together. But lately I've felt kind of awkward around Hope. I didn't even realize *how* awkward I've felt until I got here. Another side effect of her dating my twin, I guess. It's not that I'm worried she'll blab to Ethan. It's just that she's dating my brother. I'd been so wrapped up in worrying about Ethan that the everyday weirdness of that situation was only just dawning on me. Sharing things with her felt different now.

And until I got used to it, I needed to keep my dating problems to myself.

So we watch a movie and talk about Ethan's trip to the surgery ward. I get a blow-by-blow account of the whole adventure from Hope as my brother texts her updates every fifteen minutes. She's very excited by the first few, but after the tenth text she seems a little reluctant to check her phone. The idea of her boyfriend attending an operation is one thing; the gruesome details he keeps sending her are quite another.

My mom messages me halfway through the movie. "Come and get me as soon as you can. They said I can go home."

I return home to pick up the car and am at the hospital within the hour. The whole checkout process takes longer than either of us anticipated (so many papers and instructions), and we pull into our driveway at half past ten.

My mom shuffles upstairs, hauling her hospital bag after her. I pull some dough out of the freezer to defrost for tomorrow's dessert (I'm experimenting with eggnog pumpkin pie—Christmas and Thanksgiving in one dish!) and then walk into the living room only to discover Ethan stretched out on the living room floor in a yoga pose. It's the position I've taught him to use when I'm not around to help him with the Rain burrito. He's humming to himself in rhythmic one note beats, the droning noise drowning out the world around him. I sit down on the sofa and wait for him to rise.

When he does, he appears startled to see me there watching him.

"Hello, Rain."

"Hey, there. I just brought Mom home."

He nods silently.

"Do you want me to get your weight blanket?" I ask him.

He shakes his head and swallows loudly.

"So the surgery thing didn't go well?"

He shakes his head again. "It went very well. The surgeon said that I had a lot of promise. Liam told me he never says that about anyone."

"That's fantastic!" I smile. "Then why the yoga?"

He sighs and slowly gets to his feet. "I feel better now," he says, ignoring my question. "I'm going to my room to study."

"Okay. Are you sure you don't need anything—"

"I'm fine," he retorts. "Good night, Rain."

"Good night."

I drag my book bag to the coffee table and pull out my textbooks. Normally I study in my bedroom, but today I'm waiting for Ethan to change his mind. He seemed so fragile just now, and I'm sure that he'll come stumbling out into the hallway at any moment.

It was such a big week for him. He'd gone to his first party, seen his mother through a hospitalization, and started on his path to becoming a doctor. Until recently, any one of those things would have caused a violent short circuit. How was he handling all three together? He should need me right now; I should be holding him, wrapped tightly in the safe embrace of his weight blanket.

But his bedroom door stays closed, and the landing is quiet.

An hour passes, and there's no sound to break my loneliness. Finally, I shuffle off to my room and swing my door shut with a bang. I want him to know that I'm awake if he needs to talk. But he doesn't. There's no tap at the door, no restless movement on the other side of my wall. He's okay.

He's okay without me. And I know the thought should make me happy. It's what I've worked for, isn't it? Then why am I wishing I hadn't taught him the yoga pose, all those breathing exercises to calm himself? It's a horrible, selfish thought, and I know I would never admit it to anyone. I'm supposed to be the perfect sister. My mother is always bragging about my competence and caring; Hope even thinks my relationship with Ethan is impressive. But what would they think if they knew the real me? I used to believe everything I did for Ethan was out of love. But what if that isn't true? What if my love is a messy, twisted thing? Maybe I'm just a charming imposter who's managed to fool everyone, including myself. I can't keep pretending to be a good and loving sister, if deep down I'm dreading the day he breaks from me. It isn't real love if I need Ethan to need me.

This quiet feels so unnatural; I can almost hear my brother breathing on the other side of the wall. My phone is lying next to me on the pillow. I scroll through my friends' names and tap out a greeting to our WhatsApp group, then quickly delete it. What's the point in chatting? I can't say what I'm really thinking. Might as well just go to sleep. I slide over to the edge of my bed and tap the wall between us, count out five sharp knocks.

Like I do every night.

There's a short pause, and for the first time in my life, I'm terrified he's not going to respond. That he's fallen asleep without waiting for my good night.

I shut my eyes and take a deep breath. Let it out, in a slow, cleansing exhale, just as I've taught Ethan to do. I focus on each breath, concentrate on the rise and fall of my chest. Ten beats pass.

And then his voice comes through the wall.

"Good night, Rain."

He says it like he always does, in his clipped, low monotone, but to me the words sound almost musical, like a child's bedtime story. I feel my heart rate slow, my muscles relax. It's going to be okay, I tell myself. I can go to sleep now. My brother's still there.

## ETHAN'S JOURNAL:

The cholecystectomy was a successful operation. The predicted obstacles were not as difficult to overcome as expected. In the hallways, when the noise level became overwhelming, I utilized the breathing and relaxation exercises Rain taught me. When the surgeon took us to the operating room, it was a relief. The quiet voices, the unblinking light, the predictable, ordered routine. It's as if the room was designed for me. After Dr. Peters dismissed us, I took a much-needed bathroom break. While I was in the stall, two medical students from our team entered.

"Let it go," the one with the deeper voice said. "I don't think he was trying to show off."

"Who cares?" High Voice replied. "We're the ones getting graded. You'd think he'd have realized he needed to shut up. I kept staring him down, but he was ignoring me. What a dick."

Deep Voice laughed. "That kid sure knew his shit though."

"People like that always know their shit," High Voice said. "They're basically walking computers. It sucks for me though. Today's the end of the rotation, and I got showed up by a teenage robot."

Deep Voice zipped up his pants and stepped

over to the sink. The splashing water obscured the beginning of his reply. All I caught was his final statement: "I'd rather fail the surgery elective than spend a day in that boy's life. I wonder what it's like to live without emotions?"

High Voice made a snorting sound. "Whatever. How would he even know what he's missing?"

On the way home from the hospital, I told Liam what I had heard. He didn't say anything at first.

"Do you think I'm missing something?" I asked him.

He shook his head. "Of course not. Don't let those morons upset you."

"I'm not upset," I tell him. "Because I know they're wrong. I just can't prove it."

"You don't have to prove anything to anyone."

He's probably right. Still, I think it would be easier for me if I could explain what I was feeling. When I was little, I would just scream until my sister fixed whatever was bothering me. Rain once told me that I keep my emotions in a box, and that no one has the key to the box. I had no idea what that meant. So I said, "Rain, what are you feeling right now?" She started to answer me, and I interrupted her. "No. I want you to describe your emotions. But you have to do it in German."

Here's the thing: If she traveled to Germany she would still feel things. But she'd have to use big, weird gestures to show people what she meant because she doesn't speak German. And no one would understand her, no matter how hard she tried.

After I asked her to describe her emotions in German, Rain was quiet for a little while. Then she wrapped her arms around herself and squeezed. She does that when she wants to give me a hug but can't.

"You're always in Germany, aren't you?"

# Chapter 21

I'm supposed to be moving on. Finishing my schoolwork, studying for the SATs. Coming up with new ideas for the blog. But it's getting harder for me to concentrate on anything. I keep spacing out and forgetting what I was doing. My brain has already dismissed the drunken night as a stupid mistake. But my heart keeps hovering over what happened in the truck.

I need something to distract me, somebody to talk to. Not Liam, obviously. He's freaked out enough as it is.

My mom is out of the question for obvious reasons; even if "Hey, Mom, guess what I did in the back of a truck?" is something I could remotely picture saying, the last thing I want is to stress her out. Ethan is out because he's Ethan.

Hope would be the obvious choice, but she's linked to Ethan in my mind now, and I don't want to make things even more complicated than they already are.

I could try calling my dad, I think. What a weird conversation that would be! Hey, Dad, I know we haven't spoken for a while, but guess what I just did? That would be one way to break the ice between us.

I'm staring dully at my phone when it suddenly starts to flash. *Kathy.* With everything that had been going on, I'd completely forgotten to respond to her messages.

I heard about your mom, she texts. Are you okay? Do you mind if I come over?

I'm all right, I tell her. You can come now if you want.

I put a batch of chocolate and peanut butter wontons in the oven (*Blog idea: Chinatown meets Willy Wonka!*) and greet her with a plate of steaming dumplings. We are both occupied with the gooey, hot dough for a few minutes; she doesn't talk about anything except chocolate until the plate in front of us is empty.

"I'm sorry if I'm bugging you," she begins. "I know your mom's been sick and everything—"

"It's fine; she's getting better. They discharged her yesterday."

"Oh, that's good." She glances over her shoulder uneasily. "Is your brother at home?"

"Ethan? Yeah. He's upstairs. Why?"

She hesitates. "I wanted to talk to you about something."

"Okay… It's about Ethan?"

"Sort of." She clears her throat. "Not exactly. He didn't say anything to you?"

*What is going on?* "About what?" I ask. "Did something happen at the party?"

My baffled expression seems to relax her, and she leans back against her seat with a sigh. "I figured he'd told you. So you have no idea what happened after the Halloween party?"

"No!" My voice rises. I knew I shouldn't have left him alone all night. "Did something happen to him? Why didn't Hope say anything to me?"

"Hope wasn't there for most of it. And nothing bad happened. Not to him, anyway. Don't look so scared."

"Please just tell me already!"

"I'm trying! But it's hard, all right? I haven't been able to talk to anyone about this. My parents found out about the party and grounded me. I only got them to let me out today because I said that you had my homework assignments." She sighs, and her face crumples up.

I'm distracted from my worries about Ethan for a moment. I've never seen Kathy so upset. And she's never come to me on her own about anything before; I've rarely seen her without her boyfriend by her side. Why wasn't she talking to Marcus, instead of me?

"I know it's not Ethan's fault," she whimpers, "but I just *hate* him right now."

My confusion is complete. I can't begin to imagine what happened at the party. What could Ethan possibly have done?

"What are you saying?" I ask her gently.

She swallows and clears her throat. "Your brother—" A sob interrupts her confession. "I can't believe I had to find out this way."

I'm suddenly afraid again. A thousand crazy scenarios flash through my mind. Did someone hurt my brother at the party? It's no wonder he'd been pulling away from me recently. When he needed me the most, I'd gone off and abandoned him. How could I have let my guard down? I remember the foggy windows of Liam's truck and the bile rises to my throat. This was all my fault. I should have stood my ground and not let Ethan out of my sight. Spied on him, if necessary. "Kathy, what happened?" I whisper. I'm terrified and imagining the worst.

She takes a deep breath and the words finally spill out. "Marcus...Marcus tried to *hit on your brother.*"

I have no thoughts. My mind is a complete blank. I stare at her.

"I was upstairs most of the night," she continues. "I didn't want people to see me throwing up. But after everyone went home I came down for a drink of water. Hope wasn't in the living room—I think she'd gone to the bathroom. But Ethan was sitting on the couch. And Marcus was with him."

I can't breathe; I feel like I'm choking. "What *happened?*" I repeat hoarsely.

"They couldn't see me. But I could hear everything. Marcus—my *boyfriend*—was crying. 'You're beautiful, Ethan,' he was saying to him. Over and over. 'Do you know how beautiful you are?'"

"Oh." I'm struggling to grasp what she's telling me. "But... that was it? Maybe it didn't mean anything. He was drunk."

She shakes her head and wipes a sleeve over her wet cheeks. "And then he said, 'Don't tell Kathy what I told you. It'll break her heart if she finds out I'm gay.'"

There's a miserable silence. I have no idea what to say to her, so I just hold her hands as she cries. "I know Marcus was wasted," she continues after a moment. "But it was real. What he was feeling. He meant every word. I'm sure he did."

I feel terrible. Shouldn't I have sensed my friend was hiding something this huge? I knew Marcus's parents were super religious. It wasn't at all surprising he'd kept it from them. And of course he couldn't tell his girlfriend. Maybe he'd chosen to come out to Ethan because he was the only one who wouldn't judge him, a near stranger who would just listen. Or maybe the whiskey had chosen for Marcus that night.

I can't imagine how lost Kathy must feel now. Until now, if I had to bet on any couple surviving into adulthood, I would have picked her and Marcus.

Still, as sorry as I am for Kathy, I can't help thinking about the quiet bystander in her story. From force of habit, it's simply where my mind goes. What had my brother thought about all of this? I wonder. How had Marcus's confession affected him? And why hadn't Ethan told me what had happened? Had he kept Marcus's secret because it was the right thing to do? Or did he simply not understand what he'd witnessed?

"What did Ethan say to him?" I ask her.

She laughs and shakes her head. "I don't think he had any idea what was happening. He just sat there."

"And then what did he do?"

"I don't *know*, Rain. At that moment, I wasn't thinking about Ethan. That's not the point, don't you see?"

"No, I know." Of course it's not the point. I realize that, even as I'm dying to find out what Kathy's heartbreak looked like to Ethan. But I know I need to focus on my friend right now and leave Ethan behind for once. "I'm so sorry."

She sits back and rubs her hands beneath her swollen eyes. "I know what you're thinking. I *know* that this is not about me. There's this little voice that keeps telling me that I'm being selfish, that it's my job as his best friend to support him."

"That isn't selfish. You love him."

She shakes her head. "I'm not allowed to love him anymore. At least not the way I used to. But I don't know how to separate the Marcus I've grown up with from the Marcus I want to kiss. He's always been there for me, ever since we were little. But now I can't go to him. I don't even know how I'm supposed to feel. It's not like a regular breakup, you know? He didn't do anything wrong, so I can't be angry at him. I *want* to be angry at him because it would be easier than what I'm feeling. It would be so much easier if I didn't just want him to hold me."

"You can still go to him, Kathy. I'm sure he misses you."

Her face crumples up again. "Then don't you think he would have called? He knows I overheard. He looked up just after I came in. God, Rain, the expression on his face—"

"Did he say anything?"

"He didn't have a chance. Hope walked in right after me. But I don't think she heard what Marcus said. She hasn't said a word to me about it."

"Or maybe she just thought that Marcus was drunk," I suggest. "He *was* drunk, you know."

"Obviously! But no amount of alcohol will make you come out of the closet if you aren't...if you aren't in one to begin with."

There's no way to answer that. She lets out a weak sigh. "Yeah, well. And you know what the strangest part is? After I got over the shock of it, the only thing I could think about was why did I have to find out like *this*? Why hadn't he trusted me? Why hadn't he told me?"

"Kathy, you're the *last* person he'd want to tell. He didn't want to hurt you."

She frowns and slowly gets up from the sofa. "He's been my best friend since elementary school. I'll get over losing my boyfriend if I have to. But do I have to lose my best friend too? Why won't he call me? He hasn't been in school since the party. I've tried calling him, but he's not answering. And he always answers!"

"He's probably terrified," I tell her. "Look, maybe I can talk to him for you—"

"No," she snaps. "No way. I'm not sending messengers. He knows how to reach me if he wants to."

"But are you sure he's okay? It's been days since the party."

She waves her hand, dismissing my concern. "I talked to his mom. She told me that he's suffering from migraines and the doctor prescribed some meds and rest. I didn't get a worried vibe from her. I don't think she has any idea what's really going on."

"She thinks you're still together?"

"I guess," she replies with a shrug. "Look, I have to go. My parents gave me half an hour, and I'm already late. But thanks for listening."

I can't help admiring her strength then, the way she squares her shoulders and stubbornly lifts her chin, even as tears stream down her cheeks. When she was part of the Octopus I'd always thought her a little needy. But now that her supporting other half is gone, she hasn't collapsed. She seems to stand taller; there's a quiet dignity in her dark eyes.

"Kathy, anytime you want to talk—"

"Just don't tell anyone, okay? Not Liam. Not even Hope. It's Marcus's secret, not mine. I came to you because I assumed Ethan had told you. And I was desperate to talk to someone."

I promise not to say anything, and she gives me a quick goodbye hug. As the door closes behind her I hear a rustle on the stairs. My mother is shuffling down the steps, holding on to the railing and swearing softly under her breath. She's dressed in a long robe that's fallen open to reveal her jutting bones. Her long blond hair hangs like a matted blanket around her face. She's looking a little more alive today; her face has lost some of its deathly pallor, and her cheeks have begun to fill out. But she's still extremely weak, and I run over to help as she stumbles and grasps at the banister.

"The doctor said you were supposed to stay in bed," I scold. "I can bring you whatever you need."

"What I *need* is for people to stop telling me what to do," she retorts. "And maybe a breath of fresh air. I can still taste the hospital disinfectant."

I want to argue with her, but I'm not sure if that counts as adding to her stress. The doctor was very clear about the importance of peace of mind. I can't upset her now, even if I think it's for her own good.

"Would you like a papaya mango smoothie?" I ask her. "I've been reading that papaya is a great natural digestive aid." But she waves away the suggestion, just like she's waved away every one of my colon-friendly concoctions over the last two days. "Just tea, thanks," she says, and heads off to the living room.

"Hello, Rain." Ethan's voice startles me, and I turn around to see him wavering on the top step. "Has Kathy left?"

"She's gone. Why? Were you hiding from her?" The question comes out a bit snarkier than I intended.

"Yes," Ethan says. "Kathy told me she hates me."

My mom whips around and zips back to stand behind me. "*What?*"

"After the party," he says. "When Marcus left and Hope went out to look for Rain. Kathy said I ruined her life. Then she threw up."

"What *party?*" Mom says, her voice darkening. "I thought it was a small get-together." Oh, crap. Stop talking, I warn him with my eyes. Of course, he doesn't hear me.

"Kathy had a party on Halloween," he continues innocently. "But it was important for me to go. Because it's one of my steps. It was worth five points."

She ignores him and turns to me. "Kathy threw up?" she demands. "Was there alcohol at this party?"

I could simply admit it. A couple weeks ago I probably would have and taken my punishment. How bad could it be, anyway? A grounding, some extra chores? But I'm not scared for myself now. I need my mom to trust me; not just for me—but because I can see the stress flushing up her face as she glares at me. I'm supposed to be protecting her too, just like I've always protected Ethan. And yet I've managed to do just the opposite.

"It wasn't... I didn't—" I falter. She's tapping her foot.

"There was alcohol," Ethan chirps. I send him another death look. "But I didn't have any. And we sat outside. We weren't around the kids who were drinking."

She doesn't appear satisfied. "Did *you* drink, Rain? Where were you during the party?" she asks me pointedly. I open my mouth to lie. I don't like lying to my mom, but I'm not pathologically truthful like Ethan. I can spin a story if I need to. Yet for some reason, at that moment the words are sticking in my throat.

But then Ethan answers for me. "She was watching me, like she always does. Even when I was with Hope." He manages to sound wounded. "It was really annoying."

I stare at him, open-mouthed, but he's looking past me at our mother. The tension drains slowly from her face, and she uncrosses her arms. I know what she's thinking. It must be the truth. Ethan's word is gold. "Still," she says after a moment. "You two were at a party with underage drinking. If someone had called the cops—"

"I know," I say, relieved to have finally found my voice. "I didn't realize there would be so many people. And that some of the seniors were bringing beer. I wanted to go home at first. But then Ethan was doing so well—"

"Marcus told me I was beautiful," Ethan remarks.

That ends her lecture. Her stern expression melts and she laughs loudly. "*Did* he?"

"Yes. I think he wants to be my friend."

The stress lines have vanished from her face, and she's beaming at him. She's so delighted that Ethan has made a new friend that she seems to have completely forgotten about the party...and Kathy's strange behavior. "Well, you should talk to Marcus," she gushes. How did Ethan just do that? He'd simultaneously gotten me off the hook and made my mother proud of him. "Maybe invite him over. It sounds like he needs a friend right now."

"Okay," he says. He appears to calculate something in his head. "I'm up to fifteen," he says triumphantly and hurries off to his room. I decide to hurry off to mine, just in case Mom has any further questions I can't answer.

Every one of my friends has gone through something huge in the last week. But out of all of us, I'm worried most about the one who's vanished since that fateful party. I take out my phone and type a quick message to Marcus. I'm here if you want to talk. Don't worry about the punch thing. I'm feeling better now. How are you doing?

He doesn't respond. When I try calling a little later it goes straight to voicemail.

Later that evening I tap on my brother's door. When I enter, he's sitting cross-legged on his rug, surrounded by piles of open textbooks. He looks up and then quickly turns back to his notes. "Hello, Rain."

"I wanted to thank you," I tell him. "For what you did earlier."

"You're welcome," he replies automatically. He has no idea what I'm talking about, though.

"When you said that stuff about me watching over you at the party. You lied for me. And you were convincing too. It was impressive. Especially the part about me being annoying."

"I didn't lie," he says.

"What?"

He turns suddenly and focuses on my startled face; he studies me quietly for a moment, his eyes narrow and then he looks back at his book. "I didn't lie."

"Of course you did. You told Mom that I was watching you and Hope…" But the protest dies on my lips. "Oh," I breathe, suddenly understanding. "You saw me. At the window."

He doesn't respond at first. He's turning the pages of the notebook in front of him. For a second, I think he hasn't heard me. But then his hands tighten around the binding of his journal.

"Yes. I saw you."

## ETHAN'S JOURNAL:

### Ulcerative Colitis Cured by Fecal Transplant in Mice

Recent studies have shown complete remission of symptoms when stool from a healthy subject is transplanted into diseased bowels.

I've begun investigating methods of delivery for my proposed therapy. Dissolvable plastic capsules or a suppository seem to be the best options. I have plenty of samples that I could donate for the trial.

When I showed Mom the article, she said, "So you want to put your poop in a pill and make me swallow it?"

Rain and Mom both laughed. "Don't you think Mom's taken enough of your shit over the last few years?" Rain asked. I understood the pun, but I didn't think it was funny. "Taking shit" is an expression for tolerating someone's annoying behavior. I was trying to help, and Rain was implying that I was being annoying. Then Rain handed me her own research article about the digestive benefits of apigenin, found in wheatgrass, and presented Mom with a glass of wheatgrass juice with rice milk. I got up and left the room.

"Don't be offended," Rain shouted after me. "It was only a joke."

I don't usually get offended by jokes. But Mom had chosen my sister's medical proposal over mine. I would have to review Rain's article immediately. If the study is faulty, then there would be a good reason for offense. I'll know how to feel after I've collected more data.

# Chapter 22

It's been days of polite lab experiments for Liam and me. Between taking care of my mom and preparing for exams, I haven't had much chance to see him. We finally carve out a couple of hours after school for "studying."

I'm sick with anticipation by the time Liam arrives. I really need this evening to be perfect. So far our relationship has been a short history of misunderstandings and screwups. I want to start again, like we've just met, like I hadn't pined after him for a year without speaking to him and then exploded at him in chemistry class; like he hadn't told me that he was leaving Montana, like we hadn't drunkenly fallen on top of one another on our second date. I need to believe we can salvage this.

My mom and Ethan are both in their bedrooms, but I suggest we hang out in mine. As I wave him over to the futon, Liam hesitates for a moment; I suddenly realize that he's never actually been inside my bedroom. The idea is sort of funny and a little embarrassing. Liam seems to feel it too. He settles next to me awkwardly, his arms stiff at his sides.

Neither of us speak at first. He's breathing heavily, and his eyes are darting between me and the framed photo of Julia Child on my desk, like he can't decide where to look. He seems to be waiting for me to break the silence. I want to be the sort of couple that can sit for an hour without speaking and be totally cool with that, the couple who can communicate through looks and body language. That's the goal, eventually. But right now, someone *really* needs to talk.

"So… I went over to Marcus's house the other day," he blurts out, finally.

I'm not sure how to respond. I promised Kathy I wouldn't give away his secret. "Oh, yeah?" I say. "I've tried calling him but I can't get through. Is he sick?" That's the best noncommittal answer I can give.

I can feel him staring at me, but I'm not brave enough to lie under scrutiny. *Does he know? How can I ask him without giving anything away?*

He hesitates again. "There was something in that punch."

I lift my head and meet his eyes. "That was some powerful stuff."

A barely perceptible smile. "Life changing, actually."

"Liberating?"

The smile finally dawns, and he relaxes against the sofa. "How do you know?"

"Kathy. You?"

"I went over to bring him his homework, and he told me what happened at the party. He was relieved that no one else found out. But it wasn't an easy visit. He's totally freaking out."

"*He's* freaking out? Kathy's heartbroken."

"So is Marcus!"

"Really?"

He sighs and moves a little closer to me. "Kathy and Marcus's relationship is over obviously. But that doesn't mean he doesn't love her."

"So why doesn't he tell her that instead of avoiding her?"

"That's what I said to him. But I don't think he's ready to face her yet. Even if it means hiding in his room for a while."

"He hasn't done anything wrong. And it's better that she find out now."

He shrugs. "He wasn't ready to come out, Rain. It kind of spilled out while he was drunk and vulnerable, and now he doesn't know what to do. He begged me not to tell anyone."

"Well, I'm sure you helped just by talking to him. He's got no one at home to confide in."

"I don't know if I did much good. You probably had better luck with Kathy, talented psychologist that you are."

I laugh and give him a playful shove. "Not talented at all, really. I'm finding out that there's way more to psychology than memorizing a textbook. My mom's been telling me that I was a born shrink ever since I can remember. But I'm not so sure anymore."

He smiles. "Why not? Your brother's a born surgeon."

I turn to stare at him, my expression suddenly serious. "You really think so? You're not just saying that?"

"No, I'm not just saying that. You should have seen him on

that surgery ward. Absorbing everything. Asking questions—*good* questions—that Dr. Peters actually wanted to answer. He really pissed off all the medical students, though."

"I bet. Still, Ethan may be great at memorizing anatomy and stuff, but there's so much more to this than he realizes. So many challenges—"

"He was happy, Rain. And he knows his challenges just as well as you do."

"I guess. It's just that I've seen him fall flat on his face so many times, and it *hurts* me each time he does. So I'm scared for him."

"I know. But maybe you need to start hiding that fear. At least from him."

He may be right, I think. That I should fade from Ethan's life a little. Stop snooping behind curtains and give my brother some room. But what am I supposed to do with the sixteen years I've spent as my twin's confidant and shadow?

"I was just trying to help." Haven't I planned my entire future around Ethan? Where do I go from here? The thought makes me feel sad and useless. What was the point, after all? What is *my* point now?

"I'm not saying he doesn't need you," he replies. "I'm just saying that you can make next year different. Follow your own dreams for a change."

"What dreams?"

He hesitates for a moment and plucks at a loose thread at the end of his sleeve. "I mean, you've said that you want to leave

Clarkson after high school, right? That you want to be free to go anywhere you want."

I cast my mind back to our earlier conversations. When had I said that? It sounded good, like something that I wanted to say. But what about Ethan and my responsibilities at home? "Well," I reply hesitantly. "I do want to go to college and then eventually to graduate school."

"Oh, I know that," he says eagerly. "But what about traveling? Seeing the world?"

"Well, of course I would love that!" I interjected. "I mean, eventually."

"I know you would. That's what I wanted to talk to you about. What do you think about applying to the international program with me?"

It's an abrupt segue; I hadn't seen that one coming. "You mean the Global Gap program?"

"Yeah. Why not? It's a great experience, and it'll look good on your college applications."

"But you were planning to go next year. And I don't have enough credits to graduate early."

"I'd wait. If you wanted me to. If it meant we could go together."

He would wait for me? He'd put his dreams on hold in the hope it would give our relationship a chance? I don't know what to say. His eyes are fixed on mine, earnest and waiting. His lips are open, as if he's paused midbreath to hear my answer. And I'm frozen too, somewhere between gratefulness and fear, between happiness and doubt. How can I accept an offer like that? I want to embrace the idea of an adventure with Liam. But I have too many people relying on me right now. How can I abandon my mother when she's sick? And who will take care of Ethan if I go?

"But we've only been dating for three weeks," I falter.

It's absolutely the wrong thing to say. The exact opposite of what he'd hoped to hear.

The light fades from his eyes, and his shoulders sag. "It was just an idea," he says quietly. "Never mind."

"No... I mean..."

I want to take it back. I want to bring that flash of hope into his eyes again. He's staring off at my desk and chewing his lip.

"Maybe I just need to get used to the idea," I tell him softly. "Liam, please look at me." He glances back at me and shakes his head.

"I'm sorry," he says. "I feel pretty stupid. Of course it's too early to think about that kind of stuff now. And I was the one who wanted to take it slow. But here I am pushing you to make this big decision. For me."

"Yeah, what happened to you?" I ask him, smiling.

He shrugs, his eyes crinkling at the corners. "I don't know. You kissed me, and then I guess you somehow got into my blood."

"Is that right?"

He grins broadly. "Yeah, you're like this unexpected, sweet..." He pauses uncertainly. "Poison."

"Wow. That's the best you could come up with? I'm like *poison*?"

"Well, there are good poisons. Look it up."

"You'd better be careful with the romantic talk. I'm actually reconsidering kissing you."

"You were considering it? No way," he says, and brings his lips to mine so suddenly that I fall back on my arms.

And then neither of us speak. Because, suddenly, he's way better with his lips than with his words. Hell, he could have called me a rabid tarantula if it meant I'd get kissed like that.

His hands run up my back as he pulls me close to him. His mouth leaves mine and travels to my chin, my neck, my chest. I brush my fingers through his curls, the little dark spirals I love. We're starting over, I tell myself. Nothing can ruin us now. We have the power to turn our mistake into a quaint story, coat the past with a frenzy of new kisses.

And yet, somehow the shadow of Halloween still haunts us. I feel it when he hesitates, I see the question in his eyes as he pulls back and looks at me. What am I okay with? Where can he touch me? How much of that night do I remember, and how much of this is new?

How can I pretend to forget when his every kiss feels like an apology? I want his questions to fade, my mind to go quiet. No fears, no embarrassment, no past or future. Just now, this moment, his warmth, and the drum of his heart against my chest.

But the harder I kiss him, the more I grasp at his shirt and press him to me, the louder my thoughts clamor. Because, now, as I lie back against the sofa and pull him on top of me, I feel the rush of a lost memory. Maybe it's the moan of his excitement, or the heat of our bodies moving against one another, or possibly the spice-wash smell of him which awakens me. But I remember. For the first time since that night, I remember every detail of everything I said and did. And it comes back so suddenly that I gasp and pull back, sliding out of his arms so quickly that he kisses the air.

He looks startled for a moment, then pained as understanding dawns. "Oh," he says softly.

"I'm sorry. I just need a second."

But I'm going to need more than that.

*It shouldn't matter*, I tell myself. Just because I remember that night doesn't mean I can't make my peace with it and move on. But the harder I try to push the memory from my mind, the brighter it gets. I don't recognize myself in that truck, don't understand how a little whiskey could have drowned out the Rain I know. What's the big deal, anyway? Hadn't I wanted to be less cautious, more spontaneous? Wasn't I the one who'd asked Liam out in the first place, who'd pulled him close to me? Wasn't I the one who'd urged him to go farther than either of us had wanted? So why can't I take a step back and start over, climb that relationship hill with him again, but slowly and soberly this time? I take a deep breath and edge closer to Liam, who's sitting silently slumped at the edge of the sofa.

But the romantic moment has passed and all that's left is a rising squeeze of nausea. My stomach lurches suddenly, and I double over, my hand going to my mouth. I don't throw up, thank God. But I gag. And he sees it. I can't bear to look at his face.

He reaches out to me, gently lays his hand on my shoulder. But my neck is damp and cold, and I don't want him to touch my sweaty skin. I pull away from him. He flinches; I can't see him, but I can sense his hurt. My insides twist, and I swallow against the urge to heave again. What the hell is wrong with me?

"Liam, it isn't you," I stammer.

I hear him exhale. "Yeah, I'm trying not to take it personally."

But every time we kiss, something seems to go wrong. If I were him, I'd take that very personally. It's like the fates don't want us to be together. "I'm sorry. Maybe I'm getting sick."

"Do you want me to go?"

I nod dully, and wipe my sleeve over my clammy brow. "Please."

"Maybe you need to go to the doctor?"

There's a note of anxiety in his voice I refuse to acknowledge. I want him stop worrying about me and leave so I can vomit alone in peace.

He finally goes, and the nausea fades as soon as the door closes behind him.

I consider calling the doctor to make an appointment, if only to calm Liam down a bit. But as I'm looking for the number, I'm interrupted by a hysterical text from Kathy: I'm driving to Marcus's right now! I don't care if I'm grounded. I don't care if his parents are there. I'm going to make him speak to me!

So I'm on the phone with her until late. By the time I hang up, I feel better, mentally and physically. The nausea has vanished completely, and I'm calmer than I've been in weeks. I'd just managed to talk Kathy out of a big confrontation in front of Marcus's family. As she headed home, Kathy thanked me for understanding; I even made her laugh a little, despite her pain, and at that moment her brief chuckle was the sweetest sound I'd heard in ages. Recently, I'd been messing up whenever I talked to Ethan and Liam, so it's comforting to know I can still get through to one person at least. I've finally managed to help someone—and I hadn't used a single diagnosis from my psychology book.

The contented feeling lasts until I get in bed. As always, I tap out my good night to Ethan and wait for his reply. But for the first time since we started our tradition, he answers me with silence. There's no greeting at all, not even the sound of movement in the next room. I rap the wall again, just in case he hadn't heard me. Five beats, and then wait.

He must have heard that time. I'd practically hammered. I press my ear against the plaster. From the other side, there's a faint rhythmic snoring sound. Then a brief cough—and then quiet.

I become slightly unhinged. I know I'm being ridiculous, but I can't help myself. I need to bake. I pad down to the kitchen in my robe and slippers and scrub my hands with antiseptic before switching on the oven. Twenty-four pumpkin chocolate chip muffins later, I've filled the house with the smell of molasses and cinnamon, and it hasn't helped at all. The house is as still as before. I place Ethan's favorite treats in a pyramid on the dining room table and return to my room. Then I lie down on my bed and pretend to sleep.

On the other side of the wall, Ethan snores away, undisturbed.

# Chapter 23

Mom isn't taking her pills. I feel stupid for not realizing this sooner, but the thought dawns on me the next day when I hear her groaning in the bathroom. I don't know what to do. I've kept everything as stress free as possible since she came home. I've cooked every colitis food on the list. I've cleaned, folded loads of laundry, forced Ethan to mow the lawn, and generally behaved like a model daughter. I've even pushed all thoughts of Liam and our mistake out of my mind, just in case stress spreads through osmosis. But I'd stopped monitoring her medicines because—well, because she's an adult. And I thought her stay in the hospital was all the convincing she needed. But apparently it wasn't. When I realize she's been in the bathroom for more than an hour I sneak into her bedroom and open her dresser. The pill bottles are neatly lined up. And they're completely full.

What else am I supposed to do? I've already argued with her, Ethan has warned her of her imminent death, and there's even the looming threat of my father coming to take over if she doesn't get well.

When I confront her about it, she lies. "I'm taking my meds," she insists doggedly. I have to bring out her untouched pill bottles before she finally admits the truth.

"Have you read about the side effects?" she retorts when she realizes I've backed her into a corner. "They're worse than any of my symptoms."

"They're *possible* side effects," I point out. "They have to list even the rarest ones. You of all people should know that, Mom. And colitis can get really serious. Don't you remember what Ethan told you?"

She shrugs. "He was just parroting medical textbooks like he always does. And you know who writes those textbooks?"

I throw my hands into the air in frustration. "The same doctors who are trying to cure you?"

She rolls her eyes at me. "Yeah. By scaring me into buying their product. I don't need them, okay? I'm getting better on my own."

She isn't though. Anyone who knew her before she got sick would barely recognize her now.

"I don't understand," I complain to Ethan. "It's just medicine. But the way she's carrying on, you'd think the doctors were trying to poison her. I don't know what to do."

"Should I explain the pharmacology to her again?" he suggests, glancing up from his computer screen. "I have these diagrams."

"That's not going to help. This block is all in her mind. It's like she thinks she's lost control of her life or something. And I guess this is how she's trying to get it back. By being stubborn."

He wrinkles his brow and nods. "Are you analyzing Mom?"

I sigh and flop down onto his rug. "Are you going to tell me to stop like everybody else does?"

"No. I like it when you do that."

"You do?"

"Yes. I understand how her colon works. And what the medicines do. But I don't understand what Mom is thinking. I need you to tell me."

I love his honesty, but even more, I love that he still needs me a little. "Okay," I say. "But only if you promise to tell me how her colon works."

His face brightens. "Do you want to see my diagrams?"

It isn't really a question. He goes on for an hour, maybe more. By the end, my mind is bursting with information about the large intestine. But I don't care. I've finally made my brother smile, and that's the only thing I needed.

"I saw that you ate some pumpkin muffins," I say after he finishes his lecture.

He nods. "I ate ten. Next time, more chocolate chips please."

I grin. "Noted."

"What did you do, Rain?"

"Excuse me?"

He shuts his laptop and looks a little past me, somewhere between my shoulder and the colon poster. "What did you do wrong?"

I shake my head. "I don't understand."

He sighs a little, and I can't help smiling at his frustration. It's pretty similar to mine when he doesn't connect the dots.

"You always make my favorite muffins before you apologize for something," he explains. "So I want to know what you did wrong."

The realization that he's right makes me laugh out loud. The unexpected sound startles him, and he jerks his head around to stare at me. "What's funny, Rain?"

"It's weird. I never noticed that before," I tell him. "I just thought baking was a stress reliever. Isn't it funny that you understand me even when I don't understand myself?"

He doesn't answer, and I'm not sure if he gets my explanation. "And I'm sorry that I don't always understand you," I continue when he doesn't respond. "I guess that's what I'm apologizing for."

I've really confused him now, but he doesn't seem frustrated by my vague reply. Instead, a mischievous smile dawns, and he ducks his head. "I hope you never understand me," he says after a moment.

I blink at him. "Why would you say that?"

His smile widens. "Because I like pumpkin muffins. I don't want you to stop making them."

I cross my arms and pretend to pout. "Ha. Is that right?"

He nods and types something into his phone. "*Mehr Schokoladenspäne bitte*," he declares.

"*What?*"

His eyes are shining with suppressed laughter. "It's German. More chocolate chips, please."

I toss a pillow at his head, and he responds by whacking me

across the back with it. He's a bit too enthusiastic and knocks me on my side, but we're both laughing at his joke, and it's the warmest sound in the world.

"You've been stuck in Germany for a long time," I observe, after our laughter dies down. "But you're finally learning German, aren't you?"

He shrugs and leans back against the wall. "It's just Google Translate, Rain."

# Chapter 24

"So Kathy agreed to wait," I tell Liam as he drives me home the next day after school. "I told her to give Marcus a little more time."

He nods absently and gives me a sidelong glance. "That's good. And you're feeling okay?"

"Absolutely."

He doesn't seem convinced. I turn my head away and close my eyes. I have been fine all day, but I'm getting tired of faking healthy cheeriness and a hearty appetite. Lunch was unbearable. He actually refused half of my food and insisted I finish it. Never mind that I'd packed my usual double portion and his favorite goat cheese balls.

I know what he's worried about. I'm not an idiot. But I don't want to keep talking about the fact that I had *one* bout of queasiness.

To stave off further questions, I pretend to go to sleep during the five-minute ride home from school.

There's an ambulance parked in the driveway of my house when we pull up. I can sense its presence by the flashing behind my eyelids and Liam's surprised "oh!" as we round the corner.

I jump from the truck and sprint across the yard before Liam even has a chance to stop the car.

My mom is sitting on a gurney and arguing with the paramedic, a large, balding man who keeps mopping his sweaty brow with his sleeve and sighing.

Ethan appears behind me. "Hello, Rain. Hello, Liam."

"Why is Mom in an ambulance?"

"She fainted again."

"I'm fine," she snaps. "I just got up too fast."

"We need to make a decision here," the sweaty EMT says. "Are you going to allow us to take you to the hospital or not?"

"No!"

"Why is there even a question?" I say. "She needs to go to the hospital."

"We can't take an adult to the ER against her will."

"I'm not going anywhere," Mom insists.

"That's fine," I retort. "Ethan, call Dad. Tell him that Mom is sick and we need him."

"Rain!" she shouts.

"Do it, Ethan." My brother draws his phone out of his pocket.

I don't care if I'm betraying my mother. She's betrayed herself by refusing her pills. This is my last card, and I'm playing it.

"Fine," she hisses, sitting back against the gurney. "I'll go."

Ethan doesn't come with us this time. Mom's patience with him has faded since he's become a walking fountain of colon knowledge. Shockingly he doesn't argue when she insists he stay home. "You two can take turns visiting me," she assures him.

It takes less time to get Mom situated for her second

hospitalization; she's in the same ward as before, just two doors down from her former room. The whole thing is depressingly repetitive, and I feel guilty for the relief that washes over me when I finally head home.

When I get home, Ethan isn't waiting for me. I run up the stairs and tap gently on his door.

Marcus and Ethan are sitting on the rug facing each other. They look up as I enter and motion me inside. "It's fine," Marcus says. "You can come in. The more the merrier."

I settle down across from him. "You okay? I haven't seen you since the Halloween party."

"Nobody has," he admits sadly. "I've kind of been hiding. But I thought I owed Ethan an explanation. I owe a lot of people an explanation. So I figured I might as well start here."

"We've all been worried about you. Kathy—"

He flinches when I say her name. "Yeah, I know everyone's been worried. My parents started freaking out when I wouldn't leave my room."

"Did you finally tell them?"

"God, no!" he exclaims. "Never! They think I'm depressed because I broke up with my girlfriend. When I wouldn't talk to them, they threatened to have me committed unless I got some help. So I've been spending some time at a mental health center. I've got a therapist now. Two, actually."

I laugh shortly. "Wow. How's that going?"

A faint smile tugs at his lips. "Well, the first one said I've made a lot of progress but that I was still 'holding something back.' Ha. No shit, Sherlock."

"And the second one?"

"She gave me pills. Two different ones. They didn't help. Obviously."

"Oh. Still gay then, are you?"

He laughs, and his face relaxes. "Yeah. Tiny bit."

"You should tell them that you're gay," Ethan says. "Your parents will be happy to know that you're not depressed."

"You think?" he retorts sarcastically. "You want me as a roommate, then? Because that's exactly what will happen."

Ethan doesn't reply. He shoots me a confused look, but I shake my head.

"Everyone says that," I point out. "But maybe they're different. Maybe it'll just take some time. You know they love you."

"You don't get it, Rain." He exhales and closes his eyes. "This isn't some talk show. That's not my life, okay? I'm not worried that they'll kill me. I'm worried it's going to kill *them*."

"Marcus—"

"No, I'm serious." He looks up at me and his dark eyes fill. "My dad's in his sixties. He's been diabetic forever; he's gone through two bypasses and then, a couple of years ago, a ministroke. And my mother... My mom hasn't been the same since my sister died. Or so they tell me."

Ethan leans over to me. "She had pneumonia and took too much medication," he informs me.

Marcus shakes his head. "That's what they told people afterward. But she did it on purpose. My father's heart pills. Twenty of them."

"Oh, God. How long ago?" I ask.

"Before I was born. I was kind of a…replacement, I guess."

"Jesus."

"Yeah. Honestly, most days I'd rather die than tell them the truth and hurt them like that. Even if it means lying to everybody forever."

"But what about Kathy? You should have been honest with her."

He puts his head in his hands. "I've been lying to myself almost as long as I've been lying to Kathy. When I finally came to terms with it, I realized I had to tell her. I'd been planning to talk to her months ago; I had the whole speech prepared and everything. Then one evening I came downstairs and found Kathy chatting with my mom. My mother worships her, you know—treats her like her own daughter, always has. Anyway, I overheard them talking." He takes a ragged breath, lifts his tear-stained face. "My mom must have had a bit too much wine because she normally never mentions my sister. But that night she was patting Kathy on the arm and saying, 'Chloe is such a beautiful name, don't you think? Such a perfect name. Maybe one day, you and Marcus, if you have a girl—'"

"Oh, no."

"Yeah. And then Kathy smiled and hugged her—and

*promised*. I was standing there in the shadows, wishing I was dead, and my girlfriend was promising to name our future child after my dead sister."

"Kathy was only trying to be nice. To make your mother happy."

"Oh, I know that. But do you understand now why I couldn't tell anyone—even the person I love the most?"

"You still love her?"

"Of course I love her! She's my best friend."

"Then you should talk to her," Ethan says.

He sighs and rubs his swollen eyes. "And say *what*? I've ruined her life."

"You want to be her friend?"

"Of course."

"Then tell her that you want to be her friend," my brother replies. "But you don't want to have sex with her."

"Ethan!" I exclaim. "It isn't that simple."

"Why not?" he asks. "One day Kathy might meet a guy who does want to have sex with her. And one day so will Marcus. But right now I think Kathy just misses you."

We're both struck dumb, Marcus and I, and for a moment no one says anything.

"If Hope broke up with me," Ethan persists, "I would miss her. And we've never had sex. We've never kissed. But I'd still miss talking to her. That's how I know."

Marcus nods, his eyes fixed on Ethan's earnest expression. "I just don't know what to say, how to start—"

"Then do it in pieces."

"What?"

"When I feel overwhelmed by something I have to do," Ethan explains. "Like checking off one of the items on my dad's list, for example, most of the time, I can't handle the entire task. I can't walk into a party and talk to my girlfriend like you can. So my father said that I should break it into pieces. I know that I can get out of the car. I can walk across the lawn. I can say hello. I can sit down. And then I can listen to her. I can do each of those things. One at a time. That's how you have to think about it."

"One thing at a time? Walk up to her." He smiles to himself. "And just say her name."

"Yes. Just say her name."

I watch quietly as Marcus considers the suggestion. It's good advice, I realize. Better than anything I could have come up with. Ethan isn't just parroting polite responses, as I'd taught him. This isn't a show of fake empathy. My brother is actually using his own challenges to help my friend cope. I could never have taught him that.

Marcus sighs. "It's not that easy, you know. I feel like I've been playing a part forever. You can't imagine what that's like."

Ethan doesn't reply for a moment. His fingers play nervously with one another. A thick lock of hair falls forward but I catch a glimpse of his expression before it covers his face. He looks unhappy—almost resentful. "But you don't have to play a part anymore," my brother says quietly. "You can tell people who you are and eventually most of them will accept you."

"Maybe. Eventually."

"Well, you're lucky," Ethan murmurs. "Because it's exhausting to be different. Especially when you know that you can never stop pretending."

## Cooking with Rain
### SERENITY THROUGH YOUR GUT

*Where I answer all your burning food-related questions!*

**Dear Rain:** I think my girlfriend is angry at me. I know I've made a bunch of mistakes. Now I'm looking for a way to start over. I want to make something for her to say I'm sorry. She loves chocolate. Do you have any ideas?

—Heartsick in Wisconsin

**Dear Heartsick:** Liam, if this is you—not cool. If not, try Rain's Chocolate and Chili, a sweet and spicy way to reignite your love!

# Chapter 25

I've already racked up almost a week in tardies and absences. But after my mother is readmitted to the hospital, school once again takes the backseat. Over the next two weeks I get up at 6:00 a.m. to drive my brother to Missoula County Hospital, return to school to attend the bare minimum of classes, then rush back to the hospital. Evenings are spent on a mountain of catch-up work. I barely see Liam. He tries to be helpful by dropping off homework assignments and texting cheerful messages, but I don't have the energy to respond. Our days on the ward are the same as last time—bewildering, exhausting, and dull. Hours of beeping machines, fluorescent lights, and dripping fluids.

This time, though, I'm far less patient with everyone around me, especially with my mother. It's one thing to get sick; it's another thing to make yourself that way. *Especially when you have children who depend on you*, I want to say. But I'm sure my accusations will just increase her stress, so instead I sit quietly and resentfully beside her.

She seems unwilling to speak to me either, but after enduring hours of my silent vigil by her bed, she finally breaks the ice. "You're mad at me."

"Yeah, well, can you blame me?"

"No. But I wish you'd see things from my point of view."

"What point of view is that? You think being sick is natural? Holistic? Just tell me so I understand."

"I don't want to be here any more than you do. I just needed to believe that I could fix this. On my own terms."

"What does that mean?"

"I mean, this isn't the first time doctors have failed me. Do you know how many physicians I went to—" She hesitates and glances uneasily at my brother. He's engrossed in a book and doesn't look up at her when she pauses. "How many different opinions I got? His first pediatrician told me that there wasn't any hope. If he didn't speak by age four, he would never speak. One doctor actually said, 'At least you have one normal one.'"

"Mom—"

"All the therapy, all those interventions, all those tests they made him go through. For what? Eventually I decided it was *enough*. I didn't want to be told how to raise my child."

"This isn't the same thing."

"It is to me. They were wrong, don't you see? They told me that I should accept his diagnosis and learn to live with it. But I refused. And, in the end, who was right?"

"Maybe you were both right," I suggest. "You have accepted it."

"*No*. I didn't accept anything." She sinks her voice and leans closer to me. "He's doing better than ever. Some home tutoring and his sister. That's all he seems to need." She takes a deep breath and gives me a weak smile. "A few days ago he told me that Hope is his girlfriend. Can you believe it? He has a *girlfriend*. I wish I could find those doctors and—and rub it in their faces." She clenches a fist and waves it in the air.

"Well, maybe you will one day," I tell her. "But you won't be able to if you're constantly in the hospital."

"You still don't get it, Rain."

"No, I think I do," I tell her softly. There's so much beneath her decision to fight her doctors, I think. I want to talk about her control issues. Her powerlessness in the face of an illness she doesn't understand, that she doesn't *want* to understand. Her belief that trusting someone other than herself will only lead to her betrayal. But I don't say any of those things. The psychology book in my head is more useful when it's hidden. "I miss you at home," I tell her, taking her hand. "Please, Mom. We both miss you."

Her large, hollow eyes fix on mine, and she opens her mouth to speak. But then her face freezes; she's staring intently at something over my shoulder. I turn around to follow her look and rise quickly to my feet.

Standing there in the doorway, partially hidden by a balloon-and-teddy bear mountain, is my father. He looks just like he did at the diner, but rougher. His gray hair is mussed, his chin dark with stubble.

"Hi, guys," he says.

"Hello, Dad," Ethan replies from the corner. "Thank you for coming. I have to show you my list. I've collected five more points."

"That's great, Ethan," he replies, smiling uncomfortably. "Let's talk about that later, okay?"

"What are you doing here?" I ask.

He seems hurt and a bit confused. "Your brother told me that you wanted me here. So I came." He's very carefully avoiding my mother's eyes.

"What's going on?" she hisses at no one in particular.

"What's going on is I took the red eye from DC last night because I thought my son and daughter needed me," Dad snaps at her.

"Rain told me to call Dad," Ethan explains. He doesn't seem concerned about any of this. As if our family being together in the same room is something that happens every day, as opposed to the first time in ten years.

"Dad, can I talk to you outside?" I interject. I've been so careful about keeping stress away from my mother, and now Mr. Stress himself has waltzed into her hospital room. I have to get him out of there. "Ethan, you can stay with Mom."

The hall is humming with nurses and half-dressed patients with IV poles, so we make our way down to the cafeteria and settle at an empty table.

"This isn't good for her," I begin. "Your being here might make her worse—"

"Well, I'm sorry about that," he interrupts. "But your mother needs to take her medicine like an adult. And stop blaming everything on me."

He's in lawyer mode now, all final statements and confident declarations. But I'm not going to let him push me around.

"You're the reason the two of you split up, remember?" I point out. "Ethan may not know that, but I do."

"You've only heard her side of the story, Rainey. But I have my side too. Even though you've never bothered to listen to it."

"I never bothered? Dad, you abandoned us!"

"No. Your mother left me. She took the two of you and just...*left*. And I was too ashamed to challenge her decision. Too embarrassed to fight for you."

"You should have been. You were the one cheating!"

He sighs and rubs a hand over his bloodshot eyes. "It isn't that simple. You can try to boil it down to infidelity and divorce if you want. But it's way more complicated than that. When you're young, sometimes it's easiest to just classify people into good guys and bad guys. You were only five years old when your mom and I split. And I probably seemed like the obvious bad guy to you, so you chose her side. I get that. But, Rain, you aren't five anymore."

"Yeah, but I know the difference between right and wrong. And what you did was wrong."

"I realize that. But I've been punished for it, haven't I? And I'm trying to make it right by explaining."

"Explaining what? How you cheated on Mom?"

"Rain, I met your mother in law school. We were twenty-three years old. A few dates later, a couple of drinks, and we made a bad choice one night."

I glance down at my hands, my cheeks reddening. His story was hitting a little too close to home.

"Well, your mom got pregnant that night. When she told me, I didn't know how to handle it. I could have faked it, I guess, pretended to be supportive and then eventually, slowly drifted out of her life. That's what most guys do, you know. They hold the girl's hand, sit by her side when she pushes out their child. They smile and tell her she's better off when she drops out of school to raise the kid. But meanwhile, they're off pursuing their own careers as if nothing's happened. And before you know it, they've found a job in another city, and their role as father boils down to a weekend babysitting here and there. Well, I didn't *want* to be that guy. So when she told me that she was going to keep the baby, I asked her to marry me. She was carrying twins, as it turned out. And she had all these dreams of law school. I didn't want her to abandon her dreams."

I glance up for the first time. "So you married her out of pity?" I ask, my voice cracking. "Did you even love her?"

"Of course I loved her. But we'd barely gotten to know each other. Oh, I told myself that we had so much in common. We both wanted to be lawyers, we liked some of the same movies—I was desperately grasping for a silver lining. But it wasn't long before it started to come apart. Hell, we were bickering on our honeymoon."

"But there was another woman," I point out, maliciously. "Before your divorce." *His side*, as he calls it, is sounding a bit too innocent and accidental. "*You* made that choice. Instead of trying to work it out."

"Yes, I did. Rain, what can I say? I met the woman of my dreams as a married man. Ethan was throwing tantrums, biting us, hitting you—your mother was trying to study for exams and dragging him to a hundred specialists. And we were fighting every single night. Some days we were barely speaking. And then this girl I was tutoring—well, I suppose you know that part."

"I do." There's no forgiveness in my tone. He doesn't deserve it.

"Look," he continues defensively. "It wasn't so easy for me either. What was I supposed to do? What happens if you meet the love of your life when you're already married? Are you supposed to just walk away?"

"Yes! Yes you are!"

"Rain—"

"You had kids who needed you, Dad. Who still need you."

"I know. I realize that."

"So yes. You should have just walked away."

He nods meekly. "And been miserable?" He doesn't sound defensive anymore. Just quiet and very tired. I feel a little sorry for him, even though I'm trying not to. It would be so much easier to just judge and dismiss him like my mother has. But I realize suddenly that he's exhausted because he hasn't slept since he got Ethan's call. That he dropped everything to fly here and be with us when we needed him. I don't know how to dismiss that. I can't.

"You're looking pretty tired," I say in a softer voice.

He rubs a finger over his stubble. "Yeah, well. Deposition yesterday. Red-eye flight right after. You know."

A shadow falls across my lap, and I look up to find Ethan standing over us. "Mom needs you," he says.

I rise reluctantly. "We'll talk later, okay?" I'd like to say more; I want to be warmer, less stiff and hesitant. But I haven't decided how to act around him yet. Love for both my parents should be infinite, unbound—but it isn't that way for us. It's an equation, and I feel like every drop I give to him I must subtract from my mother's due.

"I'll be at the hotel—for as long as you two need me," he tells me before I leave. "I'm not planning on going back until your mother's well again."

## Cooking with Rain
### SERENITY THROUGH YOUR GUT

*Where I answer all your burning food-related questions!*

**Dear Rain:** Just so you know, I was not Heartsick in Wisconsin. I am and forever will be your Wacky Mac from Missoula. I miss you. What can I do?

**Dear Wacky:** I miss you too. Please stop hijacking my blog.

# Chapter 26

My phone rings five minutes after my response goes up. I smile at Liam's name on the screen, but before I can answer, my stomach twists and lurches. I run to the bathroom and heave into the sink.

When I finally stumble out into the hall, Ethan offers me a plate of scrambled eggs. I'm pretty impressed that he's made them himself, but the smell sends me right back to the toilet.

I thought I was finished with this stomach bug. But now it seems to have returned full force.

I manage to choke down a little tea before staggering off to school. But then it happens again at lunchtime when I smell the cafeteria food. Luckily, Liam is busy tutoring someone through lunch, so I don't have to explain myself to him. But I feel Hope's eyes boring a hole into my neck as I push the tray away and grasp weakly at the metal railing.

"Are you okay?" she asks.

"I need to sit down," I say and let her lead me to a corner table. I wipe my forehead and concentrate on taking deep breaths. My mouth floods with rancid spit, and I swallow the urge to gag.

"Have you caught something?" she asks me when I look up. "Brought some virus home from the hospital?"

God, I really hope so. A while back Ethan made me watch a documentary about hospital "superbugs" and the way they spread from staff to patients and visitors. Right now, I'm praying it's a superbug.

Because here's the thing. My period has been acting crazy for a couple of weeks, faking me out with a few of days of warning spots and then disappearing. But the nausea had vanished, so I hadn't really worried.

Until yesterday at breakfast. I've been nauseated since then, and no amount of lemon ginger gelato seems to help. So I've started praying for Ebola. Cholera. The bubonic plague. Anything other than what it could be.

"I have to go to the drugstore," I tell her.

"Okay." She looks blank. *Come on*, I think. *Figure it out, Hope. Don't make me say it out loud.*

"I…I need to get a…a test."

She laughs and rolls her eyes. "What, are you pregnant?"

Oh yeah, it's hysterical. Me, Rain Rosenblatt, Ms. super cautious, never-been-kissed Rain. I'd laugh too if I were her. But the smile fades from her face when she sees my expression.

"Rain…" Her lips twitch as if she's waiting for me to laugh with her, waiting for the "gotcha!" moment. "Stop joking. You're not—"

"Hope, I need to get a test," I repeat dully. I'm halfway

between gagging and crying, and if I have to say any more I'm going to end up doing both in front of the entire cafeteria.

"*Holy shit*," she says. Her mouth falls open. "Oh, God! The Halloween party?" She glances around the room and lowers her voice. "Are you sure?"

I don't reply. Of course I'm not sure. That's why I need the test.

"Does—does Liam know?" she falters.

"Of course not!"

Another tug of nausea twists my stomach, and I duck my head and clap my hand over my mouth. My shirt is clinging to my sweaty back, my skin goes hot and cold, and I close my eyes and take a ragged breath.

"After school today?" she offers. "I'll drive you to the pharmacy."

I nod and raise my head to meet her eyes. She's gazing at me quietly, her lips pursed together. Thank God for Hope, I think. No judgment, no questions, no explanation needed. There when I need her the most.

"It'll be okay," she says.

I manage a weak smile. "I know. I just want to be sure." But I have no idea what I'm going to do if it isn't okay.

# Chapter 27

I can't do it. There's no way. Technically I'm ready. I've chugged a half liter of Gatorade and am ready to go.

The procedure is simple enough. Pink cardboard box with the silhouette of a pregnant belly, white stick, and dummy-proof fold-out instructions. But there's nothing that explains what to do after, besides the obvious "consult a doctor." They don't mention what you're supposed to say to your boyfriend who had a whole life planned for himself that didn't include this, what to tell your estranged father, with whom you've just started talking again, how to break the news to your sick mom, who will be so disappointed and hurt that she might get even sicker. The box instructions don't include Ethan in any of this either. Lord, how will I tell my brother?

I can do the peeing part.

But I can't face the truth.

I drop the stick into the sink and walk out of the bathroom. Hope is standing on the other side of the door, her body tense with anticipation, her lips pressed into a thin line.

But she's not alone. Ethan is standing next to her. And Hope's hand is in his.

They are *holding hands.*

I'm briefly distracted from my own worries. What is happening in front of me? My eyes widen, and I shoot Hope an accusing glare. *Did you tell him?*

She gives a barely perceptible shake of her head. "I told Ethan that I was upset," she explains.

"I hold her hand when she's upset," Ethan puts in helpfully.

It probably never occurred to him to ask what's upset her or to wonder why his girlfriend is now staring at me expectantly. But his outstretched hand, that small, warm gesture, is enough to make her happy. She's scared for me, poised and ready to help me, but her own course is calm and clear. Hope glows as she stands there quietly waiting for the verdict. I gaze at their joined hands.

"I just need a minute—" I begin. And then my phone buzzes in my pocket.

I pull it out and touch the screen, welcoming the distraction, anything to keep me from thinking about the flat, white stick waiting for me in the bathroom.

The message is from Liam.

I see capital letters and exclamation points but the words blur in front of me, and for a moment the text is meaningless.

Call me please!!! I really need to talk to you. SOMETHING AMAZING has happened.

I stare at the phone stupidly. And then it buzzes again. It's Mom this time. Your father is staying in town, and you didn't tell me? I was counting on you to be honest with me.

And then again. From Dad: Can I come by later? I stopped by the hospital, but you weren't there. Your mother is pretty upset.

"What's going on?" Hope asks me.

I have no idea what's going on—with anyone. My mind is bouncing between the joined hands in front of me, the expectations of my mother, the hopes of my father, and the boyfriend whose life I'm about to destroy. I can barely stop to think about myself in the middle of all of them, the ticking bomb that's about to explode.

Suddenly the room begins to tilt and spin; I sway for a moment, then drop down to my knees. There's a rising, burning pressure in my chest, the air's too thick to breathe. I hear Hope call my name, but the blood is beating in my ears. My skin goes slick with sweat, small beads forming around my neck and spreading like a clammy sheet over my body.

Then Ethan's voice breaks through, and I look up to find him crouching next to me. "Take a deep breath," he instructs me.

I try to inhale slowly. "I can't—I can't—" I wheeze.

I feel his hand clasp around my arm and he brings his face close to mine. His pale eyes scan me and his fingers tighten on my wrist. "You're having a panic attack," he says.

"I can't breathe—Ethan—I can't—"

"Yes, you can, or you wouldn't be able to talk," he replies reasonably.

"Should we call someone?" Hope suggests. She's hovering over us anxiously and tapping on her phone. "It says on Wikipedia that you should inhale and exhale very slowly. Try to count to five."

I don't know what she's talking about; I can barely remember how to breathe, much less count my breaths. "Ethan—please—"

"Lie down," he commands.

"What?"

"Lie down. On the carpet, on your side." There's something reassuring about his detached voice. I collapse on the rug and close my eyes. "Now make your hands into fists and squeeze," he instructs me. "One, two, three, and release your hands—then squeeze again—one, two, three—" I do as he says but it doesn't help; it still feels like I'm drowning. A moment later there's a rustling noise and the sound of shuffling footsteps.

Hope murmurs, "Ethan, what are you doing?"

I don't care what he's doing. It's too much of an effort to try and stay alive. My brother will take care of me. He'll make this awful feeling go away. Somehow, I know this.

There's a grunt and then a soft weight comes down on me, warm and tough and heavy.

And so familiar.

My eyes fly open and I lift my head. He's covered me in his sensory blanket, his burrito wrap. I want to argue with him, push it off me. This is *his* therapy—*his* comfort. But then his familiar smell floods my panicked mind with echoes of the words I used to say to him. *You're okay, now. I've got you now. You're okay.* Only this time, I'm the one inside the wrap, and Ethan is muttering the phrase over and over, carefully tucking the edges around my shoulders. It feels so strange; I'm on the wrong side of this. *I'm* the one who should be taking care of *him*.

But even as I think it, I feel my heart slow down, and I let out a shuddering sigh; I bury my head in the shaggy rug and close my eyes. Ethan's wiry arms tighten around my shoulders, and he places his head against my neck. Strands of long, pale hair fall against my cheek and tickle my nose.

I take a deep breath and let my mind go still.

"Are you as good as new?" he asks me finally. He's using my words. That's my expression.

"I'm getting there, Ethan. Thank you."

"You're welcome."

After a few minutes, I'm ready to sit up. But I let an extra moment pass before I do. This is the closest I've ever been to him. This is our strange version of a hug, but today Ethan is the one giving it. And for just a second I want to hold on to that, the only bright part of this day. I know that when he lets me go, I'll have to go back to being me; I'll have to look them all in the face and disappoint them. It's safe inside this blanket, and for now, I'm happier pretending to be Ethan. I've fought my brother's battles all my life, but I've never really seen the world from his eyes. And now I realize I don't want to be unwrapped. I want to stay under my brother's blanket forever.

I shift beneath his weight, and he relaxes his grip and moves back to let me rise. Hope kneels beside me and extends a hand to pull me up. "We'll get through this, Rainey," she murmurs into my ear. "And I'll help you, no matter what you decide—"

"I didn't do the test," I reply. I can feel Ethan staring at me. "But I'll go do it now. I'm ready."

She gives me a reassuring squeeze and lets me go. On the way to the bathroom, I brush past my brother. But I can't look at him. When he calls my name and asks, "What test?" I shake my head and shut the bathroom door behind me.

I grab the stick from the counter and hold it up to my face. The little window teases me. Clean, white, and perfect.

I take a deep breath and do the deed. Then I close my eyes and wait. Ten seconds, twenty seconds, thirty.

I count to a hundred and brace myself.

There's just one line. *One line.*

I squint at the miracle stick. I have an overwhelming urge to kiss the little pee-soaked test. I was ready for disaster, and this little window of truth just saved me.

I can move on now. The nausea was probably just from stress; the weird spotting was just a messed up period or something. I'm going pick up the phone and call Liam back. And I'll be happy for him. And when I'm finished fixing our relationship, I'll go to the hospital and help my mom get better. And after that I'll find a way to talk to Dad and be the daughter I should have been before.

And I'm never, ever going to need Ethan's blanket again. I'm done with that. I'm putting that chapter behind me.

With a quick motion, I reach my hand out and flush the toilet, then toss the stick into the trash. Hope is hovering outside when I open the door, and she lets out a relieved sigh when she sees my calm expression. "It's okay?"

"Yep. Everything's fine. No worries."

Ethan still looks confused.

"I'll tell you one day when I'm ready," I say. "Right now I have to call my boyfriend."

# Chapter 28

Liam and I meet up at Milly's Diner on Saturday. He hadn't wanted to tell me his news over the phone, and I'd spent Friday evening at the hospital so we'd put it off until the weekend. I settle at a corner table to wait for him and order a soda to calm my stomach. The smells coming from the kitchen are nauseating on a good day—and I've been more than usually sensitive to strong odors recently. Maybe it's the soothing effect of the cool bubbles and sugar, but I'm surprisingly cheerful when he walks in. He grins happily when he sees me and rushes over. "Rain, I have so much to tell you."

"It's been forever since we've talked."

It occurs to me that I should have a lot to tell him too.

I shake my head and push the thought away. He doesn't need to know about the negative test. That panic attack is behind me forever. I deserve a normal first relationship, after all. And I never want to ruin Liam's sweet smile again. "So what's your big news?"

"Well, you're not going to believe this." He leans across the table and takes my hands in his. "You remember I was telling you that I'm trying to raise money to go on the international program? And that I'm only about halfway there."

"Yeah?"

"I have the money now. I can go whenever I want."

I stare at him. "How? What happened?"

"You remember Dr. Peters, the surgeon I was telling you about? The one who met with Ethan? Well, he put my name forward for this scholarship a couple of months back. I never mentioned it to you because I was sure I wouldn't get it. There are like, thousands of applicants and only *one* grant!"

"And you got it!" I can't believe it. I don't want to think about what his news will mean for us. If he can go next year and I can't…

I shake the thought out of my mind. "Liam, I'm so happy for you!" I exclaim, slipping out of my chair and sliding over to his side. "That's just unbelievable!" He pulls me close to him and gathers me in his arms. I'm lost for a second in his warmth, in the spice-wash sweetness of him. His cheek is rough against my skin; his lips touch mine.

Then our food arrives with a clatter, and Liam pulls back from me. We'd both forgotten where we were. Cheeseburgers and making out don't go together very well. But I don't want to stop kissing him. I sigh and rest my head against his shoulder. "More later," I whisper in his ear.

He pokes absently at his plate of fries and studies me for a minute. "You know, I meant what I said before. About waiting for you. I don't have to go next year. I asked Dr. Peters, and he said it's fine if I'd like to defer."

"I couldn't ask you to do that!"

"Yeah, but I'm not ready to leave you."

"And I'm not ready for you to go." The thought of next year without him—of nothing to look forward to. I can't begin to imagine. "But it'll be worse for me than you."

"How can you say that?"

"Because you'll be distracted by the adventure you'll be on, while I'll be staring at the empty seat you left behind."

His smile rewards my frankness. "So, you've thought about what I said? About applying together? I know that it's expensive, but I can talk to the fellowship people and maybe—"

"Money isn't the problem," I interrupt. "My dad put aside a trust fund for our education when we were little. I could probably use some of it for the program if I wanted."

He beams, and his arms tighten around me. "You *have* thought about it, then! I wasn't sure—I felt like such an idiot for asking you before. I know we've only been together for a little while, and you have your family to consider…"

I think about Ethan and Hope standing calmly in front of me, their hands joined. "My family will be just fine. They don't need me." I try to keep my voice light and casual, but the words are laced with regret. "I'm sure they'll be very happy for me to go."

"So then—" His eyes are so hopeful that it breaks my heart. "So there isn't anything stopping you. Right? I mean, we deserve this future, don't we? And there's nothing holding us back now."

I drop my head and concentrate on pouring too much

ketchup on my burger. The smell of fried onions is suffocating me. But he's right. He does deserve a perfect future. And I won't let anything stand in his way.

"I can't wait," I assure him, and press my lips to his. "I'll tell my family about it today."

We sit that way for the rest of the afternoon, my head resting on his shoulder, hands tucked into the pockets of my jeans. I've made my boyfriend happy, I tell myself, as I watch him cheerfully attack his burger. The faint nausea that's been following me around is no longer terrifying and menacing. The test was negative, so I don't have to worry. Just a stomach bug or stress or everything combined. I can deal with that. At least it's nothing life-changing.

"You're not hungry?" he inquires between chews.

I shake my head and push my plate over to him. It's been a while since I've appreciated the smell of food. And worse, I've lost the desire to cook.

For the last few days, I've even put the blog on hold. I'd already posted about vegan and gluten-free macaroni and cheese, but that has been the only thing I can stomach recently. A few messages from new followers trickle in, but I can't muster the energy or appetite for conversations about innovative food cures. I hadn't realized how much I loved my little corner of the internet. I miss shouting my recipes into the cyber void and waiting for someone to shout back.

# Chapter 29

They're predicting a nor'easter by the end of the week. At the hospital, the TV is on 24–7. The coming blizzard is supposed to blanket the state with several feet of snow, and everyone has predictions. I'd been hoping Mom would be discharged before the snow hit. As much as I'd like to think my arguments swayed her, I suspect Dad's sudden arrival is what actually frightened her into trying to get well. She seems determined to pull herself together, if only to push him out of our lives. Her medications have finally started to kick in, and she's showing steady signs of improvement. Today she started walking around without the assistance of the IV pole.

Last night, the doctor had been optimistic about getting her home, but then he was called away on a family emergency, and the covering doctor changed the plan. Mom threw a fit and declared that she would leave against medical advice, but then Dad stepped in and threatened to sue for temporary custody if she didn't follow the doctor's orders. They were still arguing about it when I left.

When I get home from school, Ethan and I head out for a run. Because of Mom's hospitalization, we'd been skipping our afternoon tradition. But tonight, with the forecast warning the state of the arriving snowstorm, we're forbidden from visiting the hospital. Even though he hasn't complained about it, I know the disruption to his routine has bothered Ethan, and I realize suddenly that it's bothered me too. I've missed this, the rhythmic pounding of our rubber soles on pavement, the bite of the wind on our cheeks, the burn of cold air in our lungs, the smell of the mountain firs.

So much has happened since we last ran together: Mom's illness, Marcus and Kathy's split, Liam's scholarship, my brief nausea scare, our reunion with Dad.

"Are you going to see Dad?" Ethan asks me, as we round the corner and circle Manny's shop. "He said he wants to come by later. Before the snow starts coming down."

"Yeah, of course I'll see him. I've talked to him a few times since he got here. I assumed you knew."

He hesitates and slows his pace. "I thought you hated him."

"Oh, come on, Ethan. I don't hate him. It's not like that."

"Okay." He comes to a halt and stretches his long back. "What is it like?"

"I...I don't know, really. I'm starting to understand that our parents' relationship wasn't black and white. I used to think that the difference between good and bad was obvious. Responsibility and loyalty. But I guess it isn't as simple as that anymore."

I've completely confused him; I can see it before I'm finished speaking.

"You thought Dad was bad?" he asks.

"No, not *bad* exactly. But…unworthy."

"Because he cheated on Mom?"

I shouldn't be surprised that he knows. Over the last few weeks Ethan has shown he knows far more than I thought he did. "Mom told you about that?"

"No, Dad did. He said that was the reason you weren't speaking to him anymore."

"Oh." I'm not sure what to say to that. "I was just trying to do the right thing. I didn't want to hurt Mom."

"I know."

"But now I wonder if maybe I was missing out." I hesitate and squint at the approaching mass of gray clouds. "We should head back. It's going to start snowing soon, and my legs are cramping from the cold."

"Mine too." Our breath is making the air foggy.

"My side hurts."

"We've gotten out of shape," he remarks. "You must have pulled a muscle."

"Yeah, probably." But the pain is deeper than a muscle sprain and seems to spread upward every time I inhale. "I don't think I can run anymore."

"What did you mean before?" Ethan asks me as we limp back to the house. "When you said you were missing out?"

"I don't know. I guess I feel like I'm fading out of your life. And you're talking to Dad almost every day; he's giving you all this advice. It seems like you spend more time talking to him than to me—"

"That's not true," he protests. "On average I talk to Dad about fifteen minutes a day, excluding the week when he comes to visit. And I talk to you—"

"I wasn't speaking about quantity, Ethan. I meant that Dad knows more about what's going on with you than I do. And all these details like his visits to Montana, his advice to you about becoming a doctor, even your relationship with Hope—I find out all this stuff after everyone else. It's not that I mind that you're getting close to him. It's fine. But I'm sad that we don't talk anymore. Not like we used to."

He doesn't answer me. I hear his heavy breaths as he plods along next to me, but there's nothing else coming from him: no admission, no explanation, nothing to comfort me. I'm not sure what I was expecting, but I was hoping for something more than total silence.

"Never mind," I say after a few minutes. "Sorry to bother you with my issues."

"It's okay," he replies. "Does what you just told me count as a problem?"

I'm briefly pissed until I remember that Ethan doesn't do sarcasm. He's asking me because he wants to know.

"Yes, Ethan, I do think of it as a problem."

"That's good. Then it's an extra point." He does a quick calculation. "I'm at sixteen," he announces triumphantly.

"What are you talking about?"

"I'm collecting points for Dad. Every time I do something on his list I get a point."

"I've been meaning to ask you about that. What list are you talking about?"

"Here." He thrusts his hand into his pocket and shoves a crumpled up sheet of notebook paper at me. "You can read it."

I scan the scribbled lines. *For a future surgeon*, my father's written in the corner. I smile at the title on the top. "The Dreams of Ethan?"

"Yes."

"So it's a dream of yours to…change the time of a meal?" I remark, pointing at the first item.

"No. But each time I do it, I get a point. So far I've changed my lunchtime six times. So, six points."

I hadn't even noticed. "And the points you accumulate will get you…what? Closer to being a doctor?"

He nods. "That's what Dad says. He told me that I have steps I need to go through if I want to get there."

I shake my head and squint at the blurry writing on the page. "I'm sorry, I don't get it. How many points did Dad say you have to collect to become a doctor?"

He gives me a strange look. "Dad's not stupid, Rain. He knows I have to go to medical school to become a doctor. The points are not about that."

"What are they about then?"

"They're just motivation. When I collect a hundred, Dad gives me a prize."

"What prize?"

"I get to visit him in DC. *By myself.*"

There's no hint of maliciousness in his last words, but they smart anyway, almost as if he'd said *without YOU*. I duck my head and focus on the letters in front of me. The last line catches my attention, but I'm not sure whether it's too personal a point. So instead I tap item three on Ethan's list. "So are any of these actually dreams of yours? Like, *listen to someone talk about their problems without interrupting*. I guess that's what you did just now. When I was complaining about us."

"Yes. Also when I listened to Marcus. I think I should get two points for that. His problem was really long."

I can't help laughing. "You're probably right. But it's not a dream of yours exactly, is it?"

"No. That's just one of the ways I can pretend."

"Pretend? Pretend what?"

"Pretend to be neurotypical," he responds quietly.

"But I thought you didn't *want* to be neurotypical."

"Of course I don't. But Dad said that sometimes I'll have to pretend. To get through the day."

"I guess so. Especially if you want to be a doctor."

"Yes. And if I want to get to the last step on the list."

I fold the paper and hand it back to him. The last line was just two words, scrawled boldly across the bottom in fluid script.

*Kiss Hope.*

"Is the last step also a way to pretend?" I ask him.

"No," he says. "The last step is my dream."

## ETHAN'S JOURNAL:

### Biological Theories behind the Human Kiss:

In humans, Wedekind et al. (1995) found that ovulating women preferred the scent of men who had MHC genotypes that were different than their own.

MHC is a gene complex that plays a critical role in immune responses. So when two people with different MHC genes mate, their offspring would have a more diverse immune system and a better ability to fight disease. Increasing evidence indicates that MHC genes also influences body odor and mate choice based on body odor attractiveness. Therefore, kissing may be an evolutionary behavior to literally "sniff out" the best mate.

### My Observation:

When I showed Hope this study and told her that it explained my desire to kiss her, she smiled and said, "I guess opposites really do attract." Then she put her head against my shoulder. I thought this indicated her readiness for our first kiss, but she shook her head no. It's likely that she was at the latter part of her cycle, and her hormone levels were not at the optimal level for attraction to my MHC complex. Or maybe I'm just too opposite for her.

# Chapter 30

**My father and Liam are standing** on the front porch when we get home from our run. I freeze at the bottom of the stairs when I see them, but Ethan breezes past me and offers each of them a bland greeting before going inside.

"How long have you two been waiting out here?" I ask them anxiously. I'm not sure what I'm afraid of exactly, but I know I'm definitely not ready for these two parts of my life to collide. I'm just getting comfortable with Liam. And as for Dad, I thought it was going to take months before I was ready to introduce him to my boyfriend. Liam hasn't even met my mother yet, and surely she's the one who deserves the first introduction.

"I got here five minutes ago," Liam says. "I was about to text you."

I let them into the living room. The warm air bites my frozen ears and makes my head ache. We pull our coats and gloves off and stomp the feeling back into our toes.

"I guess I should introduce you—"

"No need," Dad interrupts. "We've been talking. Do you mind making us some tea or coffee? I'd forgotten how cold it gets up here."

"Sure." I cast an uneasy glance at the two of them, and head off to the kitchen. Ethan and Dad settle on the sofa next to each other, and after a moment, Liam joins me by the stove. He holds his chapped hands to the range and shivers. "God, it's freezing out there. Sorry to just drop by without warning—"

"It's fine," I assure him. "I'm really glad you're here."

"Thanks." He pulls four mugs out of the cabinet and sets them on a tray. "How's your mom?"

"She's taking her medicine now, but she's had such a setback and lost so much weight that the doctors are still really vague about her discharge date. I hope they'll let her go after this storm is over."

He hesitates and glances over his shoulder. "That's why I'm here, actually." His eyes don't meet mine; he's suddenly very preoccupied with spooning large amounts of sugar into the mugs. "The storm, I mean."

"What's going on?"

"I really hate to ask you this—" He clears his throat, then dumps another spoonful of sugar into the mug.

I place my hand over his. "Liam, look at me. Stop with the sugar and just tell me, please."

He smiles and his face flushes. "Rain, I need...I need somewhere to stay tonight."

"Oh." That was the last thing I expected him to say. "No problem," I falter. "Really, it's fine."

"I wouldn't ask normally," he explains. "I know your mom is sick, and you've basically just met your dad again, and it's a really awkward time for you. But I'm stuck. My father took the truck two days ago, so I can't go out to Missoula to my grandmother's. And the heater in the trai—in the house just broke. I couldn't get anyone out to fix it, and the local hardware store is out of space heaters. I didn't know what to do."

"God, Liam," I exclaim. "Of course you can stay here. That's awful."

"No, no it's fine. I'll take care of it after the storm. I don't have anywhere else to go."

"Did you tell your father about the heater? It's ten degrees outside. He can't just leave you in a freezing house."

"He knows."

"He *knows*?"

"Yeah," he says shortly. "He broke it."

"Oh." I'm too stunned to speak. The idea of a parent abandoning their kid in weather like this—with no way of getting help—is horrifying. My mom had warned me that Liam's father wasn't a nice guy, but *this*—this was criminal. "Liam, you could report him—"

"No, that's why I didn't want to ask for help," he interrupts. "I *know* I could report him. I've known that for years."

"So why don't you? Look, both my parents are lawyers, they could advise you—"

"That's the last thing that I want, okay? I just need a little help. For a couple of days, that's all. Please don't offer more than that. I don't want it."

The tea has finished brewing and is giving off a strong chamomile and lavender scent. I cradle my mug in my numb fingers and take a tentative sip. It's sickeningly sweet, but I swallow it anyway. "I don't understand. It's neglect."

"Yeah," he counters. "And I'm almost seventeen. What are they going to do? Send me to live with my grandma again? She sold her house and is moving into a retirement home next month."

"Oh." I'm secretly relieved, even though the thought of Liam shivering in a lonely trailer is heart-wrenching. I don't want him moving to Missoula.

"You don't want me to go, do you?" he continues, reading my thoughts. "Because she's the closest relative I've got. I have a couple of distant cousins in Salem, but I haven't seen them in years—"

"Okay, okay. I get it. I just can't believe he broke your heater."

"He was pissed at me. And drunk. He breaks things when he's drunk. And then he disappears for weeks. Usually he'll leave some money as an apology. Or his pickup truck when he's on the road. This time he didn't."

"God."

"It's *fine*. You don't have to look at me like I'm some poor, abused kid. He doesn't hit me or anything. And he's on the road for months generally or with his girlfriend somewhere. That's probably where he is now. Drying out. It has nothing to do with me, all right? He has *nothing* to do with me."

I can't help admiring his stubborn pride. If my parent abandoned me that way, I wouldn't be able to brush it off so easily.

I steal a guilty look at my father. His back is to me, but I can see the absorbed posture of his body as he listens to Ethan chatter about the latest documentary on ovarian diseases. Dad is nodding thoughtfully, his lips compressed, his eyes fixed on his son's animated face. He really wants to hear what Ethan has to say, I realize. He cares about him just as much as I do.

Maybe even more than I do. I doubt I could muster up that level of interest in ovarian cysts.

"I'm glad you're here," I tell Liam. "It'll be fun. You can get to know my father." I pick up the tea tray and head out to the living room. "We both can."

# Chapter 31

**It's the most fun I've had** with my family in a long time. As the wind whistles in the chimney and the darkening clouds cover our town in heavy snow, we sit on the rug, wrapped in furry sweaters, cradling mugs of steaming tea and cocoa, playing games and making jokes. I fry up a pan of gluten-free cranberry skillet cookies.

Liam slides into our family easily; I'm grateful my dad says yes when I ask if he can stay with us through the storm and I wonder, in spite of myself, how differently the evening might have been if my mother had been there in his place. Deep down, I know the answer, and it hurts that I'm secretly relieved she isn't here. Mom would have asked Liam why he was homeless during a winter storm, would have dug to the bottom of his history, bared the embarrassing details, and then insisted on justice. I would have had to wrestle the phone from her hands to keep her from calling social services. And Mom would probably have been right.

But I'm not sure I want to be right. For now, I just want Liam to be happy.

"Who knew you could fry a cookie?" Liam remarks, taking a bite. "They're delicious."

"Really?" I smile, breaking off a piece. "I'm so happy you like it! You guys want another batch?"

"I am not eating that," Ethan declares. "It looks like petrified fruitcake. And it smells like cranberries and feet."

Liam chokes, spewing crumbs across the rug, and my father cautiously sniffs the edge of his plate.

"Oh, yeah," I say. "Sorry about that. I didn't have gluten-free cornflakes crumbs so I crushed up a bag of corn chips instead."

"Thank God. I was wondering what that odor was," my father says. "I thought it was me."

"You're inventive, Rain," Liam asserts graciously. "No one else would have thought to do that."

"That's true," Dad says. "Very resourceful."

"Maybe," Ethan persists. "But this cookie makes people question their hygiene. So I'd call that a failed experiment."

"Yeah, well, my experiments are all for *you*," I point out acidly. "Mom says that these recipes are good for you."

Ethan opens his mouth to answer, but Dad cuts him off with a smile. "Okay guys. Ethan, you don't have to eat it if you don't want to."

"Good for me *how*?"

"You know, Rain," Liam chimes in, ignoring Ethan's protest, "your skills will be very useful when we're abroad next year. These cakes can probably last for weeks. They're perfect snacks for backpacking."

"Wait, what's happening next year?" my father asks.

It's an awkward segue. Liam seems embarrassed when he sees me hesitate.

"Where are you going, Rain?" Ethan asks.

There's a heavy silence. I swallow and cast a frustrated look at Liam. A moment later, the stillness is broken by the whistle of the teakettle on the stove. It's a welcome distraction, and I rush to fuss over the brewing pot. I can't avoid the questions forever, though; after a couple of minutes of stirring, I have no choice but to return to the living room.

"I'm sorry," Liam stammers as I fill their mugs. "I didn't realize you hadn't told them."

"Told us what?"

"There's nothing to tell yet," I say, settling down next to Ethan. As I cross my legs, a sharp pain shoots up my left side, cutting off my breath. I clutch my hip and exhale slowly. "I really must have sprained something pretty badly during our run."

"Where are you going next year?" Ethan repeats.

I sigh and shift to my right. The pain subsides to a dull ache, but it continues to throb, deepening as I breathe. "I haven't decided yet. And anyway, it's more than a year away, but Liam was talking about maybe doing a gap year abroad together—"

"It's a wonderful opportunity," Liam breaks in eagerly. "It looks great on college applications. You get to work with needy communities all over the world—"

"Liam, it's okay, you don't have to sell it," I say shortly. "They know it would be a good experience."

It looks like my father is already on board. "Just let me know what you decide, Rain," he tells me. "If it's a question of money—"

"Thanks, Dad. But I wasn't exactly thinking of the money, not yet..."

I was thinking about my brother, I want to add, but everyone can see that. I don't need to finish the thought. Ethan's expression does it for me. He doesn't speak for a moment; he appears to be glaring at some point between the sofa and the coffee table. Then he scrambles to his feet.

"I need to study."

"Ethan—" Dad gets up and reaches out to him, then stops, his fingers an inch away from Ethan's shoulder. "This could be a good thing for both of you. We talked about this, remember? You two may not end up in the same college. So this will prepare you—"

"I need to study."

"Ethan, I haven't actually made up my mind yet—" I begin.

"I need to study!"

And then he's gone, and the three of us are left blinking at our coffee mugs.

"I'm really sorry," Liam says. "I thought that you'd talked to him already. I didn't realize."

"It's okay. I probably should have told him."

"So you've thought about your options after graduation?" Dad asks.

I can see the eagerness in his eyes. He's asking about *me* now. This isn't about Ethan anymore. He wants to know what *I* want to do.

"I'm going to get a degree in psychology," I reply. For some reason, the statement comes out like an apology. "That's the plan, I guess."

"Oh." He looks puzzled, as if I'd just declared a sudden interest in space travel. "I didn't know you wanted to be a psychiatrist."

"I don't want to be a psychiatrist." I have no idea why I said it. All I know is that it's the first time anyone has asked me what *I* wanted to do. And for first time, the answer I've carried inside me for years doesn't feel like the right one anymore.

"Okay," Dad prompts me gently. "A psychologist then? School counselor?"

I look at Liam's face, at my father's eyes. "Maybe," I reply softly. "That's what I'm supposed to be good at."

Liam shakes his head. "Supposed to be good at?"

"Because of Ethan," I explain. "Mom's always said that I have so much experience, that I was literally born to do this—"

"No one is born to do anything, Rain," Dad says. "You should choose what excites you, not what you think you have to do. Would being a psychologist make you happy?"

The truth is that I don't know. All of this was predetermined since the day I was born—the day *we* were born. I've been carrying Ethan for so long, pulling him along with me. He'd decided my future without saying a word. State school, morning classes, our afternoon run, carefully prepared dinners, therapy sessions, bed—repeat. The same, unvarying routine stretching far off into the future. But when did I decide to become a psychologist? Whose idea was that? Why had I started memorizing that giant psych manual? Who had chosen that for me? Had it not been me after all?

"I have no idea what I want," I say. And it feels like a relief to say it.

Dad shrugs and breaks off a piece of cookie. "That's good. Most people don't."

"I'm sorry I brought up the gap year idea," Liam says again. "I didn't know you were still thinking about it."

"I *was* thinking about it," I tell him earnestly. "I really was. I just didn't know how to tell my brother."

But why had I been thinking about it? Was I just trying to make Liam happy by going along with the idea? Or was I really trying to dream big?

What if all I want is the *option* to dream, but I'm too scared to make it happen? What if Ethan has always been an excuse to stay on the familiar path? To never take risks?

"Do you want me to go talk to him?" Liam asks.

"No, it's okay. He needs to be alone right now. I'll check on him later."

I hate to admit it, but a small part of me is glad Ethan is upset. Not because I ever want him to be hurt—not for a second. But recently I'd been scared he wouldn't react at all if I told him I was leaving. That he didn't need me anymore. And that, for me, would have been worse than the loss of any dream.

After an awkward silence, my father declares that he's tired. There's a brief discussion about where he's staying (Mom's bed is out of the question) and we finally settle on Dad sleeping in my room, me in Mom's, and Liam on the living room couch. Everyone's clothes and toothbrushes are shuffled around, and my father bids us good night before shutting the door.

"I'm sorry," Liam says when we're alone. He flops down on the sofa next to me. "I didn't mean to put you on the spot like that."

"It's okay. I'm glad that everything is finally out in the open."

"Is it?"

"Yeah, of course." I smile to hide the quiver in my voice. "Ethan had to know that I'd be leaving him eventually. Maybe he was just in denial or something—"

"Was he the only one? In denial, I mean."

Am I that easy to read? Liam's dark eyes focus on mine, and I drop my head. "I don't know what you're talking about. I've always expected to—"

"One day go to a state school," he interrupts. "And board at home. Next door to your brother. Take classes with him. And then what, Rain? Are you ever going to tell me your real plans? Or do I have to ask Hope?"

"Ask Hope?"

He sighs and rubs his hands over his temples. "We were chatting in the cafeteria a couple of days ago, when you weren't in school. Hope told me that you've always planned your life around your brother."

I sigh and look away from him. "What choice have I had? Ethan freaks out when I push off our running hour. Are you surprised I couldn't tell him that I was thinking about moving halfway across the world?"

He takes my hand in his. "Maybe there are different sides of Ethan that want different things? Just like there are different parts of you. Your brother has autism, Rain. And even he tells his girlfriend about his dreams. While I seem to have absolutely no idea what you want, what you dream about."

"But I've told you—"

"No, you haven't. Not really. You told me that you want to study psychology. To study abroad. To leave Montana and go to college—"

"I never said I wanted to leave Montana." I'm pretty sure I didn't say that, anyway. But I'm so confused, I can't remember. If he was kissing me, it's possible that I promised to fly with him to the moon.

"Well, it was kind of implied, wasn't it?" His voice rises. "I mean, the international program isn't in Montana, right? And you told me that you wanted to go. Or was I just hearing what I wanted to hear?"

"I don't know, okay?" I explode, throwing up my arms. "You were so excited about the idea, and I liked making you happy. But then my mom got sick and my Dad reappeared, and suddenly I don't know who to listen to anymore. And now Ethan is changing. He's the one person who isn't supposed to change! So I don't know what he needs anymore or where I need to be. I don't know what anyone wants from me!"

"What do *you* want?" He asks me so softly that I don't hear him at first. "Forget everyone else for a second. If you could do anything—go anywhere, what would you choose?"

I shake my head and close my eyes. "You're looking for some kind of magic answer. You want me to 'listen to my inner voice' or some TV movie bullshit? Well, we're not going to have that breakthrough moment, okay? I'm not suddenly going to fall into your arms and sob, *Oh my God, I want to study in Paris! Thank you for showing me the way!* I'm not that girl, Liam. *You* may be alone in the world, so all your dreams are yours. But my dreams—they've always been tangled up in other people's lives. I am my brother's lifeline. I can't just abandon him."

"You're so used to being Ethan's voice," he points out, "that you've forgotten how to listen to your own."

I cross my arms and pull away from him. "Look, I don't want your pity, okay? And I don't want to end up all alone, like…"

He flinches, and I pause, embarrassed. I had been about to say "like you," but I'd stopped myself. Still, it isn't hard for him to fill in the blank. "Like me?" he suggests.

I hadn't meant it the way it sounded. It's not his fault that his family abandoned him. "I know it wasn't your choice," I amend.

"I didn't realize I was all alone," he says. "I never thought of myself that way."

"I know. It came out all wrong. I didn't mean to hurt your feelings."

He raises his eyes and meets mine head-on. "I'm not hurt. I'm trying to explain. I've always thought of myself as a kind of traveler. Like a person on a train. People on a morning commute don't think of themselves as alone. They're on their way somewhere, that's all. And when they get there, someone will be waiting for them. Maybe a lot of people. I guess I've just been waiting for my train to arrive."

I hesitate and drop my head. "Am I on that train with you?"

He gives me a look halfway between an appeal and an apology. "Yeah. You're the girl that made me want to pull the emergency break. Hard."

I'm briefly struck speechless. "Wow," I breathe after a moment. "That was so *poetic.*"

He grins proudly. "I know, right? I just came up with that."

"You should write greeting cards."

"I should! Like maybe the front of the card would be a train hurtling through the countryside? And the inside would be a picture of a large cow stuck on the tracks. And the caption would read 'You're worth stopping for, baby.'"

My eyes narrow. "Wait, so now I'm a stranded cow?"

His lips twitch. "You're the first one I've stopped for."

I laugh and take his hands in mine. "Maybe you should quit while you're ahead."

"Maybe you should kiss me." He shrugs. "Or I can just keep talking."

# Chapter 32

We don't solve anything in the next couple of hours. The wind wails and rattles the windows, but everything inside is quiet—as quiet as two people making out on the sofa can be.

I know we haven't fixed our issues. I'm worried that we want different things, possibly because I have no idea what I want yet, and possibly because Liam's "train" isn't going to stop while I figure it out. But at this moment, we can both agree that kissing each other is what we want to do.

My father and brother are in the next room, so we keep things PG. No activities that can't be reversed quickly if someone interrupts us. I end up tiring first; my hair is wild, and my lips are raw and puffy—and he looks more battered than sexy. We settle into each other's arms, and after a few minutes, I feel Liam's chest rise and fall.

I can't sleep, though. The things we talked about are still bothering me. As I shift to find a more comfortable position, a sharp pain shoots up my left side and makes me catch my breath. The ache seems to be getting worse, even though it's been hours since our run. I struggle to my feet and dig out a bottle of Motrin from my book bag. My mother is firmly opposed to any kind of pain medicine because she thinks pain strengthens the body. So I keep a secret stash for times when my period becomes unbearable or a migraine strikes before a test.

This is the first time I've needed pain medicine in a long time. Maybe it's this weird period that won't go away. Probably the reason my side hurts too. There's a whole chapter in my psych textbook about emotional distress that can cause physical symptoms. The book doesn't say that psychosomatic pain could cause one to double over, though, or that it could make you dizzy and light-headed.

Maybe I just need to get some rest.

My mother's comfortable king-sized bed seems to do the trick. Stretched out, with my feet propped up on half a dozen pillows, I'm able to doze off for a little while. The pain doesn't wake me right away; I think I dream through it. *Mom is standing over my bed and poking me with a sharp stick. "Why did you take the medicine?" she hisses. Poke. "Why is your father sleeping in my house?" Two pokes. "Why didn't you tell me you were leaving us?" Stab. "What is Ethan going to do?" Deep stab.*

I gasp and open my eyes. My mother vanishes, but she's ripped a crater in my belly while I slept.

It hurts even if I lie still, and as I push my body off the bed, I have to bite my lip to keep from crying out. I'd intended to walk into the hallway and call for help, but when I try to rise, the room pitches and sways and I sink back onto the bed. I yell for Liam, then my father, then Ethan. No answer. The clock beside the bed says 3:00 a.m. No wonder it's so quiet.

I grab my phone from the nightstand and dial Ethan's

number. It rings five times before he answers, his voice muffled and rough. "Hello?"

"I think I'm sick," I tell him urgently. "It hurts to move."

"Hello, Rain." He still sounds like he's asleep. "What?"

"My left side. It hurts worse than before."

"You sprained it," he explains patiently. "When we ran, remember?"

"I know. I can't stand up. And I can't lie down either. It hurts too much."

There's a brief silence. "You can't lie down?" He's echoing me, as he sometimes does.

"I guess I can if I try. But then my entire side hurts. All the way up to my shoulder. I've never sprained a muscle this bad before. Can you bring me more pillows so I can sit up? I can't get them myself."

"I'll be right there." He's wide awake now. I can hear worry in his voice. A moment later, the lights flick on and he's sitting next to me on the bed. "Where does it hurt?"

I point to the spot, right above my hip. He places his finger over the area and pushes lightly. My shriek makes him jump.

"I'm sorry," I gasp. "I didn't mean to yell. Please don't do that again."

His hand closes over my wrist and he counts to himself, his eyes fixed on the clock beside the bed. "You're tachycardic and possibly anemic," he observes after a moment. "And diaphoretic."

"I'm *what*?"

"You're covered in sweat."

"Oh. I'll shower later." My words feel muddled and disconnected. "I'm trying to sleep. Can you get me more pillows, please? It hurts my shoulder to lie flat."

"You're going to the hospital," he says.

"Not now," I protest sleepily. "When I feel better."

"I'm waking up Dad." There's an urgent tremor to his voice. "We need to call an ambulance."

"For who?" I don't understand the expression on his face. Strange, I think. Usually Ethan doesn't understand what I'm thinking. Now it's the other way around. "Why are you looking at me like that?"

But he's already gone. There are voices in the hall and then my father is sitting next to me and placing his hand on my forehead. "Hi, Dad. Did Ethan wake you up?"

"She seems fine," he murmurs groggily, looking up at my brother. "She doesn't have a fever or anything."

"We need to get her to a hospital," Ethan insists. "I'm calling an ambulance."

"Have you looked outside?" Dad exclaims, waving his hand at the window. "A bulldozer couldn't get through. There's like two feet of snow out there, and the roads haven't been cleared yet."

But Ethan's already dialing. There's a brief delay and then a confusing one-sided stream of words. "We need transport to the hospital," he says, "—abdominal pain, severe tenderness, confusion, diaphoresis, pallor, concern for shock—" He pauses. "No, I'm not a doctor. High school student. Yes, my father's here. No, you can talk to me. I have more medical knowledge than he does."

"Give me the phone, Ethan." Dad says, reaching out his hand. "Now."

"Please don't fight, guys," I protest over their arguing. "I'm trying to sleep."

"Maybe we should let her rest," Dad suggests. "It'll be hours before we can dig ourselves out of here. She'll feel better in the morning."

"She'll be dead in the morning," Ethan snaps.

"Hello? Is someone there?" The operator's voice screeches from the cell. "Who am I speaking with?"

"Can everyone please leave my room?" I gasp, wincing. "You're making it worse!"

"Ethan, don't exaggerate," Dad replies. "What could it possibly be? A stomach virus?"

"She's not vomiting. No diarrhea."

"What then? Appendicitis?"

"Can someone answer me, please?" the operator demands.

"Her pain is on the left," Ethan says into the phone. "Not appendicitis. When will the ambulance getting here?"

There's a long silence; my father paces and Ethan bites his lip. I try to lean back against the headboard, but every movement feels like a kick to the gut. I end up balanced on the edge of the bed, my arms supporting me on either side.

"That's almost a mile away," Ethan tells the operator. "We can't get there."

"What's going on?"

"I know about the snow!" Ethan continues, his voice rising. "My sister can't walk a mile. She can barely get up off the bed."

"I can get up! Just give me a second."

"Is this really necessary?" my father chimes in.

"What about a helicopter?" He shakes his head. "A snow plow? Firetruck?" I've never heard him sound so desperate. "What do you do during snow emergencies? What's wrong with you? This can't be the first time!"

"Ethan! Give me the phone!"

Ethan swings around to face my father. He'd been standing with his back to us, his hair shielding his face. As he turns I see that his cheeks are streaked with tears. I've never seen my brother cry. Ever. His frequent tantrums as a child had been of the howling and shrieking variety. But the earth would have to be shaking beneath us for Ethan to produce an actual tear. What could possibly be wrong with me? Why is he so worried?

"Ethan, really, it doesn't hurt that bad," I begin, but my head begins to swim and I pitch forward into my father's arms. Dad steadies me and carefully props me up against the headboard. He's fully awake now, and his scared expression mirrors Ethan's. But at least we're all on the same page. Something's obviously not okay. My stomach pain waxes and wanes, and I can dismiss it when it eases. But the simple effort of standing up had almost made me pass out. Maybe my brother was right.

"How am I getting to the hospital?" I whisper.

"We need to go now," Ethan informs us, clicking his phone off. "We don't have a choice."

"Are you kidding me?" Dad exclaims. "Where are the emergency snow vehicles? This is Montana! They don't have snowplows?"

"They have a whole fleet of snowmobiles. There was a roof collapse an hour ago and they've been called to dig people out and take them to the hospital. Ten minutes ago, she dispatched the last vehicle to rescue people stranded on the highway. The operator said they would come to us next, but it might take time. We don't have time."

"So what are we supposed to do? Walk to the hospital?"

"She said that if we can make it to the fire station, she can get someone to us much faster."

"How far is that?"

"Three-quarters of a mile."

"That's insane! In this weather, with her limping along it will take us more than an hour! We'll just wait here until they come. How long could it possibly take them?"

"Gather up all the blankets. I'm going to get the sled out."

"What?"

"We can pull Rain on the sled."

"Ethan, really, I can wait," I insist weakly. "I can handle the pain."

"The pain doesn't matter," he says sharply. "It's the bleeding that's dangerous."

"*What* bleeding?" my father demands.

"I'm not bleeding," I protest.

"What's going on?" Liam appears in the doorway; sleep creases zigzag across his cheek. "Is everything okay?"

"We're taking Rain to the hospital," my father tells him. "On foot." He sounds like he can't believe what he is saying.

"Why?"

"Because my son thinks that he's a professional doctor, apparently," Dad mutters under his breath.

"Are you okay?" Liam leans over me, his fingers close over my wrist. "Your hands are cold."

My eyes focus briefly on Liam's crooked glasses, the concerned look in his eyes. I reach up sleepily and straighten his frames. "Good night," I whisper. And the room goes dark.

# Chapter 33

I'm not supposed to be asleep. That's as much as I understand as I'm bundled into a thick overcoat and carried to our plastic sled in the front yard. There's a lot of arguing, some swearing from me (it hurts every time they move me, and everyone keeps forgetting that), and Liam seems to be stuck on one phrase which he repeats over and over again, "Rain, don't go to sleep. Please don't go to sleep." Apparently, Ethan came back from the shed, and, finding me passed out in my boyfriend's arms, began screaming at him to wake me. Liam's taking his job very seriously now.

They pad the sled and I'm laid down in it; Ethan grabs hold of the rope and pulls, while Dad and Liam push from behind. There's an awful jolt as we begin to move, and I bite my lip to keep from crying out. The pain is tolerable as long as I keep absolutely still and don't breathe too deeply. But as we head out, the sled tosses me from side to side, and it gets harder and harder to keep quiet.

My father seems to have reconciled himself to Ethan's ridiculous plan (as he calls it) but that doesn't stop him from grumbling every time the sled hits a bump or someone falls over in the snow.

"It doesn't make sense," he says. "If she's so sick, shouldn't she be inside? It can't be healthy to be out in this blizzard."

Ethan stops responding to him after a while. I can see him straining against the weight of the sled, grunting as the twine cuts into his hands, ducking his head against the biting wind. Behind me, I hear them panting and groaning, I see them sigh as we round a corner and face a sharp incline. I feel so bad for them all, and I ask them to let me walk, at least the uphill part. But our progress is too painful and slow and we abandon the effort after a few excruciating steps.

Liam presses his lips to my cheek as he lowers me back into the sled. "Stay awake, okay, Rainey? Promise me you'll stay awake."

I promise him, and he smiles at me, and then my eyes close and he disappears.

ETHAN'S JOURNAL:

When we get to the hospital, they tell me I'm in shock and that I should sit down and calm myself. I try to explain that it's Rain who's in shock. Then (in case they've forgotten their training) I list the symptoms of shock for them: cool, clammy skin, pallor, rapid pulse and breathing, dilated pupils, confusion, weakness, and fainting. I can't tell if they're taking me seriously. I don't know what their smiles mean. They tell me it's under control, that she's going to be okay. I ask Liam if they're lying to me. He shakes his head and says, "You did great, Ethan." He hasn't answered my question, and he's lied to me too. I haven't done great. I failed my sister. She'd been complaining of pain all day, and I disregarded it until it was too late. This is the only thing I'm good at, and it wasn't enough to save her.

# Chapter 34

**Someone is forcing me to breathe,** and I can't stand it. It's the worst feeling in the world, like my lungs have rebelled and decided to expand and contract on their own in a rhythm that chokes me. I can't handle it. I have to take my breath back.

I lift my hands to my mouth and pull. Somebody has sealed my lips shut with tape and a piece of plastic is pushing air into me against my will. I give a desperate tug and the tube in my throat comes free as I cough. There's a rasping noise and a harsh gurgle, and then someone is shouting next to me. My eyes open, and people are hovering over me, blurry familiar faces calling my name. I search for my brother, but I don't see him, so I close my eyes and let the world go black.

Later I open my eyes again, quietly this time, with no shouting faces or tearing tape. The room is hushed and peaceful except for an irritating high-pitched beeping next to my head. I crane my neck around to locate the source of the noise, and as I do, there's a rustling sound next to me and a low gasp.

"Rain! You're awake!"

Liam materializes by my bed, but he looks so strange that for a moment I don't recognize him. His chin is rough with stubble, his dark curls hang damp and wild, one eye is bruised and swollen shut. His glasses are gone.

"What happened to you?" I whisper. My voice comes out in a smoker's wheeze.

He seems surprised by the question. Then his hand goes to his injured eye. "Oh, this. That's nothing."

I nod and try to swallow. "Water."

He hesitates, then glances over his shoulder. "Okay, just a little," he holds a plastic bottle to my lips. I gulp gratefully, letting the water slide over my cracked lips and dry tongue.

"Thank you."

"Just don't tell anyone I gave it to you, all right?"

"Why?" I motion for another sip.

"The doctors haven't given permission yet," he tells me in a hushed voice. "And everyone hates me enough already."

I stare at him. "What? Why?"

"I guess you might as well know," he says. I've never seen anyone look so miserably guilty. "You're here because of me. This is all because of me."

I'm too exhausted to feel much of anything; even my surprise is weak. "Huh?"

"Rain!" My father and brother appear in the room and crowd around my bed. "Why didn't you tell us she was awake?" Dad hisses at Liam, who visibly cowers before him.

"She...she just opened her eyes," he stammers.

"Call your mom and let her know," Dad instructs Ethan.

"Mom's here?"

"You're at Missoula Hospital," Dad explains. "Your mother's just downstairs in another wing."

"What happened?"

"Good morning, Rain!" a loud voice booms out. My brother steps aside. A broad shouldered, gray-haired man in a white coat bends over the bed and grins at me.

"You're looking great, you're looking great!" he bellows. "Much better than when you came in." He chuckles to himself. My father manages a weak smile. Ethan stares at the large man in awe.

"Are you my doctor?" I ask him.

"No, no," he replies genially. "I'm Dr. Peters. The OB team is taking care of you, and they'll be by to check on you in a little while. I just stopped in to say hello and congratulate this brilliant young man here." My brother winces as the doctor claps him on the back.

"He doesn't like that," I blurt out.

"It's fine," Ethan mutters.

Dr. Peters raises his eyebrows and lets his hand slide off Ethan's shoulder. "You're lucky to have this boy as your brother," he says in a softer voice.

"I know." I feel vaguely ashamed of myself, but there's no way to explain. My tongue is still sticking to my teeth and my words are slurred. "What happened after I fell asleep?"

"You didn't fall asleep," Dr. Peters corrects. "You passed

out from the internal bleeding. When you got to the local hospital your blood pressure was dangerously low. They stabilized you and transferred you here. And not a moment too soon. They had you prepped and ready for surgery within the hour. If you hadn't gotten here when you did; if your brother hadn't insisted on bringing you in—"

"Surgery? I had surgery?"

He looks confused. "Wait. She doesn't know?" Dr. Peters asks. "No one's told her why she's here?"

"She just woke up," Liam whispers. He won't meet anyone's eye.

I try to push aside the covers, searching for some explanation, some clue about what happened to me while I slept. There's a lot of sheets over me, but I finally get underneath them and stare at the crisscross of bandages that cover my belly. A thin plastic tube attached to a bottle protrudes from a hole in the dressing; the sight of the murky mess in the drain makes my stomach lurch.

"Ugh."

Dr. Peters throws a sheet over me and clears his throat. "Never mind that. It's temporary. They did a fantastic job stopping the bleeding. That's what's important."

"*What* bleeding?"

"Your left fallopian tube ruptured," Ethan explains softly.

"My... What? Why would it do that?"

"Because you had an ectopic pregnancy," Liam says.

Nobody speaks after that. I stare at him, then at Dr. Peters, then at my father who looks like he's aged ten years in a day, then at my brother who is the only one meeting my eyes. And suddenly I understand.

An ectopic pregnancy. A baby. But in the wrong place. The weeks of nausea, the recent stomach pains, the weird spotting I was ignoring.

"Did you know?" Dr. Peters asks me finally. "Most people don't even realize that they're pregnant because an ectopic can burst pretty early on."

"No. I took a test a while back. But it was negative." I can't bear to look at the expression on Liam's face. "I thought I was okay because the test was negative."

"You probably took it too early. And sometimes the first test is negative. That's pretty common too."

Nothing about this feels common. I have a plastic tube sticking out of my belly, and according to Dr. Peters, I almost died. And he's just implied my brother saved my life.

"How did you know, Ethan?" I ask him.

"I didn't guess the diagnosis," he admits. "There were other things it could have been. But I knew that your abdomen was extremely tender. And you looked like you were going into shock. So I realized that we didn't have time to wait."

"I shouldn't have argued with you," Dad says. "I'm glad you didn't listen to me."

"The important thing is she's okay," Liam ventures, but my father cuts him off.

"*You* don't get to say anything after what you did to her!" he snaps.

"Dad! Stop it!" It hurts me to shout; the area under my bandage aches and my throat feels heavy and raw. "He didn't do anything to me. We made a mistake. One mistake."

"In this day and age, teenagers should know better—"

"In this day and age, people still make mistakes!"

"Legally, this isn't a mistake, Rain. He told me that you were both under the influence. So your judgment was impaired, and you have the legal right to charge him—"

"What? I don't want to charge him, okay?" I catch a glimpse of Liam's face, and my voice breaks. "It wasn't like that. Please don't make this more painful than it already is."

He opens his mouth to answer, but then he seems to reconsider; with great effort, he grits his teeth and swallows his response. "Okay. But we're going to keep talking about this."

I can't talk anymore; I need to be alone. The shock of waking up in the hospital all covered in bandages, the realization that I'd just been through a life-threatening surgery, the knowledge that I'd actually been pregnant, even if only for a short time—

It's too much. I want everyone to get out and leave me alone. I ask them to go as politely as I can. And to my surprise, everyone begins to file out obediently. Only Liam lags a little; I see him dragging his feet and throwing hesitant looks over his shoulder. I nod quietly and gesture for him to come back, but my father steps between us.

"You're going now," he insists. "You've done enough."

"Dad! I asked him to stay."

"Rain—"

"There are no good guys or bad guys here, okay? Just people. Those are your words, Dad. Your lesson, remember?"

He pauses and seems to consider. My Halloween mistake is not all that different from the one he made years ago, and I've just made him see that. I feel briefly powerful, despite my exhaustion.

"Fifteen minutes," he mutters finally. "She needs her rest."

"Yes, sir."

God, I feel bad for Liam.

"I'm really sorry about that," I say after my dad leaves the room. "And for that." His swollen eye somehow looks worse than before. "Did my father do that to you?"

He settles down on the bed and gingerly touches his brow. "Yeah. Right after you came out of surgery and the doctor told him what was wrong. I didn't get a chance to duck." He tries to laugh, but it comes out like something between a hiccup and a sob. "It's okay. I deserved it."

"I'm so sorry."

This time he actually does laugh. "Why do you keep saying that? What do you have to be sorry about? I'm the one who practically killed you."

"Oh, for God's sake! Killed me how? With your extremely lethal sperm?"

He looks like he's fighting a smile. "Look at you. You're like the poster child for unprotected sex."

"It's a little extreme, don't you think?" I point to the plastic bottles on the bed rail and the three tubes in my arms. "Kids, screw up once and this could happen to you! I don't think anyone would believe me."

"Maybe not." He tries to smile, then sobers. "Rain…" His voice cracks. "Why didn't you tell me? I never even knew you'd taken a pregnancy test."

"You texted me about that scholarship while I was peeing on the stupid stick. When it came back negative, I figured you didn't need to know. I didn't want to ruin your big news. Anyway, things have worked out perfectly for you. You can still use your scholarship and go wherever you want. This doesn't have to change anything."

If he wasn't hurt before, he definitely is now. "Are you serious? I haven't thought about the scholarship since I told you about it! All I cared about is whether you wanted to come with me. And then when the doctor came out and told us why you were sick, I was actually glad that your father knocked me down! It distracted me for a while, otherwise the guilt would have driven me crazy. For the last three days, all I've heard, repeatedly, is that you might not make it. That you'd lost a ton of blood and that even if you did wake up, you might never be the same. Do you have any idea what that was like?" He nearly shouts the question but then, realizing his voice has echoed around the empty ward, he takes a deep breath and continues in a softer tone. "I argued with your brother, do you know that? Just before you passed out in the snow. I was pissed and cold and tired. I told him that you were going to freeze to death because of him. God, if he had listened to me—"

"Ethan never listens to anyone when he thinks he's right."

"Yeah, but he hasn't said anything to me about it since then. Even when we all realized he was the one who saved you. I wanted *him* to punch me, you know? He had every right to. Or maybe just a simple 'I told you so.' But he hasn't talked about it."

"He's not exactly the biggest talker."

He shakes his head. "I don't know about that. He explained the operation to me in exhaustive detail. And then afterward we talked about kissing."

"What?"

"He wanted pointers."

I forget everything else, as I always do when Ethan eclipses my life. And for a moment, I'm happy, despite the miserable state of my own relationship and the countless tubes sticking out of me. I'm happy my brother wanted advice on how to kiss.

"So what did you tell him?"

"Do you really want to know?"

"Ew, no. Forget it." I grin and shake my head. "Hurray for Ethan! Making it to the bottom of the list."

"What?"

"I mean that he's doing fine without me."

There's something liberating about the feeling too, as if Ethan's success has set me free. But strangely, for the first time, the freedom doesn't seem terrifying and depressing. It's like lifting an anchor and drifting off into unknown waters. The weight of him is still with me, but it doesn't pull me under. It's a welcome weight, a grounding force, reminding me where I came from. The problem is, I'm not sure where I'm going now. All I do know is that I want a chance to find my own way for once, without restrictions or obligations.

I realize now why I never told my family about Liam's international program and my desire to join him. It wasn't my dream. It was his. And as much as I care for him, it's too soon for me to share someone else's dream again. I need to find my own first.

"Have you spoken to Dr. Peters about graduating early?" I ask. "Can you still use that scholarship to go next year?"

His face falls; he sits back in his chair. "Is that what you want? You want me to go?"

"No. But I want us to have a chance. And I know that we'll never have that chance if you stay for me. Any more than we will if I go with you."

He reaches out, interlacing his fingers with mine. "But I want to wait for you."

"Why?"

"What do you mean why?"

"*Why* do you want to wait for me? You were the one who didn't want a long-term anything, remember?"

"I know," he murmurs brokenly. His head drops over my extended hand, and his face crumples. "But that was before I fell in love with you."

The words hurt. They're not supposed to hurt, but they do. My heart begins to pound, but I'm not overflowing with excitement and joy like I should be. I can't breathe because I realize, suddenly, I'm trapped, bound by the ropes I've carefully wrapped around myself. It's the first time he's said he loves me. The first time he's meant it. And I can't think of anything to say to him. I have no idea how I feel.

"Liam—"

"No, I do. I love every crazy, random part of you. I love how you keep baking truly weird food because your mother's convinced that it'll help your brother. I love your fierce and constant loyalty to your family. I love it, and I don't understand it, and I'm jealous of it because I've never felt it for anyone…until I met you." He doesn't meet my eyes as he speaks; the words fall from him like a miserable confession. "And I was willing to wait, Rain. I was willing to wait for your face to light up when you looked at me, the same way it lit up just now when we spoke about Ethan."

"But we've only been dating for a couple of months," I say softly. "I've loved my family for sixteen years."

"I know, and I'm not blaming you for not feeling the same for me."

I open my mouth to protest.

"No, don't argue. I know, deep down, you don't think that this is real. That I'm too young to know what love is or whatever. That's what the psychology textbooks would say, right?"

I watch him quietly for a moment, then gently brush the

tangled curls off his forehead. "If you weren't expecting forever, you must have known that we'd eventually go our separate ways."

He lifts his face a little so I can see his expression; his eyes are damp and bloodshot, his smile defeated.

"I wasn't looking for forever. But I guess maybe I was hoping for it."

I don't answer him. There's nothing I can say that will make any of this better. For a moment, I'm tempted to lie. To push away his desperation with a false promise. But I'm too numb and weak to find the words.

"I knew I was being stupid," he admits after a pause. "But I guess it didn't really sink in until just now when you told me that you wanted me to leave you."

"It's not that I *want* you to go. I just don't think we should be building our lives around each other. It would be a mistake. We've screwed up enough already."

He doesn't answer me right away. His head is bowed over my hand. "So it's really over."

"Don't…don't say it like that."

He nods and slowly gets to his feet. "I love you, Rain," he says simply. He leans over and kisses me, then straightens and walks out of the room.

It doesn't hit me until the curtain falls back into place and the sound of his footsteps fade. Until this moment, I was like an amateur actress reciting my lines. My face was sad, I understood my motivation, and everything I said rang true.

But I was just going through the motions of a breakup, not really feeling it.

Until he walks away and it actually hits me.

Liam told me he loved me, and I broke up with him. It was the adult, responsible thing to do. I'm sure my mother would have approved my coolheaded choice. I'd picked the right path without getting too emotional. In her book, I'd get high marks for that decision.

Except that none of it counts. Because I wasn't being coolheaded at all. I was simply cold. I'd shut down my heart, just as I'd been trained to do since I was little. When the person I loved was breaking in front of me, I wasn't meant to feel scared or helpless or angry. I didn't have my own pain. My job was to put out the fire—fast.

And that's what I'd done. Liam's feelings had gotten out of control, and I'd put them out. But in the process, I hadn't noticed my own, didn't feel the wrench of a broken heart, the sting of my loss. I was too busy doing the right thing; I was too worried about protecting his future to care that I'd just stabbed him. And underneath the neat bandage of an adult decision, I was bleeding too.

I wasn't actually ready to let go of the hope. Liam was my hope for love, the excitement at the start of a new day. He was the jolt of a heartbeat, the space between a held breath, the spill of color in my cheeks. Each morning, I'd waited, counting minutes, for him to appear. I'd dreamed, pined, and overanalyzed. And then I'd spoken to him and discovered he was better in person than in my imagination. He challenged me, made me laugh at myself, even taught me to flirt—badly. And I'd danced like a giddy child after our first kiss. But that was all over now. I could exhale finally.

I didn't want to though. I'd replaced hope with predictability, just as I'd always done. And for once, I hated my own good sense. It didn't matter what the world thought or what the probabilities were. I wanted Liam back. I wanted to be breathless again.

But there's no sound from the corridor, and the beeping sound of my heart on the monitor chirps out the same old rhythm. I stare up at the screen; the reading is steady and undisturbed: seventy beats per minute. Ethan would probably inform me my vitals are normal. He'd roll his eyes if I told him the monitor was wrong, that I believe my number should be zero and the line should be flat. It feels like something inside of me has flickered out, and I don't understand how the rest of me is still ticking away. My heartbeat is a liar.

I want to sleep, let this dull ache fade a little. If I could drift off for a few minutes, maybe I could forget I'm miserable. Maybe when I wake up, Liam will be sitting next to me, just where he was a moment ago. I close my eyes and slowly count the beeps.

And then Hope bursts into the room, flinging aside the curtain that separates me from the rest of the ward, and rushes over to my bed. "Ethan told me you were awake," she bursts out. "I was downstairs with your mom. The doctors are finally discharging her. She's coming up to see you now."

I have to brace myself for more visitors, it seems. But I can't handle any more questions right now. I can't explain any of these tubes and bandages to my mother. I'm supposed to be healthy and strong for her. But all I want to do is rip these machines off me and go running after Liam.

"What's wrong, Rain?" I haven't spoken yet, but she reads my eyes and puts her arms around me. "Did you just talk to Liam?"

I try to swallow against a rising sob. "I have to find a new lab partner," I tell her. The words are totally inadequate, but my tears speak for me, and Hope holds me close as I cry on her shoulder.

"What happened?" she asks me.

I lift my head from the messy tear stain on her shirt. "I don't know," I tell her. "But I think I just made the stupidest smart decision in my life."

"Oh. You broke up with him." There's no judgment in her voice, only the sad ring of a prediction that's come true.

"We were going in different directions," I explain desperately. She's nodding like she understands, but I'm not actually trying to convince her. I'm trying to convince myself. "I had to break up with him, didn't I?"

She doesn't respond right away; her head is bowed over her hands, and I can't see her expression. "It depends," she says finally. "Did Liam make you happy?"

I know the answer, though I can't bring myself to say it. But my eyes tell her what she needs to know.

"Then why not be happy, Rain?" she suggests quietly.

I shake my head. "Because I'm scared. I'm scared he'll leave, and it will all fall apart. I'm scared I'll end up hurting him."

She pulls back a little and takes a deep breath. "Hold on. So you're protecting Liam? By breaking up with him?" There's a faint smile beneath her question.

I try to laugh, but it comes out like a strangled hiccup. "Well, when you put it like that—"

"Or are you just protecting yourself?" she asks me. "Because you're scared."

"What do you mean?"

"You're scared of losing control. Of letting someone unpredictable into your life."

"That's not true. I wanted to be with him! I wanted to try at least..." I protest. But I don't bother to finish the thought. I don't have to strength to argue anymore. How can I explain why I decided to break Liam's heart and mine as a precaution against our future heartaches? It didn't even make sense to me.

"Sometimes different parts of us want different things," she says. "The question is, which part of yourself are you going to listen to?"

I have no idea how to answer her, but I don't even get the chance to think about it. It's almost eerie the way my mother's voice echoes through the hallway just as Hope finishes the question. I sit up and quickly wipe away my tears.

"Are you okay?" Hope asks. She reaches out to grab my hand. "What's the matter?"

"I can't deal with my mom right now," I whisper hoarsely. "Can you tell her that I'm asleep? Please."

She nods and doesn't let go of me.

"She's going to ask me why I've been so irresponsible," I explain. I need Hope to understand why I'm turning away my mother. "She's going to blame Liam, and then judge me, judge him, judge us—" My voice breaks. "And she's not going to say it, but I know that my three adjectives are stupid, stupid, and stupid, and I don't want to see that in her eyes." I can sense Hope staring at me as I bury myself beneath the mess of bedsheets and tubes. "I just went through surgery," I babble. "It's not wrong to sleep after surgery. Tell her that. Tell her that I wanted to see her but that Dad was here when I woke up. I didn't choose him. He was here already!"

"Okay, Rain, calm down—"

"No! I know what my mom's thinking. And I don't want to be here when she comes in and starts *thinking* at me—"

"Rain, you're hurting me," she gasps. I realize I'm squeezing her hand; the plastic knob on the IV is digging into her skin.

"What am I thinking?" My mother is standing at the entrance, just beyond the curtain. It's too late to drop my head and pretend I'm asleep. Hope falls back a little as Mom approaches, but I don't release her hand.

"What am I thinking?" she repeats as she settles in the chair next to my bed. Her face has filled out a little since I've last seen her. "Why are you freaking out at your friend? None of this is her fault."

"No, I know, it's mine. I really screwed up. I'm sorry." But my apology is edged with defiance, not regret.

"I was referring to that boyfriend of yours. The apple doesn't fall far from the tree with that family."

"Don't talk about him like that!" I snap. "He didn't mean for any of this to happen. And I'm the one who just hurt him!"

"Never mind," Mom replies. "We'll discuss things when you're feeling stronger. Your doctors say that you'll probably be ready to go home by the end of the week. And I'll be able to take care of you." There's no trace of judgment in her tone anymore, just quiet concern and love.

"Okay…" The fight begins to drain from me, and I relax my grip on Hope's fingers. "I'm glad you're coming home. I've missed you."

"I've missed you too. I'm really looking forward to things getting back to normal."

"Me too."

"Your father will be returning home on the next flight out. I've thanked him for bringing you to the hospital."

Her tone suggests no thanking actually occurred and Dad was being dismissed from our lives now that Mom was strong enough to stand.

"I want to see him," I say.

"That's fine. He's downstairs. I'll tell him to come up before he leaves."

"No. I mean, I want to see him when he comes to Montana. And I want to visit him in DC."

She stares at me for a moment, then, as I tighten my grip on poor Hope's hand, she seems to reconsider. "Your father's always had the right to visit you."

"I want to fly to DC and stay at his house for spring break," I continue doggedly. "So does Ethan."

Her eyes narrow, but she doesn't argue. "That has always been your choice to make."

"And I want you to stop judging me for that choice."

"Excuse me?"

"You know what I mean."

"You want me to stop *thinking*? Or you want to tell me what to think?"

"Neither. I just want the right to love you both."

"Rain, I never told you that you couldn't—"

"That's all I want to say," I tell her. I point to the heavy dressing on my belly. "I have to get some sleep now. My surgery is hurting me."

The last bit isn't exactly true, but it's close enough. I am hurting, but it's the kind of hurt there are no bandages for. I want to shut my eyes and hold on to Hope's hand forever.

When I open my eyes again, my mother is gone, but Hope is still sitting next to me on the bed.

"How long have I been out?"

"A few hours."

"Did I yell at my mom?"

"You made your point," she assures me. "You also amputated my fingers."

I glance at her puffy hand. "I'm sorry."

She shrugs. "Part of the job description."

I smile. "Then you should have fired me by now."

"What are you talking about?"

"I mean that you've been my best friend through everything. And I've been just the opposite."

She laughs and squeezes my arm. "What is this? Rain's hospital confession? You're not dying, okay? And we're fine. You don't have to apologize for anything."

"No, I do. You watched me screw up over and over with Liam. And you were still there for me. Like a real friend."

"Okay—"

"And I watched you build a relationship with Ethan. And what did I do?"

She doesn't reply, but her silence is answer enough.

"And it isn't because I was scared that you would hurt my brother," I persist. "I trust you more than that."

"Come on, Rain. You don't have to do this. I'm not upset."

"You should be. I tried to keep you away from him. I talked about you behind your back. I overanalyzed your feelings for Ethan. Even when, deep down, I knew you were for real, when I could see that you really cared about him."

"I'm over it. It's fine. I knew you meant well."

"No, I *didn't*. That's what I'm trying to tell you. I *didn't* want your relationship to work. I was...I was actually jealous of you two."

She doesn't answer right away; her bruised fingers play with the corner of the bed rail, plucking and pulling at an errant piece of tape. "I knew you were jealous," she says finally.

"You did?"

"Yeah, of course," she sighs. "We all knew that."

"We? Who's we?"

"Ethan and I. Your parents. Even Liam."

"But—"

"Look, none of us blamed you. You just needed time to adjust. Your brother used to be the center of your world. And then one day he wasn't. That must have been hard to accept."

I stare at her silently.

"He was talking to me," she continues. "And shutting you out. He'd never shut you out before."

"Yeah." I'm silently grateful she's explaining my own feelings to me. In her words, they don't seem as monstrously selfish.

"If I were you, I might have hated me too," she admits. "At least at first."

"I didn't—"

"So I kept away for a bit. To give you time to reconnect with Ethan and, maybe, in the process, to forgive me a little."

I shake my head. "Hope, you're not just the better friend. You're a better psychologist too. Better than me, anyway."

She laughs and pats my hand. "Don't worry, I'm not trying to take that from you too. That's still your thing."

"No. No it isn't. I don't think it ever was."

"What do you mean?"

"Well, it turns out that I don't really want to analyze people's feelings for a living. I'm actually not that good at it. Even with Ethan. I thought that I knew what I was doing, but I just ended up pushing him away. And I pushed you away too. I'm really sorry."

"Don't be. It's because of you that I'm so happy."

"What do you mean?"

She smiles shyly. "I have you to thank for the Secret Rule. It's brilliant, you know."

I feel a brief sting of resentment as my stomach knots up. That isn't *yours*, I want to tell her. Ethan and I invented that when we were little. The Rule only applies to us.

"Ethan told you about that?" I ask in a tight voice.

"He did. And I thought it was beautiful."

"Oh."

Thankfully, she's staring out of the window so she doesn't observe my expression when I answer her. I imagine it isn't pretty. *Stop it*, I tell myself. *This is a good thing. Ethan is communicating with his girlfriend. And you made that possible.*

"I said the phrase once just to see his reaction," she muses. "*Secret Rule*. He looked confused at first, but then he replied immediately, like it was part of a script. 'What can I do?' I didn't understand, so I asked him what he meant."

"He was asking 'What can I do to make you happy?'" I conclude softly.

"Yes," she says. "It was so sweet. Like an algorithm for showing love."

I nod. "It was how I taught Ethan to ask for help. And how I told him when I needed him. He couldn't read my emotions, and I couldn't always sense when something was hurting him. The Secret Rule was our private code. We were only allowed to use it once a day. So whenever one of us invoked it, the other knew to pay attention."

"Well, I think everyone should use the Secret Rule. It's an amazing idea."

I laugh shortly. "Most people just tell each other what they need."

"No, they really don't," she says. "Most people are afraid to be that honest."

There's a rustle of activity outside, and a moment later, Marcus and Kathy push the curtain aside and slink into the room. They seem embarrassed when they see my IV and plastic hardware. Kathy takes a step back into the hallway. "We weren't sure if you were okay to have more visitors," she whispers. "Your mom said you were pretty tired."

"But I thought we should have a peek anyway," Marcus adds.

"It's fine," I reply. "I've really missed you guys."

"Well, we've missed us too," he says, smiling at Kathy. "It's been a while."

They pull up two chairs next to Hope and exchange anxious looks. Kathy peers at the nasty bottle of murk hanging from the bed rail and Marcus pretends to study the beeping monitor behind me. They're not the Octopus anymore, I note. But Kathy looks happy. And Marcus seems at peace.

"Are you two okay?" I inquire after an awkward silence.

"Are *we* okay?" Marcus echoes. "You're the one with all the holes and tape and shit."

"We're getting there," Kathy assures me. "Still figuring out this new friendship thing."

"Friendship is cool," Marcus chimes in.

His ex-girlfriend shoots him a dirty look.

"It's going to take time," he adds.

Hope glances between the two of them. "Maybe we should let Rain sleep."

They rise reluctantly, and as he turns to go, Marcus reaches out and pushes a button on my monitor. It makes a squeaking noise, and Kathy roughly pulls him back. "What are you doing? Are you trying to kill her?"

"I just wanted to see what it did!"

"All right, guys, take the crazy outside!" Hope commands. "Rain needs some rest."

I do need a break, and it's a relief when they finally wave goodbye and leave the room. So much has happened since I woke up in the hospital. I finally confronted my mother, I broke up with Liam, I learned that Ethan saved my life, and most unexpectedly, I found out a tiny life inside of me had almost killed me. I don't know how I'm supposed to feel about any of that. Would others grieve for it? Is it strange that I'm just relieved that it's all over, that it was never meant to be?

I could try to force myself to feel something, to shed a few tears. But I've been borrowing other people's pain my whole life. Now I just want to mourn the death of what I thought were my dreams. And so, I bury my face in my starched white pillow and let myself cry—for losing Liam and for the love I'd drowned before it could take its first breath.

# Chapter 35

My nasty plastic tube and bottle are removed that evening; the bandages on my belly are trimmed down to a little square. I get a glimpse of the red scar underneath, and to my great relief, it's much smaller than I'd imagined it would be. The surgery resident seems optimistic I'll be home by the weekend, and he carries the news to my support group in the waiting room. They file in and out over the next two days, bringing teddy bears and oversized flower baskets and stories from the snow emergency outside. Nobody mentions the reason I've been hospitalized; they take their cue from me and respect the fact that I don't want to talk about it. Everybody focuses on me—at least when they're in front of me. Occasionally, ripples of an argument between my parents travel up to me, but they're careful to keep that stuff muted when I'm around. Mostly they come in separately, and one leaves when the other walks into the room.

I begin to take small trips around my bed after the bottle is removed. The IV pole has wheels on it, and I use it as a movable crutch, leaning on it when I get light-headed. I'm alone when I decide to take my first steps into the hall. Everyone's gone down to the cafeteria for dinner. The ward is very quiet; it's a shift change so the nurses are busy signing over their patients to the next team. I hobble over to the curtain and draw it aside, squinting down the corridor at the nurses' station. I'd hoped to take a walk to the dining hall to join my family, but my loose hospital gown gapes in some embarrassing places. No one answered my call button; I wanted another robe so I could drape it over my back and stop mooning the other patients.

I'm about to call out when I hear voices down the hall. Hope and Ethan round the corner and stop a few feet away from me. I'm partially hidden by the curtain, and they don't look up to see me standing there.

"Can I have one of those?" Hope asks and Ethan holds out a bag of cookies.

"You can take the rest."

"Are these gluten free?" she inquires between bites. "They're really good."

"They're not gluten free."

She stops chewing and gives him a strange look. "You just ate half a bag."

"Yes."

"But I thought you couldn't eat this."

He shakes his head. "That diet was my mom's idea. There's no medical basis for it. I was tested five months ago, and I'm not sensitive to gluten. So I can eat whatever I want."

She laughs. "How long have you been eating cookies?"

"Since I was tested." He reaches out and pops another one in his mouth.

"But your sister's been making all those crazy recipes for you! Why didn't you tell her?"

"She didn't ask."

"That's not the point, Ethan. She's spent a lot of time cooking those…creations for you. She has a right to know that you're ignoring the diet."

He shrugs and grabs another cookie. "I'll tell her if you want. But I think it will just make her sad."

She hesitates and rubs her hand over her forehead. I feel bad about spying on them, again. I know I should draw back into the room and give them their privacy. But it's the first time that I've heard Ethan predict someone's emotional reaction. I'm dying to know how he's come to it. Just one more minute, I tell myself, and then I'll leave them alone.

"Why do you think it'll make Rain sad?" she inquires.

He considers for a moment and brushes the crumbs from his lips. "Every time she brings out a new recipe, she's smiling. If I like it, she tells me how excited she is. Then she runs off to make more. I don't want to tell her to stop. It's the only way I know to make her happy."

"Oh." Hope's mouth falls open. "*God*, Ethan."

He appears startled by her reaction. "What?"

She looks like she's about to cry. "That's just… I can't…"

He starts toward her and then stops, confused. "Are you upset?" His voice is panicky.

"*No!*"

"Then what's the matter?"

"Give me a minute, okay?"

He nods and drops his head. I can see him mentally counting to sixty.

Hope only uses thirty-eight seconds.

"I think I'm ready now," she says, stepping forward and looking into his startled eyes.

"What?"

"I want to kiss you now."

"Oh." The panic begins to drain away. He swallows once and takes a deep breath. "Okay."

"Like we talked about. We'll count down from three, so you'll know what to expect—"

"All right."

"Ready?"

"Yes."

"Three, two, one…"

I step back into my room and let the curtain fall.

# Chapter 36

It takes a couple of weeks for things to start feeling closer to normal. All the roads are plowed and clear, though mini snow mountains still border the sidewalks. Christmas break comes and goes, and I don't hear from Liam even once. I eventually stop jumping when my phone rings. Marcus and Kathy come to hang out and watch movies, Hope is a permanent fixture in our living room. A couple of days after my discharge, my father returns home to his second family. I hug him before he goes. My mother watches from the kitchen but doesn't comment, and I don't make excuses. I tell him that I'm looking forward to spring break. He gives me a grateful smile.

When the door closes behind him, I walk over to my mother and give her a silent hug, a longer one than I gave my father, just in case she's counting. I wish she didn't look so wounded, but I hope, with time, that she'll get used to this new reality. The love her husband gave to another was stolen from her heart, and I understand why she can never accept that. But my love for them has nothing to do with that. I think, if I try hard enough, I can make her feel that.

We go back to school after New Year's and try to settle back into our routine. At home, things have fallen into place. At school, though, nothing feels the same. Liam is still there, but he's separate from me now. You wouldn't know it from the way he flushes when a new boy in class tries to flirt with me, or the way I stare at him when he isn't looking, but we barely speak to one another.

I try to speak to him once—I try several times, actually. I experiment with the "maybe we can still be friends" thing for a few days. He's always sweet and responsive. He answers my questions about our homework assignment, he listens patiently to bits of silly gossip, he nods encouragingly when I tell him about a new idea for my blog. I admit I'd secretly been hoping I could somehow salvage what I'd destroyed, that maybe we could slowly find a way back to each other. But he's shut himself off from me. I may have broken up with him because I was scared of getting hurt, but it doesn't change the fact that I'd actually hurt him. And he was protecting himself now, just as I had tried to protect myself.

He tells me random details about his life, when I ask him. I know that his dad is still away and that his heater is fixed. He's accepted the scholarship and is leaving Montana forever in a few months. But I don't know how he feels about anything. When I press him, he tells me he's excited. But his eyes give him away.

There isn't much I can do, I realize. I was the one who'd pushed him to go. What can I say to him? I can't destroy his dreams—again. So I stay quiet and try to focus on other things. I bake obscene amounts of cookies and record the recipes in a journal.

I'm searching for the perfect chewy/chocolaty combination to post to my page.

There was an old message waiting for me on my blog, sent by a new reader while I was in the hospital. I don't see it until I've been home for a few days, and I disregarded it as spam until a follow-up message pops up a few days later.

> **Dear Rain:** A college buddy sent me a link to your blog, and I've been following your column for a while now. Your recipes and serving suggestions are both inventive and fun; I've tried several of them with excellent results. I was wondering if you've had formal culinary training. If not, I'd like to recommend some of the evening courses at our culinary program. I think you could learn a lot from our instructors. My contact information is below, and I've attached a brochure. We've trained some of the best chefs in the area and have placed our students in some of the finest restaurants in the country. I hope we will hear from you soon.

There are about a thousand things wrong with the letter, so of course I don't believe it. What are the chances that the head of a culinary program would find my obscure blog? How did he even know that I live in the area? And how do I know that he is who he claims to be and not some creepy sixty-year-old dude who gets off by triggering useless cooking fantasies in teenage girls?

Still, I can't help daydreaming. Cooking classes with actual experts! Talking to classmates about unusual food and *not* getting puzzled (or disgusted) looks! Sharing ideas, swapping success (and horror) stories, bringing in edible homework assignments!

*What excites you, Rain?* my father had asked me.

I knew the answer; I'd known it forever. It had always been there, dangling at the tips of my sugar-coated fingers. For years, my mom had pushed me in a direction that ran parallel to my dream. She had the right instincts, maybe, but her plans for me were too concrete. Yes, I wanted to help people. But I was *excited* about working with food. So why couldn't I do both? Maybe I could invent new recipes that were a cross between gourmet and healing. A menu tailored to a customer's medical history, lifestyle, or mood—their choice. A groundbreaking eating experience. A restaurant that merged Rain's rules of cooking with customers' dreams of health and happiness.

I start working out the menu in my mind. But I don't answer the blog message. It seems too good to be true.

A few days later, I get a suspicious submission to my blog:

**Dear Rain:** I plan to visit my daughter in Montana next month and I want to make her something special. I know she's partial to unusual recipes and chocolate. Can you help me?

—Lawyer from DC

**Dear Lawyer:** Why do people keep hijacking my blog for their own personal agendas? If you want a recipe, Dad, you can just ask me.

The reply comes a few minutes after I post.

**Dear Rain:** I just wanted to make sure you were still checking your blog messages. Just in case important people write to you. Also, I really do want to make you something.

—Dad from DC

**Dear Dad and Important Cooking People Stalking my Blog:** Rain's Chocolate Chip Cardamom cookies, because nothing says love like cocoa and spice.

After I post, I look up the number of dad's important chef friend and tap it into my phone. I don't call him right away though. There's an experiment I've been working on, and I haven't perfected it yet. It involves a plate of nachos, an artichoke head, sage, cheddar, and a large blowtorch. *(Next blog post: Blowtorches! They're not just for crème brûlée!)*

I can't wait to heat up the kitchen and present the culinary master with my perfect charred creation.

# Chapter 37

A few weeks after we return to school, I finally feel ready to resume my daily run with Ethan. The recovery from my surgery took longer than we expected. At first, I got winded just walking up the stairs to my room. My tennis shoes sat next to my bed as a hopeful hint, placed there by Ethan after my discharge. "Baby steps," I'd told him. In the beginning, that's exactly how it felt; a baby could have outrun me.

But by the end of the first week, I don't need to take breathers every few minutes. And by the end of the second, my energy level rises. I'm starting to get restless.

Ethan looks surprised when I knock on his door and hold up my running shoes.

"It's going to rain," he says, glancing at the forecast on his computer screen.

"So what?" I say. "It's never stopped us before. Rain doesn't change the rules, remember? Only you can do that."

I think he misses the joke, but he smiles anyway. "I'll get my shoes."

The air is heavy with the smell of a coming downpour, but

the earth is dry when we set out. We run quietly for a few minutes, but to my surprise, it's Ethan who eventually breaks the silence.

"Why did you split up with Liam?"

I jog for a few moments before I answer. "Why do you think I broke up with him?" It isn't a fair question, especially for my brother who isn't the best at predicting or understanding romantic relationships. But then, he's still in a relationship, while I'm the one pathetically staring at my ex-boyfriend's back and trying not to cry.

"Did Liam cheat on you? Or lie to you?"

"No. Of course not."

"So what did he do?"

I shake my head and slow down to a walk. It takes me a moment to catch my breath. "We wanted different things," I say finally. "And he was leaving town in a few months. It wasn't going to last."

"Okay." He hesitates and then turns to look at me.

"Does that answer your question, Ethan?"

"No."

I laugh and shake my head. "Well, it's the best that I can do."

"But he wasn't leaving today. You could still be together until he goes."

"I know." I sigh. "But we'd always know that the end was coming. And it would ruin whatever we had left."

"Why?"

"Because it just…would. It's hard to explain. Wouldn't it

bother you if you knew that you and Hope were definitely going to break up at a certain date?"

"No. Every relationship breaks up eventually. We're all going to die. And you, as a female in the United States, have an average life expectancy of eighty-two years. Which is nine hundred and eighty-four months."

"Okay. So?"

"So if you can be happy for six of those months, why wouldn't you be?"

I stare at him for a moment. "I...I never thought about it like that."

"Well, that's how I think about it."

I study him quietly for a minute. We've stopped in the middle of our run, and he's bouncing on his heels impatiently, staring off at some point behind my tennis shoes; his chapped fingers tug nervously at his jacket hem. On the face of it, he seems shut off in his own world, oblivious to everyone around him. But he isn't. He's closer to me now than I've ever been to him.

"You know what?" I say. "You and Hope aren't so different."

He nods and his eyes flicker up to meet mine. "I know. I made it to the bottom of the list."

He hadn't just made it to the bottom of the list. He'd blown us all away.

"I'm going to take your advice," I tell him. "I'll talk to Liam."

It doesn't seem like such a crazy idea, suddenly. I'd found a space for myself between my warring parents, hadn't I? They were both right and wrong, and I was discovering a way to love them both. What if there was a gray area between this black and white too? A friendship after a breakup might be too much for both of us—if Liam stayed in Montana. But what if it was a long-distance friendship? We still cared about each other. Did I have to stop caring about him because he was a thousand miles away? He was eventually coming back. That could be the start of a whole new adventure for us.

Ethan and I start off again, and we jog side by side in silence while I think about my last conversation with Liam. It isn't the most encouraging memory. He'd been really polite, but so, so guarded. "I'm still scared," I admit after a moment. "I'm not sure what Liam wants now."

"He wants you," he says. "Hope told me."

I can't help laughing at the matter-of-fact way he says it.

"Well, thank you for talking to me about this."

"You're welcome."

"And you can add that to your points, right? You've just discussed somebody else's problems."

"Yeah, that's true!" he remarks, with a pleased smile. "That's not why I asked, though. I really wanted to know."

We've slowed down outside of Manny's Ice Cream Shop, and I take the opportunity to stretch my aching legs.

"We should head back soon," I say. "I told Mom I'd start dinner."

"Make it a high-calorie one. She promised me that she would actually eat today."

"I think she's finally getting better. And she's been taking her meds religiously, did you know that?"

"I know. I've been counting them."

"Me too!" I chuckle to myself. "I guess she's paranoid that we'll ask Dad to come back if she gets sick again."

"Probably."

"Speaking of which," I say after a short silence, "Dad's invited me to come visit him for spring break. I know he asked you to come too."

"Yes."

"So I've been looking at tickets for both of us. You can take the first flight, if you like. Stay with him for six days and then come back. Then I could fly out there for the end of the break."

He seems confused. "You're not coming with me?"

"I wasn't planning to. I thought that you wanted to do this alone. Be independent from your sister. That's been the point all along, hasn't it?"

"No. It hasn't."

"Really? Because I was just trying to make you happy."

"Okay." His brow wrinkles, and he drops his head so his hair falls over his face. "Rain?"

"Yeah?"

"Secret Rule?"

My voice catches on the words. "What can I do to make you happy, Ethan?"

"You can come with me to DC," he says. "That's what I want."

"Okay," I tell him. "I'll buy the tickets tonight."

"Thank you."

It's started drizzling, and I'm about to suggest hurrying back when Ethan suddenly steps forward, and silently, abruptly, throws his arms around me. I stop breathing for a moment; my arms are limp and heavy, frozen at my sides, my mouth is hanging open in surprise. Then, very cautiously, I raise my arms and wrap them around his shoulders. It's an awkward and short embrace, yet it's the sweetest hug I've ever gotten. I have to blink away my tears before I let him go, or he'll think he has somehow made me sad.

"Secret Rule?" I whisper as I step away.

"What can I do?" he asks me.

"Tell me what you've been studying today. I want to hear about it."

He smiles broadly. "Brain transplants."

"*What?* You're kidding! That's actually possible?"

"No! Of course not!" He bursts out laughing, and suddenly his whole body is shaking, he's doubled over with hysterical glee. I feel my face flush red, and I give him a playful shove to hide my embarrassment.

"That isn't fair, Ethan!" I protest over his peals of laughter. "I always believe everything you say. I don't know what to expect from you anymore!"

He takes a deep breath and wipes his eyes with the back of his hand.

"Well, maybe that's what I want," he says and breaks into a run.

# Rain's Chocolate Chip Cardamom Cookies

1 stick (½ cup) butter, softened (not melted)

¼ cup white sugar

¼ cup light brown sugar

⅓ cup dark brown sugar

¼ cup cream cheese

1 egg

2 teaspoons vanilla (or chocolate liqueur)

½ teaspoon cardamom

2 cups flour

2 teaspoons cornstarch

1 teaspoon baking soda

¼ teaspoon salt

¼ cup milk chocolate, grated

½ cup chocolate chips

Combine the butter and sugars in a large mixing bowl, and cream until fluffy (the fluffier, the better!). Add the cream cheese, egg, and vanilla (or chocolate liqueur). In a separate bowl, mix the cardamom, flour, cornstarch, baking soda, and salt. Add the flour mixture to the creamed butter, and blend. When well mixed, fold in chocolate chips and grated chocolate. Refrigerate 4 hours or overnight.

When ready to bake, preheat oven to 350°F. Drop rounded spoonfuls onto a cookie sheet, and bake until lightly browned, about 10 minutes. Let the cookies cool before enjoying!

# Rain's Gluten-Free, Dairy-Free Chocolate Chip Cookies

2 tablespoons coconut oil

3 tablespoons maple syrup or date honey

⅓ cup dark brown sugar

1 egg

1 teaspoon vanilla (or chocolate liqueur)

2 cups ground almonds

½ teaspoon baking soda

¼ teaspoon salt

½ cup chocolate chips

In a large mixing bowl, combine the coconut oil, syrup (or honey), sugar, egg, and vanilla, and mix until well blended. Sift together the almonds, baking soda, and salt, then add to the mixture. Gently fold in the chocolate chips.

Refrigerate 4 hours or overnight. When ready to bake, preheat oven to 350°F. Drop spoonfuls onto cookie sheet, and bake until lightly browned, about 10 minutes. Let the cookies cool before enjoying!

# ACKNOWLEDGMENTS

I'm grateful to many people who helped me during the writing of this novel: Rena Rossner, for her invaluable advice and encouragement over the last four years. She truly is a superagent; Annette Pollert-Morgan, for her vision. A great editor is like a mother to her characters. Her suggestions help their story grow because each comment is given with love. I am so lucky to have worked with Annette on two novels; Cassie Gutman and Katelyn Hunter, for their incredible attention to detail; the entire Sourcebooks team for believing in my books; my mother, for being my most enthusiastic beta-reader and my father for his wonderful critique about the ending (thank you for making it so much better!); my sisters, to whom this novel is dedicated, for their high-pitched and clamorous support; my husband, Eric, for answering multiple questions about medical procedure, and for more than twenty years of patient listening; and to my three daughters, Aviva, Miriam, and Talia, whose teenage voices fill my novels and my life.

# ABOUT THE AUTHOR

Leah Scheier is a pediatrician and the author of *Secret Letters*, a historical mystery featuring the daughter of the Great Detective, and *Your Voice Is All I Hear*, a contemporary young adult novel about a girl whose first love is diagnosed with schizophrenia. During the day she waves around a pink stethoscope and Smurf stickers; at night she bangs on her battered computer and drinks too much caffeine. Feel free to contact her through her website at leahscheier.com or on Twitter @leahscheier.

Read on for a peek of Leah Scheier's
*Your Voice Is All I Hear*

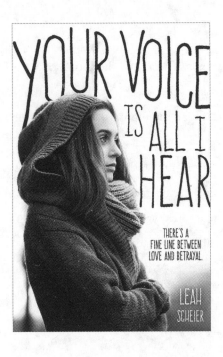

# PROLOGUE

I KNOW MY WAY AROUND THE MENTAL HOSPITAL.

I doubt most of the girls in my neighborhood could claim that, even though many of us lived just a few minutes from its leafy, sterile grounds, and some of us picnicked on the lawn outside its gate during summer break.

By the end of tenth grade, I knew Shady Grove Hospital better than I knew my school. I knew that the security guard's name was Carla and that she'd worked at her depressing post since the place was built. I knew the quiet path behind the topiary garden where I could wait until visiting hours began and she let me in. I'd memorized the shape and color of his shadow behind the dark-red curtains, and I knew where I had to stand so he could see me from his eleventh-story window. From that distant spot, I could even guess how well the medicine was working for him that day; I could tell what kind of visit it would be by counting the paces of his shadow.

I had the place mapped out, his daily routine memorized, the doctors' names and call schedule, every pointless detail carefully recorded in his special little book. He'd given me those notes as if they were classified secrets, the papers wrapped in strips of hospital linen sealed together with bubble gum, long wads of partially chewed Wrigley's tied into a crisscrossed mesh. That tattered spiral notebook was crammed with data he'd gathered over months: patients' names and histories, nurses' phone numbers, the cleaning crew's shift hours. I would never know how these bits of information came together for him or how he even found them out. But somewhere in these random nothings, he'd put together a story for me, a clue of how to get to him, a coded message that, for some reason, he believed only I could read. I was the one he trusted, the only one who had not betrayed him. I was the one he loved, the only one who believed him, even when his own mother had locked him up and thrown away the key.

And now, nearly three months after they'd taken him away, I was finally ready. I was going to march up to the security window, look into the tired guard's blurry eyes, state my name and the name of the patient I was visiting, and hear the buzz and click of the locked gate sliding open. I was going to walk down the white-tiled hallway, knock on his doctor's office door, slam his secret notebook on her desk, and make her read it, make her understand what he was hiding, make her see what only I had seen.

I was finally going to do it.

I was going to betray him.

# CHAPTER 1
## SIX MONTHS EARLIER

I'D LOST THE HOMESCHOOLING ARGUMENT AGAIN. ALSO THE SCHOOL TRANSFER argument, the study abroad argument, and finally (in a pathetic, last-ditch effort that stank of desperation), the chronic fatigue syndrome argument.

The truth was that I hadn't really expected to win. I knew what my mother was going to say before she said it. Simplified, her points were: single parent, can't afford it; can't afford that; can't afford that either; you don't have that illness or any other, April, so stop being ridiculous and get your books ready for school and don't forget to set your alarm, please, good night.

"But I can't, I just *can't* go without Kristin," I wailed, unleashing my last and final weapon—honesty. *That has to get through to her*, I thought. She couldn't ignore her only daughter baring her soul. My mom was all about "sharing your emotions," "listening to your primal voice," and "nursing your inner baby"—or whatever. (She reads *a lot* of self-help books.) So maybe if I dumped a buttload of truth and suffering on her, she'd celebrate my personal growth, shed a couple of cleansing tears, and let me stay home. "Mom, *please*, you know how hard it's been for me to make friends at Fallstaff High,"

I pleaded. "I just can't go back there tomorrow; I need a little bit more time—"

I should have expected the next part, I guess. She'd just gotten through her latest favorite: *Face Your Fear* by some celebrity healer. What did I think was going to happen? Fast-forward half an hour, and we were still in the same position on the living room rug. I was tired. She was just getting started. Somewhere between "fighting back against the darkness" (*you've never been to Fallstaff High, have you, Mom?*) and "knotting the spiritual umbilical cord" (*knotting my spiritual what?*), I humbly admitted defeat. Or exhaustion. Same result.

Bottom line: I was going to start tenth grade tomorrow (Mom's words).

I was going to "connect with others" and "strengthen my inner immunity" (Mom again).

I was going to end up sitting alone at lunch, everyone was going to treat me like I had leprosy, and I was going to be miserable (me—obviously).